Glimpse Of Eternity

Evanell

A Wings ePress, Inc.
Paranormal Romance Novel

Wings ePress, Inc.

Edited by: Diana Greenwood
Copy Edited by: Leslie Hodges
Senior Editor: Elizabeth Struble
Executive Editor: Lorraine Stephens
Cover Artist: Regina Brytowski

All rights reserved

Wings ePress Books
www.wingsepress.com

Copyright © 20xx by: Author
ISBN 13: 978-1-59088-759-2

Published In the United States Of America

Wings ePress Inc.
3000 N. Rock Road
Newton, KS 67114

Dedication

To my husband, William,
for his love and support
and for making sure my computer always works

* * *

One

London, England-The Present

"It's pouring rain," Kacy Rose said to her best friend while they collected their backpacks and umbrellas from the attendant near the front door and prepared to leave London's National Gallery.

"I'm not surprised," Jennifer replied. "It's been cloudy all week."

Clutching her pink umbrella with both hands, Kacy dashed down the steps beside Jennifer.

"Harrods, here we come," Jennifer sang merrily, as they skipped puddles and skirted Trafalgar Square, where people fed pigeons in spite of the storm.

Kacy grinned. "London's famous department store will probably be a stark contrast from the sixty-eight galleries of art we just saw."

"We didn't see all sixty-eight." Jennifer laughed. "Besides, your grandmother said Harrods is as good as a museum."

"I'm sure it is." Orphaned at the age of four, Kacy had grown up with her grandparents in southeast Denver, near Jennifer, and the two had been best friends all their lives.

"And," Jennifer frowned as they sloshed through an unexpected puddle, soaking their feet, "it'll be nice to go indoors again, where it's warm and dry."

"I love being here," Kacy said cheerfully. "London's so exciting!"

"Yeah. Everywhere we look we see history."

Behind them the National Gallery, built in 1838, a long stone building of off-white, looked as gray as the overcast sky. St. Martin's in the field, adjacent to the gallery, boasted a slightly darker shade of gray. Across the Strand stood Charing Cross Station. Sandy in color with white trim, the French Renaissance structure contained both the railroad and underground stations, plus a hotel on top.

"Something smells good," Kacy said when they stopped at the traffic light, waiting to cross the busy Strand so they could catch a bus.

"Must be our perfume," Jennifer said. "Or somebody else's."

"Maybe," Kacy laughed, envying the two girls behind them who sipped steaming drinks from uncovered Styrofoam cups, "but it smells like hot chocolate."

Two pigeons flew down and landed by her cold, wet feet. A sense of *déjà vu* descended. Shivers of excitement wiggled through her. "I feel like I've been

here before. Not in this life, but in another."

"I have the same feeling," Jennifer said. "Kinda creepy, isn't it?"

"Yes." They both shared a belief in reincarnation and felt that they had each loved one special man in prior lives but never had a chance to fulfill their love.

Unable to shake the strange sensation, Kacy clutched her pink umbrella tighter, straining to read the numbers on the approaching red double-decker bus. "I think that's the one we want."

"C'mom. The light's changed." Jennifer grabbed her arm.

Still not used to traffic driving on the left, Kacy saw the speeding black taxi too late. She realized Jennifer was looking the wrong way. Terrified she might get hit, Kacy shoved her back toward the wide sidewalk. But before Kacy could dash to safety too, the taxi smacked her. Hard—and sent her sailing through the air.

Pain so sharp she nearly blacked out rattled every cell. Her breath whooshed out in a loud gush. Umbrella and backpack scattered. But instead of crashing on the ground, Kacy kept right on soaring.

Dazed, she realized she didn't hurt anymore. Why? Was she numb? Or was something weird was going on? The impact should have broken bones. Knocked her out. Maybe even crippled her for life.

In a stupor, she peered down through the rain. Traffic on both sides of the Strand had come to a complete stop. Jennifer, along with a crowd, had begun to encircle somebody lying on the dark, rainy road. Before Kacy could see who, a powerful gust of wet wind swept her higher, up above the uneven rooftops that bordered Trafalgar Square and Charing Cross Station.

The pleasant sensation of flying without exerting any effort captured her attention. She'd dreamed about flying before. It always felt like this. Ethereal. Easy. And very real. She no longer felt cold. Now she felt warm, relaxed. Yet expectant, as though something wonderful was about to happen.

Suddenly, somebody seized her arm.

Startled, she turned her head and stared into the kind, gray-blue eyes of the white-bearded personage she had conjured as a child to be her guardian angel, then at the two-inch fairy perched on his shoulder, her fairy-godmother. Surprised that she had conjured them now, when she hadn't for years, she exclaimed, "Rey and Fey. It's great to see you!"

"Yes, 'tis." The adorable fairy, dressed in pale green and shimmering silver, beamed.

A little nervous, Kacy fingered the tiny scar on her right cheek. She'd had the scar since her sixth birthday when she tripped and fell on her grandfather's miniature Ferris wheel and rammed a tinker toy clear through her cheek. "When will I fall and hit the ground?" she asked, thinking she must be dreaming.

"Your mortal shell never left it," Rey said.

"Th-That's me," she stammered, "ly-lying down there?"

"It is," he confirmed.

She jabbed her chest with her thumb. "Then what's this?"

"Your immortal soul."

"But I don't feel immortal. I still feel human."

"Of course you do." With a nod of his brilliant white-haired head, Rey guided her higher above the Thames, now nothing more than a narrow, murky ribbon far below.

Unable to believe she was up in the sky with Rey and Fey, who didn't have a drop of rain on them, Kacy asked, "Am I dead?"

"No." Fey fluttered her tiny, silver-tipped wings before she folded them behind her slender shoulders.

"Am I dreaming?" Kacy asked.

Fey smiled, her green eyes sparkling. "No, sweetling."

Her thoughts in turmoil, Kacy swiped her wet face with the sleeve of her London Fog, a Christmas gift from her grandparents. They'd be worried sick when they heard she'd been in an accident.

As though he read her mind, Rey said, "The accident cannot be undone." He veered right and Kacy's attention jolted to a huge, cone shaped tunnel that suddenly loomed before them.

She blinked, then glanced at Rey, who looked somber and upset.

"Is something wrong?" she asked.

"Could be." His tone reeked with disapproval.

In her other fantasies the five-foot wingless angel and two-inch winged fairy were always cheerful and whenever Kacy had had nightmares, they'd helped her through her fear. Now, although Fey appeared quite pleased, Rey looked seriously worried and concerned. Confused, Kacy asked, "If I'm not dead or dreaming, what's going on?"

"You're in a coma," he grumbled.

"But I feel so alert," she objected. "And free. In fact..." she spread her arms and glided effortlessly, "... I've never felt this free before."

"Because you haven't been." Rey clasped her arm more firmly as the gigantic tunnel twisted closer. The colorful interior of spiraling pink, lavender, orange, yellow, green and blue contrasted sharply with the various shades of gray that made up the turbulent sky.

Drawn inexorably toward the stretching, yawning cone, Kacy shivered. "Where are we going?"

Fey winked. "On an adventure."

Concerned about leaving her grandparents and Jennifer, Kacy mentally resisted, although an imaginary adventure held more appeal than waking up and facing the injuries she was bound to have. "Could you be a little more specific?"

"Fey," Rey said as they paused at the mouth of the tunnel, "thinks you should visit the man in your dreams."

Too stunned to comment, Kacy gaped at the swirling vortex of kaleidoscopic colors they were apparently about to enter. The tunnel looked scary. It also held a certain hypnotic appeal. And it smelled pleasant. Faintly sweet. Like daffodils. Honeysuckle. Fresh flowers in the spring.

Trembling with a mixture of excitement, fear and reluctance, she squeaked, "Where is the stranger who haunts my dreams?"

"In 1854."

Before Kacy could draw another breath, Rey dived headfirst into the colorful, sweet smelling, whirling, twirling tunnel.

<h1 style="text-align:center">Two</h1>

Morning of The First Day
Surrey, England 1854

Claythorne Banes, tenth Earl of Havenhurst, reined his black stallion to a halt in front of his ancestral mansion. Small puffs of dust settled around Blade's hooves as a dozen stable lads rushed out from the stable, followed by half as many grooms.

"Kin I tend Blade?" Timothy asked while the others shoved and pushed to get closer to Clay's favorite stallion.

"No, lemme," they begged, elbowing and jostling each other.

Clay dismounted and turned the reins over to Timothy, who stood beyond the skirmish. The serious young French lad he had brought with him when he returned to England three years ago grinned at the honor bestowed on him. Clay affectionately tousled Timothy's dark brown hair then watched him lead Blade away before he turned and walked toward his ancestral mansion.

Depressed by the conditions of the earldom, Clay gripped his rifle. His uncle's diabolical will compelled him to keep too many stable workers and servants. The will also forbade him to use his own personal wealth to improve the conditions of the earldom, the tenants' lives and the rundown mansion.

The creaky front portal opened. For the umpteenth time Clay realized why villagers thought the mansion was haunted and fed the rumor that ghosts lived in his woods. He harbored no such thoughts, but did nothing to dispel the prattle that ensured privacy and kept visitors to a minimum.

"Welcome home, m'lord," his aging butler, Montfort, said.

Clay nodded a greeting, then strode through the dreary foyer. Still gripping his rifle, suicide crossed his mind. If he were dead, the Crown presumably would appoint a new earl and the restrictions in his uncle's will might cease to prevail.

Deep in thought, Clay blinked when he reached the library and saw a strange young lady standing before the fireplace. Her back to the door, she stared up at his portrait, the only painting in the room. *Deuce take it. Why hadn't Montfort announced he had a visitor?*

"What are you doing in here?" Clay demanded, his tone curt.

She turned and smiled.

Sheer shock froze him. Never had he seen a lovelier lady. And never before had he been tongue-tied. His brain could not form words. His senses were too busy devouring her.

Small of stature with alert blue eyes, a perfectly shaped nose and delicate cheekbones that highlighted her elegant features, she tempted him to do things he hadn't considered for months... years. He drew in a calming breath. It didn't help.

Her smile faded. A small scar dented her right cheek, but rather than detract from her appearance, the tiny flaw added to her appeal. Tension tightened his muscles. He wanted to reach out, touch her and ensure she was real and not just a figment of his imagination. He moved his gaze from her face.

She wore neither cloak nor bonnet, merely a pink, long-sleeved, day gown. The fitted bodice molded the enticing mounds of her full breasts and the skirt flared over her slender hips to the floor. Black shoes peeked out from beneath her hem.

Good Lord. What was wrong with him? Why was his body reacting as though he hadn't seen a woman for decades? Stunned by the unwelcome emotions boiling inside him, he found his voice and bellowed, "Who the bloody blazes are you?"

"Most people call me Kacy."

He watched her scrutinize his black knee-high boots, red-jacketed, white-trousered hunting togs and tightly gripped rifle.

"Dare I hope your hunting trip was successful?"

He had just left two deer with Bardsy, his bailiff, to divide between the tenants, but he didn't think that
was any of her business.

"I understand your bailiff's coffers are far from empty."

Clay still didn't comment. He had no idea who kept Bardsy's coffers filled. Perhaps the vicar and his wife. Their daughter, Sarah, was married to one of his tenants and the couple had two children with another on the way.

"Has the cat got your tongue?"

Unable to give a sensible reply because he didn't know what his visitor meant, Clay folded his arms across his broad chest before he said, "Kacy is an unusual name."

"It's a nickname. Short for Kathryn Cassandra. My initials, although I spell it k-a-c-y."

Rather than commenting, he repeated his first question with less hostility. "What are you doing in here?"

She gave his features the same thorough inspection she'd given the rest of him. "Perhaps you should sit down."

"I do not wish to sit."

Why did he feel like he knew her? That some elemental chemistry bound them together? And why this need crying out, as though he must have her at his side or perish? He didn't even know her, yet his soul felt as though it would never again be complete without her. He took another calming breath and forced himself to think. Having seen no conveyance outdoors, he concluded she must have wandered here by mistake.

"Are you lost?"

She shook her head. Her long, blonde hair billowed becomingly. Clay chastised himself for noticing. Perhaps she was a guest of his nearest neighbor, the Marquis of Rotherhile and Valerie, his granddaughter, whom the marquis repeatedly urged Clay to offer for. Valerie was lovely. Also quite spoiled. With the earldom in dire straits, Clay didn't need another burden added to his insoluble problems.

"Are you visiting the Rotherhiles?"

"No. I came to visit you. And I traveled a great distance to get here."

Her enchanting smile punctured the hard shell that encased his lonely heart. Unwilling to dwell on that or even own up to it Clay asked, "Why?"

"Because I wish to help you."

"A task for which I consider you singularly ill suited," he said, unable to control his body's continued reaction to hers.

She eyed his clenched rifle. "You contemplated suicide."

Cold chills crept down his spine. How did she know the secret thought he had entertained mere moments ago? Although he didn't believe in their actual existence he asked, "Are you a ghost?"

Another smile turned the small dent on her cheek into a dimple. "No. Are you?"

He didn't bother to answer. With all of the problems he had due to being trapped by his uncle's will, polite conversation seemed a waste of time and intelligence. Clay pondered how to dismiss her.

"You can't send me away," she said, as though she divined his thoughts.

Startled, but doing his best not to be affected by her uncommon appeal and his equally baffling attraction, he asked, "Why would anyone wish to visit this monstrosity I am compelled to call home?"

"To meet you."

He stepped closer and inhaled her sweet feminine, flowery scent. With one gloved hand he tilted her chin. Her blue eyes, as unfathomable as the depths of the ocean, locked with his. She reminded him of someone. Someone he knew very well. But he couldn't recall whom. "Who are you?"

"My surname is Rose."

"You speak like a foreigner."

She smiled, her cheek dimpling again. "Is that a crime?"

Clay resisted the temptation to smile himself. He rarely smiled anymore. "Where do you hail from?"

"Far away."

When he found himself wondering what her chin would feel like against his bare palm, he dropped his gloved hand to his side. "Are you an American?"

"Yes."

"How did you get here?"

"My guardian brought me."

"Who the blazes is your guardian?"

"His name is Rey. However, you don't know him."

"Where is he?"

"Beats me."

Clay blinked. "I beg your pardon."

"I'm sorry. I don't know where he is right now."

Beats me? Right now? Did all American's speak so strangely? He cleared his throat. "Why did your guardian leave you in the home of a man you have never met before?"

"Because I've dreamed about you and wanted to meet you."

Clay sucked in a sharp breath. Every instinct he possessed warned that if he didn't pack her off quickly, he might lose the ability to send her away at all. Ignoring the other questions begging for answers, he stated, "I do not entertain guests, therefore, I suggest you leave, Miss Kathryn Cassandra Rose."

"I like the way you say my name." She startled him with her comment and another bewitching smile. "And I think you look real cool in red, white and black."

"Cool? Real cool? What the devil does that imply?"

She smiled, her eyes sparkling with good humor. "Handsome."

Clay almost gnashed his teeth in frustration. She was flirting, but a man should be the one to initiate flirtation. "Do not attempt to flatter me," he growled. His resentment mounted as her smile grew, implying she knew something he didn't. *Where in the hell had she come from?*

"I didn't come from hell," she astounded him. "Actually I came from the future."

Shocked, he frowned again. "What?"

"I said I came from the future."

"Impossible," he snorted. Did she think him a dimwitted nodcock?

"No. I don't think you're dimwitted. But what I said is true. I live in the twenty-first century."

Clay dragged his fingers through his hair. He didn't know which bothered him most. The fact that she guessed his thoughts, announced she had dreamed about him, said "hell" out loud, or claimed to come from the future. "Now see here, Miss Rose..." he gripped his rifle with both hands to keep from touching her again, "You will surely wind up in hell if you tell more preposterous lies."

She smiled. "I know what I said boggles your mind. It boggles mine too, but I know this adventure isn't real."

"What?" Baffled, he shook his head. *Was she a ghost in spite of her denial and his ability to touch her? Fancy her?*

"I'm not a ghost," she startled him yet again. "And Rey said I'm not dead or dreaming, so I decided I must be hallucinating."

Rey? Her guardian? Short on patience, Clay didn't ask. And his glare didn't seem to bother her one whit. "You must go," he said in his most stern, severe tone. "Take your hallucination elsewhere."

She laughed.

He didn't recall ever hearing laughter in this solemn house before, and hers reminded him of music as it jingled merrily through the library, bouncing off shelves filled with leather-bound books, tomes and family histories.

With mirth still brimming her eyes she said, "I don't think I can leave until I help you."

He furrowed his brow. "Why the devil not?"

"Because I gave my word."

Before he could comment, she rushed on. "We're not at cross purposes, Lord Banes. Rey said that every night you go to bed silently cursing the will, which precludes the use of your personal wealth to improve the appalling conditions of the earldom. Your huge staff of servants and stable workers require a small fortune to feed and clothe, but the wretched will forbids you to dismiss a single one until five years after inheriting.

"Servants aren't the only problem plaguing you. Failed crops have made it impossible for the estate to support your tenants and their families. Their cottages are near hovels, mended clothing little better than rags, yet the will stipulates only money earned on the estate may be used to improve and support it. Since all you're allowed to spend is fifty pounds a year, I think you definitely need help."

What she knew was common knowledge. Clay's friends considered the manipulative will a challenge he'd eventually overcome. Thus far he'd managed only to keep starvation from his tenant's doors, and he'd been aided in that by an unknown source. A source he feared might stop any day. Too proud to accept help from a woman, he said, "I have no need of help."

"Yeah. Right."

Startled again by her odd choice of words, he said, "I beg your pardon."

"I apologize for upsetting you."

"I am not upset."

"Good." She eyed the rifle he held in a stranglehold. "Then you won't shoot yourself while I'm here."

Although he sensed she might be an interesting diversion from the solitude of his lonely life, he said, "You have no right to be in my library."

To his surprise, she genuflected. "Please forgive me." Then she crossed the room and damn if she didn't smile once more!

"When your mood improves, maybe we can talk again."

She raised her fingers to the small scar on her cheek, the only indication she might be nervous. For the first time he noticed the diamond clustered necklace that adorned her pale throat. Matching earrings decorated her earlobes. Were the jewels a family treasure or a gift from someone especial? Clay chastised himself for wondering as he watched the graceful sway of her pink day gown before she stepped into the corridor.

After she closed the door, he swore. "Damnation!" Nothing had gone right since he had inherited the bloody title three years ago—a title he had never wanted and wanted even less each day.

He stared at the door a full minute before he plunked his rifle in a corner, peeled his gloves off and stalked to the window to gaze out at the overcast sky. How in the blazes had a beautiful, bold American come to be in his home? *Why was she here? What the devil did she want? Where had she gone now? Were his unmanageable servants involved?*

Three

Outside the library, Kacy leaned against the cold salmon hued wallpaper and waited for her thudding heart to calm. This hallucination eclipsed everything that had come before. Claythorne seemed so vibrant. Alive. *Real.*

The tall handsome hunk she'd dreamed about since her sixth birthday, the day she rammed the tinker toy through her cheek and had been rushed to the hospital, had glossy black hair, brilliant green eyes, an aristocratic nose and a build that almost made her drool. He had made her heart pound and her body tingle from head to foot.

Expecting her guardian angel and fairy godmother to appear, Kacy grinned when Rey did just that. As always, his cherubic face looked kind, his gaze thoughtful. "You have questions?"

"Yes. The Earl doesn't want me here, so what am I supposed to do now?"

"While we traveled through the time tunnel, you promised to help him," Rey reminded her.

"And you promised to try to have me restored to my normal, healthy state in the twenty-first century
and returned there."

"You cannot wake up in the future until I confer with the powers that be. Your mortality is in question."

Kacy's thumping heart dived to her stomach. "Does that mean I might die?" she gasped.

"Not exactly. However, there's no need to discuss what might happen until I know for sure."

"Where's Fey?"

"With her own kind. Time travel depletes her energy and she must spend time in fairyland to renew it. So, you may as well relax and enjoy this adventure. That's what Fey had in mind."

Kacy attempted a cheerful grin. "I'll try." She looked around the dreary old corridor. "You didn't answer my first question. What should I do now?"

"Whatever you think will most help the Earl." Rey blinked and disappeared.

A vision flashed before Kacy's eyes. *She saw herself tied to a horse, wrists and ankles bound. The men leading her away looked dirty, unkempt, evil. Then she saw her beloved, dashing to her rescue on a beautiful white horse. His name was Theo and he wore rich purple garments, the color of royalty. He vowed to love her all the days of his life. Unfortunately she was ill and died a few days later, before they consummated their marriage or their love.*

The vision ended. Kacy shivered. Her beloved in the vision was the man in her dreams. The man who was no longer a stranger. *Claythorne Banes. Was it possible to have a vision within a hallucination?* The answer really didn't matter. She was more convinced than ever that reincarnation was more than just a belief. It was a reality.

At the far end of the long hall she spied a pack of rats playing tag, scattering dust balls. Goose bumps pimpled her arms. This hallucination had already lasted longer than expected. Nervously, she fingered the small scar on her cheek. The best way to help Claythorne might be to organize his servants and get them to clean his filthy home. Rey had explained that Claythorne's eccentric uncle had deliberately let the mansion go to ruin because he resented the fact that his nephew would inherit. The uncle had also ordered the servants not to clean. He'd even threatened to return and haunt them if they disobeyed. But Rey and Fey had both assured Kacy the mansion wasn't haunted. So why hadn't Claythorne put the servants to work when he assumed the title?

Puzzled, yet dissatisfied with their inactivity, she pushed away from the dank wall. The challenge of motivating the servants might take her mind off the Earl and her impossible attraction.

As she wandered through the mansion, she resisted the urge to roll her sleeves up so she could show the servants how to work. Surely they knew. Eager to discover how much could be cleaned and disinfected before she woke up, she hastened her steps. The mansion was old and dirty, but it wasn't decrepit. If clean, it might be fun to live in.

~ * ~

In the library Clay continued to stare out the window. He couldn't imagine why a foreigner would come to Havenhurst uninvited. Who might send a beautiful lady here? An answer clicked. The solicitors who had prepared his uncle's will. Had they sent her to spy? Brew trouble? Tempt him to ignore the will and do as he pleased?

Clay slapped his gloves down on the wide, low windowsill, then marched out with purposeful strides. Usually so many servants wandered about he couldn't walk down a hall without a near collision with two or three. So where were they now?

It occurred to him that perhaps no one had seen his visitor and he had either lost his mind, or was having a hallucination of his own. She couldn't be a ghost. Spirits existed only in people's fickle imaginations. Besides, he had touched her, inhaled her sweet, unique scent. *A scent that seemed oddly familiar. How strange.*

He looked in half a dozen dreary, empty rooms before he found his butler Montfort, in the kitchen, gumming a dry crust of bread.

"Have you seen my visitor?"

The stooped manservant blinked his rheumy eyes. "I believe she be in the music room, m'lord."

Grateful he hadn't lost his mind, Clay stormed up the curved stairs. Once a masterpiece of fine craftsmanship, the grand staircase now reminded him of an old ship, listing on its final journey home. The swaying balustrade stood in dire need of repair. Rail and posts required the hand of a skilled carpenter, the application of turpentine, beeswax and a very thorough polishing. In addition, the worn carpet runner begged to be replaced. Clay would dearly love to restore his ancestral home to its previous glory.

He dismissed the dismal state of his home when he reached the music room. Thirty servants sat on worn silk brocade chairs while Miss Kacy Rose listened to Bertha, his downstairs housekeeper.

"I been in service many years here at Havenhurst, milady."

"How many?" Miss Rose queried gently.

"Too many ta count. Me mum worked here a'fore I be born."

Clay cleared his throat, noisily.

All heads turned to the doorway. Although his servants looked nonplused, Miss Rose gave him a dazzling smile.

"Did you wish to see me, Lord Banes?"

"Indeed." To counter the riot taking place inside him, he dredged up an ominous expression.

Apparently unconcerned, she said to his servants, "Excuse me, please. Perhaps we may continue our discussions another time."

Her refined speech with its pleasant American accent bespoke an educated, gently reared maiden. Clay told himself not to be impressed and spun on his heel, leaving her to follow.

Part way down the corridor, he opened the door of a room that had been the nursery years ago.

"What a sweet room." His unwelcome guest touched the black spindled high chair before she floated across the room and examined the matching cradle with theatrical grace. "These are like the pieces I saw in George Washington's ancestral home, Sulgrave Manor in Northamptonshire. Elizabethan, aren't they?"

"I did not summon you to discuss furniture," Clay ground out, startled by her mention of America's first president's ancestral home, which he had never heard about before.

Miss Rose turned to face him. "I didn't assume you did, Claythorne." She arched a delicate golden eyebrow. "May I call you by your Christian name?"

"No," he snapped. "You may not."

"How then, do you wish me to address you?"

"I do not wish you to address me. I want you gone."

"Impossible," she said.

He blinked. *She had the temerity to disagree?*

"If my presence disturbs you," she added, "I'll stay out of your sight until you get accustomed to having me here."

"Perhaps you misunderstand." He stepped closer and assumed an intimidating stance. Her scent, a faint mixture of roses and gardenias, wafted through his senses. The urge to reach out and caress her, kiss her, descended. Instead he growled, "You are not welcome here."

She didn't look the least bit daunted. "I don't think I can leave until my guardian is ready to take me away."

Her smile revealed even, pearl-white teeth and the sparkle in her radiant blue eyes rivaled the diamonds she wore. Incapable of ignoring the pretty picture she presented, or his desire to touch her, he said curtly, "I shall provide you with the use of a carriage."

She shook her head. "Won't work."

"All my carriages work," he said, annoyed that she might think they were in the same state of disrepair as the mansion.

"I meant I can't leave."

"Rubbish!" he snarled.

"Please don't obsess or freak out over this."

"What?"

"Sorry. Where I came from we use that kind of jargon."

"Jargon?"

"Slang."

He hiked his brows. "Slang."

"Nonstandard language. Meaningless talk."

"I see." But he didn't and he almost forgot his anger when he saw the pleading in her pretty blue eyes.

"Please don't send me away. I promised to help you." She didn't give him a chance to object, but rushed on. "I know when you first became an earl you wanted to return to your business ventures in Europe and Africa and have your bailiff manage the earldom. But you discovered he's a harried old man with as much energy as a sleepy dog."

"When you learned the estate was in dire straits, the mansion riddled with rack and ruin and some of its treasures sold by your pence-pinching uncle, you felt as though you'd been robbed."

Still without giving him an opportunity to comment, she continued, "Your uncle bled the entire estate and placed the considerable funds in the hands of a trio of London solicitors who'll acquire the wealth if the earldom fails to make a profit within five years. With three down and two to go, the solicitors expect you to fail and the earldom to revert to the Crown. You care about your servants and tenants though, and the thought that you might fail them bothers you more than the potential loss of the earldom or your uncle's wealth…"

"Stop!" Clay thundered, his jaw rigid with fury. "From whom did you obtain your information?"

"My guardian. Personally I think only a man with a sick mind would attach the monstrous conditions to a will that your uncle attached to his. But maybe…"

Clay seized her arm. "I do not wish to hear another word." He pulled her from the old nursery, along the dreary corridor to the stairs. Before they were halfway down, conflict battled inside him. *Bloody hell!* Had he ignored women so long he had forgotten how quickly one could kindle a man's lust?

As the subtle scent of her perfume attacked his senses again, he fought the urge to pick her up, carry her back up the stairs and lose himself in her. He cursed himself for being tempted. If the solicitors had sent her here to beguile, they had chosen well. She was every man's dream come true. Small enough to bring out his protective instincts and so desirable he feared he might make a fool of himself.

Determined not to succumb to her charms, Clay clamped his hand more firmly around her small-boned elbow and concluded ruefully that she most certainly was not a ghost. She was flesh and skin and bones, put together in one delectable package.

At the bottom of the grand old staircase he escorted her through the cavernous entry and stopped before a clothes tree near the front portal. "Do you have a cloak, Miss Rose?"

She shook her head.

He hiked his brow in question. "A bonnet?"

She exposed a melancholy smile. "No."

Disturbed by his reaction to her sad half-smile, he grabbed his own cape off a hook and draped it over her slender shoulders. The cape dragged on the floor. She had the good sense to lift her hems when he opened the door. He gripped her arm again, guided her outside and led her across the cobbled drive to his pungent smelling stable where he barked at his lazy stable lads and grooms, "I need a carriage put to."

Eight lads scrambled to obey.

Feeling deuced awkward, Clay regretted the sadness that clouded his guest's pretty eyes. Had he not lost his temper, he might have reconsidered sending her away. After all, it was better to know where one's enemies were rather than to wonder.

But he didn't trust himself to let her stay. She was too lovely, he too lonely and he didn't know whether he could keep his hands off her if she remained. And if she had London connections, he didn't wish to compromise her, or suffer the consequences.

A gangly groom opened the carriage door. Another scrambled up to the driver's perch.

"Where is your accommodation, Miss Rose?" Clay asked.

"I don't have one." She lifted her hems again.

He caught a glimpse of her silk stockings and trim ankles and inhaled sharply.

She wiggled her nose with distaste and stepped around a heap of fresh dung, belatedly making him aware of the filth and stench in his stable. His uncle had encouraged the laggards who worked for him to be lazy; knowing that would drive Clay mad. Although he often prodded them, their only interest lay in caring for Blade, his prized black stallion. Like his house servants, they feared his uncle's ghost would haunt them if they obeyed Clay.

"Where do you wish to travel, Miss Rose?" he asked.

She shrugged. "Send me wherever you wish."

Exasperated, Clay ordered the skinny groom, "Deliver my guest to the Whiteleafe Public House in the village. Hire a room and instruct John, the innkeeper, to post the charges to me."

Clay handed her inside the carriage. "Farewell, Miss Rose."

"How odd to bid me goodbye without a reunion."

He had no idea what that meant, but as she leaned toward him, he had the uncanny sensation she intended to kiss him. Unable to resist such temptation, he started to reach for her.

But she didn't touch him. Instead she clasped the ornately carved ivory handle on the carriage door. "I can't say it was a pleasure, Lord Banes, but if you wanted to make me feel like a flake, you succeeded." She closed the door on his startled face and stared straight ahead.

A flake? What did she consider a flake? Something made of snow? Surrey's last snowstorm had occurred in February, more than two months ago. Puzzled, Clay watched his carriage wobble across the uneven cobbled drive. The moment it moved onto the rutted road and rounded the bend he heaved a sigh of relief. She was gone. In that selfsame instant he realized he was alone again. Feeling lonelier that he had ever felt before, he turned and trudged toward the mansion.

What had she meant by that reference to a reunion?

He squared his shoulders and looked up as the sun peeked out from behind angry gray clouds. The sudden brightness reminded him of Miss Rose's sunny smile. Although she reminded him of someone he must have once known, he knew without a doubt that he had never met the alluring American, Miss Kacy Rose before today.

Unfortunately her visit made him think of Oraline, the young lady who had betrayed him. Dear God, even after all these years he mourned the life they might have shared. But her deceit, combined with being stood up at the altar in France by Timothy's mother, had taught Clay not to trust women and he had sworn never again to become emotionally entangled with one.

Why then, did he worry about Miss Rose and feel responsible for her? Why did he regret sending her away and wish he had kissed her, tasted her tempting pink lips and sampled her hidden charms?

~ * ~

Kacy leaned back on the bench seat and tried to relax. In sharp contrast to the deplorable conditions of the Earl's mansion and stable, his carriage was clean and well maintained. The inconsistencies made her marvel that he lavished care on some possessions, yet ignored others. A guilty tremor trailed through her. She wasn't here to judge or censure, but to help. Still, she thanked heaven the horrific stable odors hadn't infiltrated the interior of the carriage.

This hallucination was getting more lifelike all the time.

"Rey..." she called, "... where are you?"

No answer came.

Kacy clasped her clammy hands together. She regretted not getting off to a good start with the Earl. When she announced she came from the future, he had accused her of lying. Too bad she didn't have her backpack. She could have boggled his mind with her cell phone, digital camera, Palm handheld, money, credit cards, driver's license, and all the other things that didn't exist in this century.

She fingered her scar. Would Rey take her back to the Earl's run-down, rat-infested mansion? She hoped so. Already she missed Claythorne. No... Thorne. That's what she'd call him because he was one stubborn dude.

Grateful for his cape and his thoughtfulness in lending it, she smoothed the itchy black wool, lined with matching black satin, over her lap. She might be hallucinating, but she certainly wasn't immune to human sensations and emotions. Besides being cold, she felt drawn to Thorne, as she'd never been to anyone else. Not a surprise, given that she was convinced he was the man she'd known and loved in prior lives.

Mesmerized by the beautiful countryside, she enjoyed the newly budding trees, green shrubbery, crooked rock walls and hedgerows that bordered the bumpy road. Then, not content to be idle, she rapped on the carriage front with her fist.

The groom jerked the carriage to a stop.

Kacy climbed out before he had time to get down.

"I don't require your services any longer."

Doubt filled the gaunt man's eyes. "Milord told me ta take ye ta the inn at the village, milady."

"I haven't time to go there. But thanks for your trouble."

Pleased with the sturdy, high-top boot-shoes Rey had provided, Kacy lifted her hems and hiked into the woods.

To her delight, Rey materialized at her side.

Before she could blink, he whisked her back to Havenhurst.

Four

Afternoon and Evening of The First Day

After the unsavory midday meal, Clay repaired to his study intending to work. Mildly aware of the warmth coming from the fireplace, he closed the door, then sensed another presence. *Hers*. His head swiveled as though it had a mind of its own.

Kacy Rose stood before the window, watching him. His hungry gaze feasted on the sight of her. She no longer wore his black cape. The straps of a brown reticule dangled from one elbow and her delicate fingers clasped the shiny handle of a pink umbrella, several shades brighter than her day gown.

How could he feel as though he'd always known her when he'd met her only this morning?

Her blue eyes twinkled until he growled, "How did you get back in here?"

She flinched at his harsh tone. "The same way as before."

Unable to stave off the desire to be near her, he eased closer, like a cat stalking a mouse. "How was that?"

"My guardian angel brought me." To that nonsensical reply she added, "I knew it wouldn't do any good to send me away. This is where I'm meant to be just now. I think I'm supposed to convince you that life is worthwhile and that you can overcome the restrictions in your uncle's will."

Startled, not only by her softly spoken words, but also by the sincerity in her eyes, Clay asked, "How in the devil am I to overcome legally binding restrictions?"

She shrugged. "Maybe with my help and my guardian angel's—"

"I do not believe in guardian angels."

"I know. You don't believe in reincarnation either."

He felt a muscle twitch in his jaw. "Re-in-what?"

"Carnation. Reincarnation. Other lives, prior lives." She raised her hand to the tiny scar on her right cheek and licked her lips.

Clay's body stiffened. All over.

"You see," she continued, "I think we knew each other in previous lives. That's why I've dreamed about you."

He didn't believe a word she said. Still, he found himself enchanted. Fascinated. Her rosy cheeks, as pink as her painted lips, matched her varnished nails. Was she a woman of the night? It mattered not. He fancied her. And imagined himself disposing of her pink gown, unlacing her corset to see how small her waist was, how full her breasts. His fingers actually itched to explore her hidden charms. How would she react if he kissed her?

Telling himself he must not harbor such thoughts, he shook his head to clear it, then shoved an errant lock of hair off his forehead. "I know not why you're here, nor what you wish to accomplish by fabricating such tales, however…"

"I'm not fabricating. I truly am from the future. And my guardian angel did bring me here to help you."

Clay decided not to argue. "What do you hope to gain from your efforts, Miss Rose?"

"I'm not sure." Her composure dwindled as she fingered the scar on her cheek again. He imagined running his tongue over the small dimple, tasting her skin, caressing her flesh.

"You see I don't know what's going to happen when I finish helping you."

Chagrined by his wayward thoughts, Clay asked, "How long do you expect to be here?"

"I don't know that either."

He found his heart softening and hardened his resolve. "Then I shall tell you. Not another moment more." He seized her arm and guided her to the corridor, struggling with the battle going on inside him.

At the front portal he saw his black cape hanging from the clothes tree. He draped it over her slender shoulders again and fastened it beneath her chin. The top of her head barely reached his shoulder. Concern tugged at his protective instincts. She was small and delicate and shouldn't travel alone.

His desire to know more about her escalated. He would dearly love to keep her with him for a good, long time, if only to hear what other tales she might spin. But if she stayed, he might never want to let her go. She was a weakness he could ill afford.

~ * ~

As Thorne led Kacy outside, raindrops bounced on top of her head and slithered down her scalp. She opened her pink umbrella, then tried to shield Thorne as well as herself. Focused on dragging her across his uneven drive, he seemed unaware of her effort.

When they entered the stable, a dozen boy's eyes bulged with fright. Kacy knew why. They'd seen her leave and the carriage she'd gone in hadn't returned. In an attempt to soothe them she closed her umbrella, then said, "I'm not a witch."

Tugging her arm free from Thorne's grasp, she moved closer to the boys, doing her best to avoid scattered, smelly horse manure. "My means of transportation was simply quite efficient." When she smiled, two boys smiled back. The others turned and fled into the recesses of the dark, dirty stable.

"Timothy and Thadius," Thorne barked at the smiling boys. "Put that carriage to." He nodded at the nearest one.

Rey had put a number of things, including candy, in her reticule. Wanting to reward the boys, Kacy spread the drawstrings and withdrew a small box of bonbons.

"After you finish, I have a treat for you," she told them.

They quickly fetched horses and started to harness them. When they finished, both boys stared at the promised treat. Kacy smiled and extended the candy.

One boy had missing front teeth. The other spoke with a French accent. "*Merci,* Miss," the latter said.

"Rose. Miss Kacy Rose," she introduced herself. "What are your names?"

"I be Thad'us," the boy missing his front teeth lisped. "An he be Tim-thee. He be from Franth. The master, he brung him back…"

"I have no time to dally," Thorne snapped. Hustling Kacy inside the carriage, he climbed in behind her and sat across the aisle. A scowl puckered his forehead.

As the carriage left the stable Kacy concentrated on keeping her knees from bumping Thorne's. She resisted the obvious solution, moving to sit beside him. That would create a worse problem when the wheels hit ruts and forced their bodies into close contact. "May I ask a question?" He glanced at her face, then her heaving chest, and she felt herself blush.

"You may."

"If I were a man, would you let me help you?"

"No," he said crossly.

"Then it isn't just me you object to. You object to help from anyone." He didn't comment. So she turned her head and didn't say another word. He seemed indifferent to her. Unfortunately, she wasn't indifferent to him. She wanted him to touch her again, but gently, as he had in a thousand dreams. She wanted more than that. She wished he would kiss her before she woke up.

It would probably be very easy to fall in love with this proud, handsome man who constantly worried about his tenants and servants and stable workers. But with her mortality in question, she knew she shouldn't complicate matters. Although she believed she had known and loved him in other lives, she didn't intend to love him now. She didn't belong here. Besides, this wasn't real. Just a weird hallucination.

When they reached the inn, she said, "I don't need your help either, Lord Banes. I can take care of myself." She slid over and opened the door. Before his groom dislodged himself from the upper driving seat, she climbed out.

As she approached the inn's door, she quietly murmured, "Please, take me away from here, Rey."

To her delight, he did.

~ * ~

Surprised she had climbed out without assistance, but determined to see her settled in a pleasant room, Clay moved to the open door. Her pink umbrella lay on the seat across from him. He grabbed it, then stared at the slick handle. What had it been fashioned from to be so smooth and shiny? It felt lighter than wood. Could it be ivory dipped in paint?

He tightened his grip and climbed out. Although the rain had ceased, the ground was muddy and slippery. In spite of that, Miss Rose had already disappeared inside the public house. Clay quickened his stride.

But when he entered, he didn't see her. Thinking she must have previously hired a room and gone directly to it, he nodded a greeting at the innkeeper he'd known all his life. "Is a Miss Rose one of your guests, John?"

John's crooked grin revealed a new missing tooth and Clay wondered how he would chew if he lost any more.

"No, milord. Me only guests be a aging couple. He hath the gout. And they asked not ta be disturbed."

Puzzled, but worried too, Clay returned to his carriage. *Where had Miss Kacy Rose gone?*

~ * ~

Back home some time later, he stood her wet pink umbrella in a corner by the clothes tree to dry out. Then he returned to his study, half expecting to find Miss Rose there. To his disappointment, he didn't. Seated behind his desk, he busied himself with correspondence and business matters. But his
thoughts kept straying to the absent Miss Rose.

After an hour his wayward thoughts turned to concern. Had Kacy Rose traveled here alone, to this foreign land? Or had she been separated from her traveling companions? Either way was unsafe. The fact that she claimed she came from the future and had a guardian angel indicated she might be the one in need of help. Suddenly Clay felt like a wretch, an ungracious wretch. He shouldn't have sent her away.

~ * ~

"This hallucination business is weird," Kacy said to Rey as they sped through the woods without touching the ground.

"You're not hallucinating," Rey said. "This adventure is as real as your life in the future."

Kacy gulped, afraid to ask what that meant. The way Rey zapped her from one place to another made it hard to believe she wasn't hallucinating.

A moment later Rey stopped in front of a small cottage, about a half-mile from Havenhurst's mansion. "What now?"

"It's time for you to meet Bardsy, the bailiff." Rey winked and became invisible. "Fear not. The bailiff's a kind soul."

Bardsy, a bent old man, answered her knock.

"I've come to help improve the tenant's lives," Kacy said after she introduced herself.

Bardsy smiled a crooked smile. "I knew someday ye'd show yerself."

Kacy smiled, too. "How did you know?"

"I dreamed it when me coffers began to stay full no matter how much food the tenants took."

She started to object, but the invisible Rey communicated silently. *"Let him believe you provided the food."* Before she could react, Rey silently added, *"Tell him you wish to visit the tenants."*

"Would you please take me to meet the tenants?"

"With pleasure, Miss Rose." Bardsy limped outside, around the side of his cottage.

Kacy followed.

"Pillow?" she heard him say when he saw a fine looking steed. "Be that ye?"

"Yes. That's Pillow." Somehow Kacy knew the nag had been named Pillow because he was so comfortable to ride, just as she knew Rey had revived the former sorry nag and provided a black mare for her. She wished Rey could do something about Bardsy's limp and marveled when he did. Suddenly the bailiff stood taller, prouder and looked years younger.

As they mounted and rode off, Kacy thanked her lucky stars she'd taken riding lessons while growing up and learned how to ride English style. She also blessed the sunshine and clear blue sky. Now that rain had settled the dust, she anticipated a pleasant outing.

Much to her dismay, the cottages at the edge of the woods were worse than she had feared and the tenant's expressions were somber. *Downtrodden,* she thought, as her horse and Bardsy's trotted away from the last dilapidated cottage.

"What's wrong with all of the tenants?" she asked.

"Failed crops hath drained their spirits and all fear the Earl willna purchase seed this year and they'll lose their livelihood."

Kacy decided help hadn't come soon enough. "Tell them to begin tilling immediately."

"That will gladden their hearts. And mine as well."

"Take these," she took her diamond necklace and earrings off. "Keep them in a safe place. You may need them to purchase seed if the Earl refuses."

"I canna," Bardsy objected, staring at the jewels like they were beyond his comprehension.

"Of course you can," Kacy disagreed with a smile. "And..." she added after another silent communication from Rey, "... Tell the tenants that tomorrow night we'll have a big feast behind your cottage."

"Who will provide and prepare the food, my lady?"

She smiled. "Let me worry about that."

"I'll spread the news in the morning."

"Go now," Kacy encouraged.

"I canna leave ye to ride alone."

"I won't be alone. My guardian's nearby."

Bardsy looked doubtful but he said, "If ye be sure?"

"I am. I'll see you tomorrow." She waved goodbye and Bardsy turned Pillow around.

Rey materialized as soon as Kacy entered the woods.

She reined the black mare to a stop. "Now what?"

"I shall take you back to the Earl's mansion."

"I doubt he'll be pleased."

"He may surprise you."

~ * ~

Clay climbed the stairs to retire. All afternoon and evening he had tried without success to dismiss the guilt he felt for sending Miss Rose away. If he knew where to find her, he'd bring her back to Havenhurst. That could conceivably create problems, but the thought of her alone without a chaperon, disturbed him. *Dash it!* He raked his fingers through his hair. *Would she return?* And why did he have the odd feeling that she ought to belong to him?

Deep in thought, he reached the music room before the strains of Mozart penetrated. Startled, he pushed the door open—and froze. Miss Kacy Rose sat at his pianoforte, playing *A Little Night Music*, while his servants, seated again, listened as though spellbound.

Unwelcome emotions swelled inside Clay as he gazed at his uninvited guest's silk evening gown, the same blue shade as her pretty eyes. Her long hair, gathered at her nape and tied with a blue ribbon, left a few short curls free to frame her beautiful face. She no longer wore the diamonds. Why? Had she locked
them away because they were an heirloom or a gift?

Irritated by his conflicting reactions, he marched to her side, then glared at his servants as Miss Rose ended her musical recital. "Who admitted...?"

"I admitted myself, Lord Banes."

He turned his glare on her before he waved dismissal to his servants, then abruptly changed his mind about staying in the music room until they all filed out. "I must speak to you in private," he gritted.

"I thought you might say that," she mumbled.

Baffled by the relief he felt that she had returned, he seized her elbow. Pleasurable jolts charged up his arm, then spread out until they suffused his entire body. Doing his best to ignore them, he drew her to her feet and practically dragged her across the hall. Once decorated with fine furnishings, the guestroom now lay in near ruin. Unable to ignore its sad state, or the fact that if it were clean he might be tempted to do more than lecture her, he said with stern regard, "Surely you know that without a proper chaperon your reputation is at risk."

She shrugged, elegantly. "I'm a lot more concerned about helping you than I am about my reputation."

Although not indecent, the neckline of her gown exposed a delectable cleavage and he found it difficult to concentrate on scolding her.

"Why won't you accept my help, Lord Banes?"

Only a miracle could help him. And miracles weren't made of supple flesh that smelled like flowers and delicate bones, which looked like they belonged to a one-dimpled angel. "Why do you wish to help me?"

"Because you need it. We both know that instead of working, your servants spend hours gazing out dirty windows blackened with soot and layers of ever-growing mildew. You needn't live amidst this." She waved her arms to indicate the pitiful state of moldy wall-coverings, threadbare carpet, tattered curtains, tapestries and bedcovers. "Put your servants to work." She nodded at the ceiling. "There's no reason to have dust motes and cobwebs strung about like tinsel decorating a Christmas tree."

Clay didn't take exception to her remark. The Queen's consort, Prince Albert, had made decorating evergreens during the Christmas holidays a popular tradition, and Clay thought Miss Rose's observation rather apt.

"Your uncle's will prohibits a number of things but it doesn't prevent me from instructing your servants to clean, or finding other places of employment for those you don't need."

"You may know my problems," Clay conceded for want of something to say, "but you know nothing about me."

"I do too," she stoutly disagreed. "Your portrait in the library was commissioned by your father before you left for Oxford in 1844. It hung in your parent's home until their unfortunate deaths in 1848. To deal with your grief, you left England. Astute investments turned your modest inheritance into a small fortune, then into a much larger one. You were in Africa negotiating the purchase of a diamond mine when your cousin, heir to the earldom, met his demise while foolishly swimming in the cold English Channel at Brighton Beach on Boxing Day."

Instead of getting mad, Clay felt flattered. She had obviously gone to great lengths to learn such details. Curious, he asked, "What else do you know?"

"When you returned to England to offer condolences, you discovered your uncle had sold your parent's home and claimed the proceeds as his own. Expecting the money to be used to improve Havenhurst, you refrained from creating a scene over the blatant thievery. You even acted pleased your portrait from your family home had been hung in Havenhurst's library."

How the blazes had she learned those personal tidbits? Not even Drake, his closest friend, knew that about him. Did she also know he had once loved Oraline? That she had professed to love him too, then scorned his love and married an old titled and wealthy lord instead?

Reluctant to ask, Clay admired the thick fringe of Miss Rose's dark spiked lashes and her beguiling eyes. With stoic control he resisted the desire to touch her. She had the dewy purity of the rose in her surname and simply looking at her eased some of the tension he had lived with for three weary years. Not wanting to sour his convivial mood, he said, "The hour grows late. Where do you intend to spend the night, Miss Rose?"

She looked uneasy. "Maybe I shouldn't answer that."

Annoyed at having to pry information from her after she had eagerly discussed him, he said, "Will you return to the inn?"

Shaking her head, she blurted, "I plan to stay here... in the blue room. On the floor above this one."

"I cannot believe your audacity," he clipped.

"I hardly believe it myself." She had the good grace to blush. "However, as long as I'm here I'm confident you won't commit suicide."

"Perhaps your confidence is misplaced."

To his surprise, she reached out and splayed her hands on his gray waistcoat covered chest. A bolt of desire slashed through him and he fought the temptation to wrap his arms around her as he stared down into her eyes.

"Please, don't do yourself in!" she implored. "That won't help your servants or your tenants. They need you."

"If I were dead," he played the devils advocate, forcing his voice to sound calm, but unable to extinguish the fire burning hotly inside him, "the Queen might appoint a new earl and the restrictions in my uncle's will would end."

"But the Queen might not appoint a new earl," Miss Rose argued. "And even if she did, he wouldn't care about the tenants and they could be worse off than they are now."

She pleaded a good case, Clay admitted, but he knew if he didn't step back soon, he might lose the ability to do so. He closed his fingers around her wrists and removed her hands from his chest. Color rose in her cheeks and she tried to pull free, but he didn't let her.

"You may spend the night in the blue room." He lifted her hands, kissed one, felt her tremble and kissed the other, all the time holding her gaze with his. Her color deepened and he experienced a vague sense of *déjà vu*. But he knew if he had ever met Miss Rose before he would not have forgotten her. She affected him as no one else ever had. Not even Oraline had possessed the power to make him want her to the exclusion of all else.

He cleared his throat, surprised at how normal his voice sounded when he spoke. "On the morrow we shall discuss finding your guardian and making arrangements for a permanent place for you to reside, or sending you back to America." He released her hands and stalked out, confident he left her gaping at him. And harboring an emotion he hadn't felt for a very long time—hope. *Or was it revenge?*

He wouldn't mind attending a London ball with Miss Kacy Rose on his arm. Not only would he be envied by friends and peers—all of England, including Oraline, would know he had found someone more beautiful than her to occupy his time and thoughts, and perhaps to share his bed as well. At least until he tired of her. And he knew he would, as he had tired of women in the past, which was the reason he'd been without feminine companionship since his return to England. Women required time, attention, and devotion; and he couldn't bring himself to pretend he cared when he didn't give a fig whether he pleased or displeased the fair, unpredictable gender.

"Why then," a quiet voice asked, *"do you want to keep Miss Rose? Why have you already decided to offer her a semi-permanent home?"*

~ * ~

In the master suite he stared at the garish decorations without closing the door. For the first time in months, he was acutely aware of the ostentatious gargoyles. His uncle may have liked them, but nothing in the room suited Clay's taste.

An ornate canopied bed, appointed with gargoyles on each corner post, dominated the wall opposite the east facing windows. A table and two straight-backed chairs occupied space on one side of the bed. Near the fireplace stood an overstuffed chair that was about as comfortable to sit on as a rock. Two gargoyles resided above the door leading to the ancient garter robe. Two more decorated the fireplace mantle. When the room was dimly lit or in shadow, as now, the gargoyles looked like hideous, live monsters.

Sensing somebody watching him, Clay turned. He expected to see his manservant, Carlisle, waiting to offer to help him disrobe. Instead Kacy Rose stood in the hall. Their eyes met briefly before she surveyed his chamber.

How could he bring a bride to share this horrible room? He knew precisely why he'd had that thought. Kacy Rose tempted him to do things he hadn't considered for years. He stalked to the corridor, dragged her inside and kicked the door shut without releasing her arm. "The room's appalling, isn't it?" he asked.

She pulled her eyes from his, looking at the big bed, her cheeks flushed. "I've seen worse."

Unable to resist temptation any longer, Clay gathered her close and lowered his mouth to hers. He swallowed her small protest, his lips demanding a response.

She didn't disappoint him. With a small moan that sounded like surrender, she wound her arms around his neck and arched closer. His tongue probed and coaxed until her lips parted.

Her sweet scent filled his senses. Coherent thought deserted him. All his concentration focused on the woman in his arms, the only woman who had ever made him forget himself. Need rose within him. He lifted her in his arms, still kissing her and carried her to his bed. Only when he sat down and she drew away did he realize what he'd done. As they stared, he considered apologizing. But he wanted to kiss her again. Giving in to the impulse, he lowered his head.

She thwarted him by scooting off his lap, jumping to her feet. Instead of dashing away, she stood before him, her mouth swollen from his prolonged kiss, her eyes blazing with unfulfilled passion.

And then to his utter amazement, she said, "Thank you."

Startled, and still on the bed, his gaze level with hers, he said, "If you like my kisses, why did you stop me?"

"Because that's not why I'm here. And I'm sure my guardian angel wouldn't approve if we did anything more."

Clay breathed in and out, slowly. "Why then, did you thank me?"

"For the reunion."

Puzzled, he frowned. "The reunion?"

She nodded, babbling, "I think we've known each other before. In other lives. But I don't expect to stay in this century. So I don't think we should kiss again. I need to try to help solve your problems, not complicate them, so I can go home."

Although he still considered her ill-suited to help him, he asked, "And how do you intend to help solve my problems?"

She folded her arms. The gesture emphasized the fullness of her partially exposed breasts. He swallowed. *Deuce take it!* Never before had he envied a piece of clothing, yet now he envied her damn blue evening gown.

As though in deep thought, she raised a hand and cupped her chin, her elbow supported by her other hand. "Does British law allow the strange restrictions in your uncle's will? Is it legal? Could you have it contested? Declared null and void?"

Clay kept his face expressionless. He had considered doing just that until he learned his uncle's solicitors knew his carefully guarded secret—He had been accused of murdering Timothy's mother in France. Although he hadn't been tried because Yvette's body had never been found, the London solicitors would publicize the accusation if Clay challenged the will. He didn't wish to have his name besmirched, nor did he wish to be the object of gossip and he wasn't all that sure he could have the will declared null and void.

"I had it researched. The will is legal," he said, ashamed of the half-lie and wanting Kacy back on his lap... in his bed.

She accepted his answer with a nod, but something in her eyes indicated she knew he hadn't told the truth. "Thanks for allowing me to stay at Havenhurst." She backed up a step, her voice softened to a near whisper. "I apologize for any inconvenience I've caused." At the door, she said, "Good night, Lord Banes."

"Good night, Kacy."

Without looking back, she slipped into the corridor.

He fought the temptation to go after her. Honor kept him in his room.

But desire tormented his uneasy sleep. He dreamed of her. In another time... another place. Bound to a stake surrounded by fire, she was about to be sacrificed to pagan gods. Clay charged through the crowd on a huge black destrier, slashed the binding cords and rescued her. Deep in the woods he kissed her with hungry, desperate passion. Then he took her to his people, promising to return. The dream ended before he did.

He woke up, stared at the dark ceiling, wondering why he'd had the confounding dream. Because she'd planted baffling bizarre ideas in his head?

Five

Morning of The Second Day

Clay slept again. His dreams were haunted by Kacy's lush curves and sweet, alluring scent. He woke up aroused. *Damnation!* Even when he didn't touch her, his body burned with need. He'd known her a mere day and could only think of one thing—possessing her. Disgusted with his inability to dismiss her from his thoughts, even when asleep, he lunged out of bed, dressed quickly, then bounded up the stairs, meaning to pound on the blue room door.

Instead he frowned when he saw the corridor. Candles burned in wall sconces and servants rushed about with mops, buckets, rags and bars of soap. Many were already busily washing walls, windows, doors and floors. It was the most activity Clay had seen since he moved in and although it pleased him, he didn't like the suspicion in his mind. Had Miss Rose taken charge of his home without his permission?

He spotted her with a group of servants. When she saw him, she approached carrying a brass lantern, the likes of which he'd never seen before. The soft glow of light illuminated her modest, high-collared, pink nightwear. Unfortunately it failed to conceal her delectable peaks and curves. His senses assaulted anew, Clay tore his eyes from her enticing form and stared at her face.

"Good morning," she greeted him with a cheery smile.

Another sense of *déjà vu* flashed. Had he seen her in bedclothes before? 'Twas impossible. Yet the feeling persisted. Disturbed by the recurring illusive sensations and annoyed that she had apparently taken charge of his servants, he barked, "Are you responsible for the commotion going on before daybreak?"

Her smile faded at his clipped tone and she nodded.

"Who granted permission for you to order my servants about?"

"Nobody, but somebody had to give them direction."

"I have two housekeepers for that purpose."

"But neither of them work. They just…"

"What my housekeepers do is not your concern." He reversed his previous decision about letting her stay at Havenhurst and resolved to lodge her elsewhere; to get her out from under his roof before he lost control, not only of himself, but also of his home. "A tray shall be brought to your room. Be prepared to leave immediately after you break your fast."

Bewilderment covered her delicate features. Suddenly he wished he could recall his harsh words and gather her close. His good sense prevailed, arguing he must not be taken in by her uncommon appeal. She could be here to create problems.

He didn't know why he pushed the blue room door open and stalked inside. But shock stopped him in mid-stride. *The room had been completely refurbished! And it looked grand. When had the work been done and by whom?*

With newly painted walls, new blue window treatments, chairs and a blue floral carpet that covered all but the edges of the polished wooden floor, the room looked more elegant than any other in the mansion. Instead of candles, brass lanterns, similar to the one she carried, graced tables on each side of a new four-poster canopied bed.

"Those are moderator lamps," she said behind him. "On the off chance you don't know how they operate, the flow of oil is automatically regulated by means of a piston."

Clay didn't comment. Ladies were not supposed to know about pistons and the flow of oil or other things mechanical. Across the room a fire burned in the fireplace. He envied the clean, cozy atmosphere and to his chagrin, imagined himself sharing the room and *bed* with her. Unable to control his thoughts or the lust threatening to best him, he demanded, "Who refurbished this room?"

"Our guardian."

"I beg your pardon?"

"I think you need to calm down before I explain."

Too agitated to agree or disagree, he marched over to inspect the wardrobe. And found it full of gowns. She had certainly made herself at home.

"Get dressed," he snapped before he strode out.

He ordered the first servant he saw, a youthful girl named Maisy, to pack Miss Rose's gowns in the trunk he'd seen in the blue room. On the ground floor he instructed Cook Edna Mae to have a tray sent up to Miss Rose. Then he charged out to the stable and ordered his largest, most luxuriant carriage put to. He intended to take her to London and he intended to travel in comfort. And he did not intend to let her sway him or his decision. She wasn't welcome at Havenhurst and he wouldn't allow her to spend another day... or night.

When he finished his half-cooked, unappetizing breakfast, he found Kacy in the cheerless entry with the trunk at her feet. A gray cloak draped her arm, a brown reticule hung from her elbow and she wore a becoming, long-sleeved yellow day gown. She had pinned her long hair atop her head, hastily it appeared, and she stood with demure demeanor and downcast eyes.

Clay reached for her arm. A pleasurable thrill, created simply by touching her, spread through his deprived body. Appalled by the sudden ache in his groin and his utter lack of control, he clamped his teeth together and loosened his grip.

She pulled away and raised her hand to the tiny dimpled scar on her cheek. "Could we talk please? In private? I need to explain some things and I don't want to be overheard."

"Come." He turned down the corridor, already regretting his hasty decision to send her away, regretting his harsh thoughts. He disliked believing she was bent on ill will, but the worry persisted. He was the earl. She was merely a young lady. He would not lose control of the earldom, or what occurred in the mansion. The servants and tenants should look to him for instruction, not to her. She had somehow refurbished the blue room and set the servants to clean. He should be pleased, not threatened. A mere slip of a girl could not harm him.

At his study, he waited for her to precede him inside, then closed the door and walked to his desk where he turned.

"I'm not leaving Havenhurst," she said.

He cocked a brow; secretly oddly pleased she had the nerve to challenge him. No other lady had ever dared. "Are you not?"

She shook her head. Some of the silky blond locks she had pinned up tumbled down. "There's so much to do and I don't know how long I'll be here."

As she fumbled with her hair, attempting to re-pin her locks, she added, "You must think I'm real spacey."

"I beg your pardon?"

"I'm sorry. That's an expression people say in the future. It means you must have a terrible opinion of me, showing up alone and unable to prove where I came from."

He considered saying something to put her at ease. Instead he said, "Can you prove it now?"

She looked nervous. His heart softened.

"I didn't lie when I said my guardian brought me here."

Curious, he asked, "Do you have a guardian because you have no family?"

She shook her head. "Like you, I'm an only child. My parents died when I was four, so my grandparents raised me."

"Did you travel to England with them?"

"No. They're not alive right now, either."

"So you're alone in the world?"

"I'm afraid so. My grandparents haven't been born yet. But I have my guardian."

Clay hiked a skeptical brow. "Who appears to be absent at the moment."

"Because he's an angel... a guardian angel. And most of the time he's invisible."

Disappointment flashed through Clay. Anger followed. He battled to remain calm. His chest heaved with the effort. He couldn't fathom why she fabricated such fripperish tales.

"He wants me to help you save the earldom," she repeated.

"How in the blazes can a mere chit of a girl help save an earldom?"

"By myself I probably can't do anything, but with Rey's help, anything's possible."

"Who the devil is Rey?"

"My guardian angel." She grinned impishly. "And I doubt he has anything to do with the devil."

Clay decided not to argue that at the moment. "Have you any place to stay Miss Rose, or are you homeless?" She looked unsure of herself. Once more his heart softened. He wanted to believe her fabrications because he didn't wish to believe her fit for Bedlam. Why? He hardly knew her and shouldn't care. But he did.

Kacy took a deep breath. This didn't auger well. Last night she'd been full of optimism. Now she felt inept. Ill equipped to deal with the earl or the attraction she felt. She moistened her dry lips with the tip of her tongue and saw Thorne draw in a sharp breath. Unfortunately, she couldn't discern any of his thoughts today.

"My home is—it's a long way off. In time and distance."

Thorne unfolded his arms, and leaned his hip against a corner of his mahogany desk. "How far?"

"About a hundred and fifty years from now." She watched him make the mental calculations. A wave of hopelessness floated through her when he scowled. Fingering her scar, she said, "I had an accident in the twenty-first century and my life there has apparently been put on hold. Rey's attempting to return me but until that's arranged, he wants me here."

"What kind of accident did you have?"

"I th-think," she stammered, "it may be difficult to make you understand."

"Why?"

"Because I got hit by a speeding taxi, which is a car and you don't know what a car is," she blurted. "They haven't been invented yet."

Thorne furrowed his brows. "Your imagination invented them, along with guardian angels. Do you fabricate tales in an attempt to confuse me? Or is your upper story unhinged?"

Kacy shook her head. More locks of hair escaped their grips. She ignored them, although they made her feel awkward and ill at ease. "I'm not fabricating and I'm not nuts."

He hiked a puzzled brow. "Nuts?"

"Crazy. Unbalanced. Unhinged. Whatever. And please listen. I can explain. Around the beginning of the next century cars will replace horse drawn carriages. They'll have four small rubber tires with air pumped inside rather than large wooden wheels with spokes, which will make for smoother, more comfortable rides. Motorized engines will eliminate the need for horses and steering wheels will guide cars on paved roads or divided highways. Fast roads are called freeways in the United States and motorways over here. Gasoline, or petrol as the Brits call it, will provide the necessary fuel and cars or automobiles, as they're also called, travel at speeds so fast people can drive hundreds of miles in a day. I'm not much of an artist but I could draw a rough sketch if you'd like."

"Do not do me any favors." Clay tried to act bored, but her ability to describe something so unusual fascinated him. *What other tales was she capable of spinning?* "I suppose there are other marvelous inventions which exist in this future of yours."

"Oh yes!"

Words he'd never heard rolled off her glib tongue. "Electricity and indoor plumbing."

He flattened his lips to a grim line as she continued. "Central heating and air-conditioning in homes, office towers and movie theaters."

While he attempted to understand what that meant, she added, "Radios, telephones, movies, televisions, automatic washing

machines and clothes dryers, dishwashers, computers, electronic games, satellites that orbit the earth and space stations. Even shuttles soar through the universe to explore. And airplanes. They're more remarkable than cars. Like huge birds, they fly through the sky, operated by a single pilot and carrying hundreds of passengers. Most people fly across the Atlantic instead of traveling by boat or ship. There are so many wonderful things in the future I can't even begin to name them all!" She
paused, stepped forward and touched his arm.

A charge of energy whipped up to his shoulder.

"I know you don't believe a word I've said, Lord Banes, but I'd like to take you there. Not only to prove I'm not lying, but also to show you things you'd consider miracles. I'd adore seeing your reaction to them. And I'd love to have Jennifer, my best friend, see you. We both believe in reincarnation and I'm convinced I knew you in another life. That's why my guardian angel and fairy godmother brought me here."

A fairy godmother? Clay frowned, opened his mouth to speak, then snapped it shut again. Only a blithering idiot would believe such gibberish. He cleared his throat. "You're right. I don't believe you." Torn between the urge to snatch her close and ravish her, and the opposing desire to turn her over his knee for manufacturing such blatant lies, he held himself in check.

She squeezed his arm ever so gently. "I have proof that I'm from the future."

He hiked a disbelieving brow. "Do you?"

Nodding, she held up her pink umbrella that he'd plunked beside the clothes tree yesterday when he'd been unable to return it.

"All of the materials used to make this won't be invented until the next century. I think iron's the most common metal in existence right now, but this frame is a blend of metals. Much softer than crude iron and soft enough for somebody to bend with their bare hands. And the fabric's synthetic, the handle plastic. Some of those words haven't even been heard of yet."

Ignoring the fact that he'd wondered about her brolly himself, he stared at her hand on his arm. "Your umbrella may be a prop a magician uses to earn his keep."

"I also have the clothes I wore before I came here."

"Which prove nothing," Clay maintained.

She looked startled. Disappointed. "Don't you want to see them?"

He shook his head, unwilling to watch her expose herself as a fraud and a liar.

Her shoulders slumped. Now she looked defeated.

"If you can't believe I came from the future, then you probably won't believe we knew each other in different lifetimes either."

"That's correct." He stared again at her hand still curled around his arm.

As though just realizing she'd put it there, she let go and offered an apology. "Forgive me, please. I suppose in this century, that's considered a *faux pas*." But rather than looking embarrassed, she held her head high, as though daring him to criticize her.

Instead, Clay asked the question he had avoided too long. "Did my deceased uncle's solicitors send you to spy on me?"

He saw her hurt. It was immediate. And he had his answer. Relief poured through him.

Before he could apologize, Kacy turned and murmured, "Take me away, Rey. Please. I can't bear to be here any longer."

Clay started to reach for her. But right before his eyes she vanished— as though snatched by an invisible giant hand.

Unable to believe what he'd seen, he blinked, then blinked again before he dashed to the door, yanked it open and stared up and down the corridor. He didn't see her, but he saw her trunk on the floor. A swirl of silver mist began to surround it, gathering momentum as it grew. The trunk changed colors—from pitch black to startling pink. Then it lifted magically off the floor and spun in the air, before it too, disappeared, along with the swirling silvery mist storm.

Servants cleaning the corridor screamed and shrieked. Some covered their eyes; others fell on the floor. Clay left them to deal with their fright and raced up two flights of stairs. He didn't find Kacy in the blue room, but her pink trunk sat near a corner by the new blue dressing screen. He raked his hand through his hair and vowed that when she returned, he'd discover what trick she had used to whisk herself and the trunk away.

And he fully expected her to return. Unless she hadn't left and had merely hidden.

With that suspicion, Clay ordered a search of the entire mansion, including the stables. Servants abandoned their cleaning posts and joined grooms and stable lads who rushed about, frantically searching for Miss Rose. Their eagerness to please impressed Clay. But how long would it take them to spread the tale of the flying trunk? He made no attempt to squelch it. If they didn't have that to gossip about, they'd find something else. At least they were diligent in their search.

But in spite of all the effort put forth, no one found Kacy.

Thinking she might have gone to the inn, Clay ordered a lad to saddle Blade and galloped there. Perhaps if he accepted her offer to teach his servants to clean his home, she wouldn't disappear or use magic again. Perhaps if she spent all her time with the servants, he wouldn't be tempted to kiss or ravish her. And perhaps horses would fly—like the airplanes she had described.

At the inn John announced, "I havena seen Miss Rose. I havena seen any ladies by 'umselves today."

Perplexed, Clay remounted Blade. During the ride home, he did his best to clear his head of the strange, worrisome notions presented by the eloquent Miss Kacy Rose and her talk of the future.

Back home, he discovered she still hadn't been found. He instructed Montfort to notify him if she returned, then closeted himself in his study to deal with correspondence, foreign business affairs and pour through ledgers.

Before the evening meal, Clay poured himself a
brandy from a crystal decanter on a silver tray behind his desk. *When would Kacy return?* And when had he begun to think of her as Kacy rather than Miss Rose? He sipped his brandy. No answers surfaced, but he knew intuitively that her lush body would match well with his.

How he knew that was as much a mystery as her unexpected arrival yesterday and his demmed attraction that grew stronger with each encounter.

Relaxed by the brandy, he held the crystal snifter up by the light and twirled it. The swirling pale amber reminded him of Kacy's golden hair. The sparkling crystal reminded him of the twinkle in her eyes and the diamonds she'd worn yesterday. Now that he believed she hadn't been sent by the solicitors, he felt obligated to take care of her. Because she'd spent the night under his roof without a chaperon, her reputation had been compromised. He felt responsible and lazily considered viable solutions.

There seemed to be only one. Marriage. But he'd be out of his mind to consider that. Twice before he had proposed. Both offers had been spurned.

Six

Evening of The Second Day

Alone in the dining room, Clay scooped what remained of the unpalatable evening meal into an old scrap of linen, then strolled outside and deposited it on the rubbish heap by the compost pit. The unpleasant odors of putrefied waste hastened his retreat. He disliked wasting food, but hated to injure Cook Edna Mae's feelings by leaving it uneaten on his plate.

It had occurred to him that his uncle's will didn't restrict his tenants from hunting game, nor did it bar Clay from providing rifles and teaching them to shoot. But first he must convince them the woods weren't haunted. Deciding to discuss that problem with Bardsy, he hurried to the stable. Neither groom nor stable lad could be found. While he puzzled that, he realized with the exception of Cook Edna Mae and the serving maid, Ellen, he hadn't seen any servants in the mansion either. Perplexed, he saddled Blade himself.

To his amazement, lights twinkled through the trees as he approached Bardsy's cottage and he heard singing. Curious, he dismounted, walked to the edge of the woods and stood transfixed. Tenants, servants, stable lads and grooms were all gathered in a circle. Moderator lamps revealed happy faces, not the somber ones he usually saw. A few men played musical instruments Clay didn't know they owned, while parents and children sang songs Clay hadn't heard since he was a lad.

Astonishment kept his feet rooted when the singing ended. Dressed in a forest green gown, covered by her gray hooded cape, Kacy stood in the midst of the crowd. Relief flooded through him. While he battled with his attraction, she organized the children around a fire pit, urged them to sit on mended bed covers and proceeded to tell stories. Still concealed, Clay listened to the most animated tales he'd ever heard of:

Jack and the Beanstalk, Cinderella, and *The Three Bears.*

Afterwards he remained concealed while parents collected their children. All thanked Kacy for the feast and accepted new kettles of leftovers and bundles of clothing along with moderator lamps to see their way home.

When Kacy and Bardsy were alone, Clay heard her say, "My guardian's in the woods with my mare waiting to take me to my lodgings."

"Good eventide then, Miss Rose."

As soon as Bardsy closed his door, Clay stepped from his hiding place, blocking Kacy's path.

She gasped as their eyes locked and emotions clashed between them. "Thorne!" Guilt shimmered in her eyes. "I didn't ex—"

"What are you doing?" he growled, displeased with the desire she inspired, yet oddly amused by the nickname.

"Getting to know your tenants and servants."

"With whose permission?"

"Our guardian angel's."

"Ours?"

She nodded.

Flooded with disbelief and nearly consumed by the need to haul her off and make love, Clay's mood turned foul. He intended to keep it that way lest he embarrass himself and further compromise her.

Kacy drew in a deep breath. She hadn't expected Thorne to come to Bardsy's cottage tonight. Had he missed the servants, stable lads and grooms? Maybe she shouldn't have invited them, but it seemed a shame to exclude them when she knew Rey would provide plenty of food. Still, unable to read Thorne's mind, she had no idea how long he'd been there or how much he'd seen and heard. But she knew he didn't trust her. And that stung. Uncomfortable she said, "You needn't worry about providing food for your tenants."

"How can you make such an outrageous claim?"

"Rey has and will continue to fill Bardsy's coffers."

Although Thorne looked stunned he said, "I did not grant permission for you to entertain my minions."

"They aren't slaves. And you have no right to dictate who they spend time with."

"You trespass upon my property," he reminded with such pomposity Kacy stiffened her spine. "In future I expect you to consult me about matters relating to my minions."

Gathering her dignity around her like a protective cloak, Kacy summoned all the poise she could muster. "With or without your cooperation, the earldom will thrive, Lord Banes. And since you're too ill-bred to thank me for attempting to help, I'll take my leave."

With that, she spun around and marched into the woods, where she wished herself far away from the obnoxious, handsome earl. To her relief, Rey transported her to a beautiful, dry forest glade, complete with a huge pink and white striped tent. Inside a canopied bed hosted a soft feather tic mattress with mounds of fluffy goose down duvets and pillows.

Delighted, Kacy grinned as she burrowed under the covers, fully clothed. "Thanks, Rey, this is great. I love camping."

"I know you do."

"And thanks for keeping the rain away from the fields so the tenant's could plow today."

"There is no need to thank me."

"Is Fey still with her own kind?"

"Yes."

"Will I see her again?"

"Presumably."

Rey had always reminded Kacy of a jolly, happy-go-lucky leprechaun, but instead of wearing green, he always wore a three-piece white suit. Posed at a jaunty angle on top of a table by the tent flap, he added, "Sleep well, dear one."

~ * ~

Ill-bred? Furious at the slur on his rearing, Clay blinked, too shocked to follow when Kacy stomped away. What manner of rearing gave her the right to criticize him, a Peer of the Realm? When he finally gained control over his temper, he charged after her, further agitated when he couldn't find her. As before, she'd disappeared. For future equanimity, he decided, rules must be laid down and Kacy must agree to stop disappearing.

Clay mounted Blade. The clouds released a gentle, misty rain. As he galloped through the woods, he passed servants, stable lads and grooms. It was foolish for them to be on foot when they could have used his carriages. They were seldom used and the horses needed exercise. He knew a number of people in London and Paris wouldn't have agreed, but he didn't consider any of them as friends. No man who treated those less fortunate than himself with scorn and disdain numbered among Clay's friends.

When he arrived home, Clay rushed up to the blue room only to find it empty except for Kacy's trunk.

Down in the master suite, the long night stretched before him. He climbed in bed, got out, put a robe on and sat in his rock-hard chair, then repeated the process. Around midnight he decided if Kacy returned, it would be to the blue room so he dressed and went there to continue his sleepless vigil.

~ * ~

The two-inch sprite appeared before dawn began to streak the sky. Her brilliant glow might have blinded Clay had she not been so small. Not quite sure he believed his eyes, he rubbed them before he demanded, "Who the blazes are you?"

"Who do I look like?" the sprite returned.

"Like no one I have ever seen before." He stroked the rough stubble on his jaw, wondering if he might be dreaming or hallucinating. "What are you?"

The wee sprite surprised him by replying with a loud disgruntled snort. "A fairy godmother."

"Whose?"

Her dazzling white, silver-tipped wings shimmered behind her tiny shoulders as she placed her hands on her minuscule waist and sprang up on the tips of her tiny toes. "Whose do you think?"

When he didn't answer, the fairy molded her features in disgust, dropping back down on the soles of her tiny, green-satin slippered feet. "Kacy's," she said in a haughty tone which far surpassed Kacy's toplofty proficiency. "However, I may help you, if I deem you worthy."

Turning her back to him, she stretched her arm and produced a wand. From where he couldn't imagine. The wand was five times longer than she was tall. She waved the wand at the pink trunk. The lid opened and gowns magically lifted themselves into the air. The fairy flew close, inspecting each gown and unmentionable that floated in the air. Apparently satisfied, she flicked her wand at the clothes, which refolded and repacked themselves inside the trunk.

Then she shook herself and grew *and grew* until she was human size. With a flick of her enlarged wand, the trunk flew across the room, dropping between the blue tufted footstool where Clay had propped his black-booted feet and the window.

He watched the entire proceeding and blinked time and again. Finally he pinched himself to determine whether he was awake before he said, "I consider Kacy's possessions to be under my protection."

"Ha," the fairy snorted again. "Do you value her possessions more than you value her?"

"Certainly not!" he bellowed, incensed by the accusatory tone.

"Kacy had nothing to do with moving her trunk up here yesterday. My magic was responsible. But she'll need her things come morning. And by the by, I removed the memory of the trunk's disappearance from the minds of the servants who saw it, so you
needn't worry that they'll spread ghostly tales."

The fairy waved her wand again. The trunk raised, landing softly on her slender shoulder. She sprang to the window, with the precariously wobbling trunk before she turned, "You have behaved as an ungrateful wretch. Kacy came to help you, but you hadn't the proper sense to realize your good fortune."

"Where is she?"

The fairy godmother fluttered her silver-fringed life-size wings, her pixie-face drawn up in a frown. "She spent the night in your woods and if any harm befalls her, I shall hold you personally responsible." The trunk wobbled again as the fairy leaped through the open window, rattling the clean panes of glass before she flew off with the swaying trunk in tow.

Clay charged down the stairs. He didn't even consider changing clothes or shaving. Out in the stable he awakened a lad and instructed him to saddle Blade. But the sleepy lad moved so slowly, Clay ordered him back to bed and completed the task himself.

Although the misty rain had ceased and the dark sky was clear, the meager moonlight failed to penetrate the wide branches of evergreen and newly budding oak trees. Clay searched methodically, but he didn't find Kacy. His frustration mounted to heights heretofore unknown before he saw an incandescent glow in the distance and nudged Blade toward it. Not wanting to startle Kacy if she was responsible for the light, he dismounted, looped Blade's reins around a bush and approached on foot.

Seven

Morning of The Third Day

Kacy awakened before dawn. A candle glowed on the table by the tent flap and she saw Rey on a wooden chair beside her bed. A potbellied stove, with a fat stovepipe that stretched up through the center of the striped ceiling, kept the huge tent warm. She smiled at Rey. He signaled not to speak by placing a finger at his mouth.

She heard voices outside and mouthed a question. "Do you know who is out there?'"

Rey conveyed a silent answer. "Miscreants who spent the night thieving."

The voices grew louder. "Let's have a look inside," one of the gruff voices said.

She mouthed another question. "What shall I do, Rey?"

"Stay where you are."

A motley crew of three entered the big tent. Each scruffy character carried a bag that Kacy suspected held their loot.

"This be 'ur lucky night," one man said, his eyes taking on an evil gleam as he stared at Kacy.

"A pretty gel ripe for pluckin'," a second man said.

A third man pointed at Rey. "Wot we gonna do 'bout 'im?"

"I'll teke care 'a 'im," the evil-eyed man boasted, setting his bag down.

"You should give up your thieving ways," Rey said in a calm, benign tone.

All three mangy men laughed. "Who be ye ta tell us wot' we oughta do?"

When Rey didn't reply, Kacy did. "He's an angel. My guardian angel."

"Ye don' say." Raucous laughter filled the tent. As it died down, one man leaped forward. Rey raised his hand. The man came to an abrupt halt, as though he'd run into an invisible wall. He straightened, plowed forward, only to encounter the barrier again. This time it knocked him down. On the canvas covered ground, he held his head and yelped.

The other two bums dropped their bags and raced forward. They met the same fate. As they lolled on the canvas floor, they moaned, holding their heads. "Wot 'appened?"

"I dunna see nothing. What'd we hit?"

"Tis a force to shield good from bad," Rey told Kacy.

The men looked baffled and she felt like she'd been stuck in the middle of a Star Trek adventure.

Without warning the tent flap opened again. Thorne stepped inside. In one swift glance, he took in the scene, then asked, "Are you all right, Miss Rose?"

Still in bed, half under the covers, she nodded.

"How did you manage to subdue them?" Thorne asked.

"I didn't. Rey did." She realized Rey had made himself invisible as a coiled rope miraculously appeared on a chair beside Thorne.

Clay blinked. "Where is he?"

One chap on the floor said, "Wot 'append ta the gov'ner?"

"Disappeared," another said, fear in his eyes and voice.

"He be dressed all in white and he knocked us down wiffout touching us," one chap told Clay.

"Mayhap he be a ghost. I 'eard these woods be 'aunted."

Scowling, Clay demanded, "What mischief are you about?"

"I think they spent the night robbing your neighbors," Kacy said. "You might want to look inside those bags."

"I'll tie them up first." He seized the rope off the chair. After he bound the three together, he secured one end to his waist, then emptied the bags on the table beside a burning candle.

"I believe most all of this belongs to the Marquis of Rotherhile," Clay said as he examined the assortment of silver and jewels. "I shall escort the thieves to the village and give their loot to the constable." He repacked the bags. "I want you to go
with me, Miss Rose."

"You don't need me to tag along," she said. "I'll probably slow you down."

"You cannot stay here alone and unprotected."

"I won't be alone. Rey's here and has been all night." She folded her arms across her chest.

Clay slung the bags over his shoulder. He didn't want to leave Kacy, but from the determined set of her chin, he suspected she might argue till midday. That peculiar sense of familiarity returned. Why did he feel he knew her so well? That he could sometimes determine her thoughts? "Are you absolutely certain you will be all right?"

Kacy nodded.

He nudged the thieves to their feet. "I shall return in the shortest possible time. Do not stray. We have things to discuss." He tightened the slack in the rope and hustled his captives outside.

Rey reappeared as soon as they left. A few minutes later Kacy heard another noise outside. Beginning to feel spooked, she asked, "What's that?"

"Tis a young lady who ran away from home to protect her virtue."

Kacy mouthed another question. "Should I invite her in?"

"I shall bring the young miss inside. Her name is Catharine Paice."

Before Kacy could blink, the girl stood beside the potbelly stove. A dark green shawl covered her head
and a damp gray cloak hung from her shoulders.

As she gasped in shock, Rey said, "Fear not. I'm a guardian angel.

This is my charge, Kathryn Cassandra Rose. We shall not harm you. We wish to help and befriend."

Catharine's startled gaze darted from Rey to Kacy, who felt as though she was staring at her own reflection in a mirror. The only difference between them was the scar on her own cheek. Her look-alike didn't have one. And Kacy envied her smooth, flawless cheeks.

Without mumbling a word, Catharine blinked, then promptly fainted.

Kacy scrambled out of bed, lurched across the tent and knelt on the canvas floor at Catharine's side. "She must have fainted from the shock of being zapped inside the tent."

"Also from hunger," Rey said. "As well as seeing you."

In an attempt to revive her, Kacy rubbed her cold, clammy hands. "Can't you do something, Rey?"

"She needs rest," he calmly advised. "Except for forty winks now and then, she hasn't slept for nigh on a week."

"Could you provide dry clothes for her?"

"Certainly." Without so much as a blink, Rey did. Then he transferred her from the canvas floor to the fluffy bed with no more than a nod of his head.

Cupping his bearded chin between his thumb and forefinger, as though deep in thought, he said, "We must concentrate on helping the earl and your return to health. I shall summon someone to help Catharine. Can you cope whilst I'm gone?"

"Sure," Kacy said.

"You may wish to know that Catharine knew of your existence some time ago."

Kacy's heart thumped so hard all she could manage was a one word question. "How?"

"She has dreamed of you for years."

Rey left and Kacy paced the floor. It looked as though she'd lack for nothing. Rey had provided all the comforts of home. And now that she'd met servants, tenants and Catharine, this adventure might turn out better than she had dared to imagine. When... if she returned to her own time, she'd have great fun telling Jennifer about Thorne, the glimpse of another life, being the hostess of an old-fashioned outdoor feast, camping in a tent big enough to house a circus, and meeting her own clone.

As she turned back toward the bed, she spied a pink trunk. And blinked. It looked like the trunk Rey had provided except it wasn't black. It was pink. Bright pink. On top lay a folded royal-blue garment. Thinking it a dress, Kacy picked it up then decided it must be a riding habit when she saw the divided skirt.

Inside the trunk she saw the gowns that had somehow been hung in the wardrobe at Havenhurst while she slept. This must be the same trunk. *But who turned it pink and why? Because pink was her favorite color?*

After she repacked the clothes, she glanced at Catharine, still asleep or in a faint. As light began to filter through the pink and white tent stripes, Kacy decided to change from the wrinkled gown she'd slept in to the new blue riding habit. Thank goodness Rey didn't think it necessary for her to wear the restrictive corsets she'd read about. She didn't even know how to put one on.

As she finished changing,Catharine stirred and opened her frightened blue eyes.

"We have each other's faces," she rasped.

"We're mirror images," Kacy agreed, "except for my scar."

Catharine sniffled as she sat up. Realizing she had a cold, Kacy rummaged in her reticule and found a hanky.

With a timid smile, Catharine accepted and used it before she said, "Which do you prefer to be called? Kathryn or Cassandra?"

"Neither. Everybody calls me Kacy. For my initials."

"Kacy. I like it." Catharine smiled.

"Thanks. So do I."

Catharine cleared her throat. "Why are you in the woods?"

"I had no place to sleep so Rey provided this tent."

"You are fortunate to have a guardian angel."

"I agree. He went to summon someone to help you."

A hopeful expression replaced Catharine's bleak, worried one. "That would be the most wonderful thing that has ever happened to me, along with meeting you at last."

"How long have you dreamed about me?"

"Most of my life. Always I thought if we were to meet, my life would improve. Why do you suppose I felt that way?"

"I haven't a clue," Kacy said and admitted, "Rey told me you ran away to protect your virtue."

Catharine nodded, then coughed and covered her mouth with the hanky until she stopped. "My stepfather betrothed me to a man old enough to be my grandfather because he… Wilbur wishes to bed me. Thus far, Mother and I have contrived to thwart him. However, if I marry an old man too feeble to stop him, Wilbur may try to have his way with me whenever he chooses to visit."

"That's awful!" Kacy sympathized.

"Yes, 'tis," Catharine said. "He mustn't find me. He's evil. And I shan't go back. I should rather die."

"He won't find you," Kacy said without knowing how she dared make such a promise.

"I am terribly afraid he might." Catharine's shudder made it clear that just talking about her stepfather filled her with dread.

Kacy reached for her shaking hands. "Don't let your bravery desert you now." The next thing she said startled her as much as it apparently did Catharine. "I think you're on the brink of discovering a whole new world."

"Truly?" Catharine's question quivered with doubt.

Kacy nodded, squeezing Catharine's hands. "I wish I could heal your cold."

"My throat feels much better and…" her eyes widened in disbelief. "I believe you have healed me, Kacy."

Rey reappeared before Kacy could comment. The red rawness at the tip of Catharine's nose was gone and her face no longer looked flushed and feverish. Even her voice sounded better. Had Rey heard her wish and healed Catharine?

Kacy's energy had taken a sudden nose-dive, but she shelved her questions as Rey folded his arms across his stocky chest. With his white hair tousled in comical spikes and his pure white, double-breasted suit rumpled, he looked like he'd traveled a great distance in a hurry.

"Unfortunately no one is available to help you at the moment, Catharine. However," he continued as tears glistened in her blue eyes, "Fear not. I shall."

He glanced at Kacy. "She needs bed rest."

"Lie down, Catharine," Kacy urged. Then to Rey she said, "She probably needs something to eat and
drink, too."

"What would you like? Hot chocolate perhaps? Or tea?"

"Hot chocolate sounds wonderful. It would truly be a treat."

A tray with two cups of hot chocolate topped with dollops of whipped cream and a platter of fresh scones with butter, red jelly and clotted cream materialized on the small table by the bed.

"Have I died and gone to heaven?" Catharine asked.

Rey shook his head. A lock of white hair fell over his brow. He shoved it aside as he said, "After you rest, Catharine, I shall accompany you to Europe so that you may check into your stepfather's bigamous background."

Catharine looked bewildered. "Wilbur is a bigamist?"

Rey nodded. "Eat your scones and drink your chocolate. Both of you."

Eight

Patches of sunlight spilled through tree branches when Clay returned to the woods. Shadows danced across the gigantic pink and white tent that rose from the forest floor like a huge monolith. He couldn't imagine how Kacy had managed to erect a tent. But then, he didn't know how she'd subdued the miscreants either. Perhaps the fairy had helped, then taken on the appearance of the man described by the thieves. Although Clay had seen the fairy change from a two-inch sprite to human size, he still didn't want to believe in the existence of fairies.

At the tent entrance, he reached for the flap.

"I wouldn't do that if I were you," Kacy said behind him. "Unless you wish to be embarrassed."

He spun around. She sat on a log beside the clear bubbly brook. With her long blond hair unbound and floating around her shoulders, she looked beautiful and desirable. He had to force himself to speak. "Why might I be embarrassed?"

"Because someone's sleeping in there."

"Who?"

"I don't think I should tell you."

"Why the devil not?"

"I don't know if you can be trusted."

Clay knew he deserved that, but he didn't like the truth one whit. He let his gaze roam over Kacy. The snug blue riding costume sent a surge of desire raging through him. In an effort to tame the hunger he said, "I expected you to return to the mansion last evening. You left your trunk in the blue room."

He expected her to say the fairy had brought it here. Instead, she said, "You don't want me in your home."

"In that you are mistaken. I apologize for suggesting you might be in cahoots with the solicitors."

"What makes you think I'm not?"

"The look in your eyes when I asked if they sent you." Pleased by the surprise he saw then, Clay walked closer. Feeling more light-hearted than he'd felt in years, he bent to hunker before her. When she inhaled and let her breath out slowly, he knew his nearness affected her, just as hers affected him.

"I regret you felt it necessary to sleep in the woods." He had no intention of allowing her to sleep here again. There was no telling who might wander through and try to harm her. "You may stay in my home, such as it is, for as long as you wish."

Kacy thought his mood much improved, but she expected no miracles where he was concerned. Careful to keep her tone neutral, she said, "Thanks, but I like it fine right here."

"You cannot stay here alone and unprotected."

"I won't. My guardian angel will be with me."

Thorne aimed a dubious eyebrow at the tent. "I did not realize angels required sleep."

Deciding not to admit Rey wasn't there right now, or explain Catharine and her need for rest, Kacy asked, "Are you hungry?"

"What fare are you offering to share?"

She feigned nonchalance, motioning at a table beside the tent. Set with a pink linen tablecloth and napkins, gold-trimmed dinnerware, crystal and sterling silver, the table looked fit for the Queen. Two cups of steaming hot chocolate and platters of toast, eggs, sausages, steamed tomatoes, and out-of-season fruit tempted the appetite.

Thorne glanced back at her. "Who cooked it?"

"Our guardian angel, Rey, provided it, just as he provided the feast last night and the food in your bailiff's coffers."

Thorne arched a brow. "You actually expect me to believe an angel has been filling Bardsy's coffers?"

"Yes. However, Bardsy thinks I provided it. Rey said that's better than trying to explain him or creating problems for you with the solicitors." Then she decided to prepare him for what he would soon learn and added, "Tilling began yesterday. Soon your fields will be ready to sow."

Instead of looking mad as she expected, he said, "Where do my tenants intend to obtain seed, my
dear?"

My dear. A volley of unexpected thrills waltzed through her. Breathless she whispered, "From you."

His stare turned fierce. "How am I to pay for seed?"

"I understand the fifty pounds you're allotted hasn't been exhausted."

He glowered, but his tone remained mild. "If I spend that, how will I feed my minions during the remainder of the year?"

Kacy considered telling him she had given Bardsy the diamonds for an emergency, but decided that might raise more suspicions. "I told you. Rey will provide food for them."

Thorne wrinkled his forehead. "If seed is sown and washed out by rain..."

"I have it on the best authority that this will be a semi-dry year."

He stared at her mouth. Kacy raised her fingers to her scar and glanced away. All during high school and college she'd fended off unwanted advances but she hadn't expected to face that here. What would she do if Thorne actually made a pass at her? She drew in a quick breath. And dropped her hand to her lap.

A grin tugged at the corners of Thorne's generous mouth as he stretched out a hand and gently cupped her cheek. His touch unnerved her. Certain that being attracted to him would only lead to folly, she asked, "What would you like to eat?"

His green eyes smoldered. "I hunger not for food."

He leaned close and claimed her lips with his. When she opened her mouth to protest, his tongue slipped inside and his arms closed around her. Sensations, sweeter than honey, sluiced through her. She'd been kissed before, but never like this and no power on earth was strong enough to stop her from responding. Her arms wound around him. He deepened the kiss. A new, untamed wildness surged through her as he tasted, staked, claimed and mated his tongue with hers in a ritualistic pagan sort of dance. The kiss tasted familiar, yet new. And so delicious!

Never in recent memory had she experienced anything so sensual, so wonderful, and so sublime! Still, the kiss, his touch and spicy masculine scent seemed as well known as her own name. In her current life she'd never wanted a kiss to go on and on. She felt deprived when this one ended.

Thorne's emerald eyes, fringed with long black lashes, filled with a combination of curiosity and pleasure as they stared. He was the most intriguing man she'd ever encountered. The silent admission made her blush.

Wow! What a reunion, she thought, as another glimpse from a previous life flashed and she saw them kissing in the woods. She knew by the unusual clothes they wore that the glimpse was of a time different from the other she'd seen. And she knew now what she had tried to deny. She loved him still. That's why he haunted her dreams.

"I should have kissed you more often."

With her heart beating triple time, Kacy disagreed in a desperate whisper. "You shouldn't have kissed me at all."

"Why the devil not?"

Unable to tear her eyes from his or make her voice work properly, she croaked, "That's not why I'm here."

He grinned, but said nothing.

"Don't look so smug, Lord Banes." She tried to look stern.

He wrinkled his forehead in mock horror. "Your words wound me, my lady."

"Well, your kiss wounded me," she fired back.

"The bloody hell it did!"

"So don't do it again," she warned, and swallowed to moisten her dry throat. "I'm sure our guardian wouldn't approve."

A smile like a conspirator's blazed in his green eyes. "Perhaps we shouldn't tell her."

"We won't have to. *He* may be watching us."

"Then let's give *her* something to see," Thorne suggested and with a wicked gleam, drew Kacy back into his arms.

Before she could even think of resisting, he kissed her again. Thoroughly. She felt like a forest fire had ignited inside her and started burning out of control. Unable to stop herself, she wrapped her arms around him and kissed him back with more passion than she knew she possessed.

In one fluid motion Thorne rolled from his knees to sit on the ground, pulling her onto his lap. Passion hurtled through her. She could only marvel, because his kisses surpassed everything she had ever experienced. Not even the journey through the time tunnel had prepared her for such pure magic.

An eternity later, Thorne pulled his head away. "If you expect an apology," his voice sounded ragged, "you shall be disappointed, my lady."

In a stupor, Kacy saw him through dazed eyes. Although he held her firmly, his powerful arms were amazingly gentle. And his hands hadn't wandered to her chest to grope for her breasts. He was a true gentleman. She didn't think she'd ever met one before.

If he hadn't lifted her off his lap, she wouldn't have remembered to eat. But he shifted her back to the log while he stood, then reached down, took her hand and led her to the table where he pulled a chair out and waited for her to sit before he sat across from her.

Because she'd eaten a scone with Catharine, Kacy wasn't very hungry, but she ate to be sociable. Thorne cut and speared a piece of sausage and chewed with apparent relish. She sampled a morsel of egg, chewing slowly to make it last.

When they finished, a gleam simmered in his eyes. Goose bumps raised on her neck and arms as the slow simmer turned to a blistering stare. When he stood and started toward her, Kacy knew he intended to kiss her again. But as he reached for her, they heard a loud crashing noise in the woods. The clamor sounded like a herd of wild animals racing toward them. Before she knew what was happening, Thorne lifted her up into his arms and carried her to safety behind a sturdy oak.

With a tree to protect her on one side and his strong body on her other, she waited with baited breath for the noise heralding potential danger to arrive. She would have run inside the tent, but as in past lives, he preferred to face danger head-on.

Nine

The noise ceased abruptly. Kacy peeked around Thorne's broad shoulder. Near the table, where they had eaten, stood his beautiful sleek stallion, his coat as jet black as Thorne's hair, eyelashes and brows.

"You have nothing to fear," he soothed. "'Tis only Blade. Something must have disturbed him."

A ghost? Where had that thought come from?

As Thorne studied her face, Kacy realized her whole body had tensed. She tried to relax, but couldn't.

"I suppose you should put me down," she said.

"I suppose I should." But he made no move to do so.

Cradled in his strong arms with his breath fanning her forehead made breathing a chore. His spicy masculine scent attacked her senses. She couldn't tear her eyes from his. He seemed more familiar each time she saw him. Would he ever recognize her? Remember her from previous lives?

Blade whinnied, breaking the spell that held her in Thorne's thrall. He started to lower her to the ground. As her body slid down his, she reacted to the delicious feel and her heart pounded so loud she wondered if he could hear it. When Thorne released her and stepped away, she swayed. He reached out to steady her and captured her gaze again.

"Explain how you wish to help me."

His hands, warm on her shoulders, churned her nerves to the consistency of melted butter. She tried to smile and had to clear her throat. "I'd like you to approve Bardsy's instructions for your tenants to plant the fields. I'd also like permission to find other employment for your unneeded servants. And I'd like to clean and refurbish your home."

"Did you bring a fortune to accomplish the latter?"

"No. However, we have the use of yours."

Thorne cocked his head to one side. The gesture—familiar and achingly dear because she'd seen him do it in her dreams, as well as other lives—made her want to reach out and touch him. As they stared, she glimpsed yet another life. She was a Scottish lass; he an English knight. They met in Edinburgh and fell in love. When he proposed, her clan forbade their union. Heartbroken, she ran away to England a few weeks after he left, hoping to find him at his home. She arrived; travel weary and ill and his family took her in. But he had already gone off to fight for the king and he died in battle and never returned.

Thorne cleared his throat, jarring her thoughts back to the present. A lump of yearning welled up inside her as his warm, strong hands slid down her arms.

"Since you know my problems," he said, "presumably you are aware of the stipulations regarding my inheritance."

"That's correct."

"Then you know I may not use my wealth to put the earldom to rights."

"Your uncle's will stipulates you can't use your wealth, but I don't think it restricts you from giving money to somebody else, who can then use it for the good of the earldom."

Thorne looked startled. She thought he might be thinking her solution too rudimentary to work—until anger clouded his green eyes.

"I suspected you of being a number of things but an outright thief was not amongst them."

"I don't want your money for my sake," she defended, doing her best to salvage her injured pride.

"Do you not?" he demanded, his tone harsh, his expression angry.

She shook her head. His fierce stare didn't alter. He looked more intimidating than anybody she'd ever met. But she wasn't afraid. And she knew why, as another near blinding flash showed him racing toward her on a magnificent white stallion. Barely slowing his speed, he plucked her from the midst of a crowd about to sacrifice her to their pagan gods. But in that life, as in all the others, they never had a chance to fulfill their love.

Her emotions in a jumble, Kacy took a deep breath. "I know your hands are tied by your uncle's
will. But mine aren't. Let me help you."

Instead of replying, his scowl narrowed.

So she blundered on. "Your tenants and servants need more than a feeder; they need a leader."

"Are you suggesting I give them no direction?" His voice stung with outrage.

Had she gone too far? Probably. But no sense backing down now. "Your tenants were upset because you didn't instruct them to begin tilling and your servants shirk their duties because nobody directs them. Did they get up early this morning to clean? Or did you let them revert to their lazy habit and sleep late?"

Thorne continued to glare. In an attempt to retain her composure, Kacy folded her arms. *Was he different now than he'd been in other lives?* In another flash she saw his tenderness and fierce devotion after he'd rescued her from certain death and she decided an apology was in order. "I'm sorry if I sounded insulting. You've been ill-treated, but maybe it's time to do something different."

"Such as?" Thorne hiked his dark brows and tightened his hands on her shoulders.

"Challenge the solicitors. Or prove changes can be made within the restrictions of the outlandish will."

"Nothing can be changed," he said, his expression cold.

"I beg to differ."

"You have a lot of nerve," he gritted.

If she had any sense, she'd be quiet. But her good sense had deserted her. "Of course I do. A meek, gentle soul couldn't help you. She'd be too frightened and intimidated even to try."

His face lost none of its anger. "You want my wealth."

"No I don't. All I want is a little faith."

He frowned, his eyes looking perplexed. "Faith?"

"Yes."

"And if I refuse to give it?"

"Then I guess I should excuse you."

"Excuse me?" He looked surprised she hadn't coaxed him. She took advantage and eased away from his restraining hands before she cast a quick glance at the tent, hoping they hadn't disturbed Catharine. Then she turned toward the woods.

"Where are you going?" Thorne sounded mad—again. Kacy suspected his gaze was narrowed in suspicion, but she wouldn't give him the satisfaction of turning around to see it.

She whistled, expecting her mare to neigh in response or for Rey to return so she could depart from the earl, but she saw and heard nothing.

Thorne seized her arm again, turning her back to face him. His long fingers closed around both arms and his eyes, as they burned down into hers, held her immobile. She couldn't resist his magnetism. Too bad she didn't have the same effect on him. Just as in past lives she was deeply attracted to him.

Shaken by his nearness, she babbled, "I understood your wealth is so vast that the amount it would take to refurbish the mansion and mend your tenant's cottages would be considered exceedingly small."

"Perhaps you were misinformed. The cottages have fallen into such disrepair that a huge fortune spent on timber, wattle and whitewash could not bring them up to snuff."

"Well then, maybe I should ask Rey to perform some more miracles and repair them."

"There is no such thing as a miracle."

"Wanna bet?"

"I beg your pardon?"

Kacy knew by Thorne's puzzled expression that she had startled him again. "If miracles don't exist, why is that word part of the English language? And what about the food Rey puts in Bardsy's coffers? I call that a miracle. What do you call it?"

"You cannot expect me to believe everything you say."

Tired of trying to convince him, Kacy shrugged. "Believe whatever you wish. Men usually do."

"Is that an insult?"

"Interpret it any way you wish."

He rubbed her velvet-covered arms with his thumbs. Butterflies darted back and forth across her middle again. She told herself she couldn't afford to be attracted to him and tried to pull free, but he tightened his hold.

"Why do you say such strange things?"

"Why are so darn stubborn?"

"I am not stubborn. I am a very reasonable man."

"Then why don't you do something about the tenant's cottages and your mansion? If you hope to someday take a wife, you might consider her comfort. I can't imagine any woman consenting to wed you and living in that run-down, rat-infested monstrosity you call home."

That failed to elicit a comment, so she stumbled on, "In any event, with or without your cooperation, Rey will ensure that your tenants are not without food and decent clothing; also that your crops, this year and next, thrive. If you don't wish to assist or believe, perhaps you should go home and drown yourself in strong drink."

"I don't intend to let you out of my sight," he said with deliberate calm, but she doubted his anger had cooled.

She raised her chin a notch. "What did I do to earn your mistrust, Lord Banes?"

"What have you done to gain my trust?" he countered.

"I've spoken only the truth."

"And melted in my arms in an attempt to seduce me," he accused in a deceptively silky tone.

Kacy jerked one hand free and raised it to smack his handsome cheek, but at the last second she regretted her anger and softened the blow. Still smarting, she retorted, "I didn't initiate a single kiss and if you think I'll stand for your unwarranted accusations, I suggest you think again."

"Where are your diamonds? And who gave them to you? A lover perchance, a man you succeeded in seducing?"

She yanked her other hand free to slap his other cheek, but again regretted losing it and barely touched his face. "I reverse every worshipful thought I've had of you. You're as obtuse, despicable and overbearing as any man in my own time." Provoked beyond reason, she raised her finger and shook it with all the outrage of a violated maiden. "I wish I could get out of my vow to help you. I can't, but that doesn't mean I must suffer your company, too."

Then, mortified by his accusations and her own stupid behavior, she dashed into the woods and didn't stop until she ran out of breath.

"Upset you, did he?" Rey asked, sitting on the low branch of a huge oak tree a few feet away.

"I don't want to help him," she moaned.

"Of course you do," Rey consoled.

"And I don't want to be here. I want my life back. My grandparents need me. How long must I be in a coma?"

"I'm working on that question. However, you promised to help the earl and the powers that be took you at your word."

Her frustration devolved to hope. "You've com-municated with the other powers involved in this?"

"Why would you think otherwise, Kacy?"

Suddenly she felt heaps better. Amazed at her optimism she decided maybe she could do what was necessary without having to be near the handsome, conceited earl again. Even if she had loved him before, she didn't want to love him now. He didn't trust her and she didn't care. Well, maybe she cared a little bit, but she didn't want to be here. She wanted to go home. Nobody in her right mind would want to give up all the wonderful conveniences that existed in the twenty-first century.

Ten

The little vixen has a temper, Clay thought while he mounted Blade. Never had he known a lady who had the nerve to display one. Lord knew he'd never met anyone like Kacy Rose before. She amused him, claiming she came from the future and that her guardian angel—their guardian angel—kept Bardsy's coffers full. Both assertions were too ludicrous to believe. Clay couldn't doubt she had a fairy godmother, though, unless he doubted his own sanity. Perhaps she had confused the two.

As Blade cantered through the woods, Clay found himself smiling. His facial muscles twitched from disuse. Had Kacy truly entertained a notion that she worshiped him? His smile faded. Now she thought him rude, obtuse, overbearing and despicable.

Had he been wrong to imply she wanted his wealth? If she could camp out in an enormous tent, eat delicious food with china and silver and garb herself in fashionable clothes and diamonds, she likely didn't need his money.

He didn't want to accept blame for suggesting she had tried to seduce him, but he knew that accusation had been unjust. She'd done nothing to tempt him, although she had responded.

Women were fickle and couldn't be trusted. He had learned that the hard way, first from Oraline, then from Timothy's French mother. Oraline deceived then married for wealth and a title. Timothy's mother sold her son. Thinking about the English and French ladies created a bitter taste in Clay's mouth. Were American women different? Even if Kacy were, how could he believe she was virtuous when she returned his kisses like a wanton? And why did he want her regardless of the doubts and confusion she put him through?

He reined Blade to a stop when he saw Kacy in a one-sided conversation—as though communicating with the oak tree, or an invisible being. Why did he think that odd? Shouldn't he be accustomed to her strange behavior by now? He waited for a pause in her one-sided conversation before he asked, "Are you talking to that tree?"

She flicked her flashing blue eyes around to him. "No."

He thought it perverse to be pleased she looked upset, but he liked being responsible for the twin flames in her eyes. To further provoke her, he said, "I don't believe in ghosts."

"I'm not talking to a ghost," she gritted.

"And I don't see a sprite," he teased. "Unless you are one."

"I'm not," she grumbled.

"What are you?"

"At the moment I'm... not sure." Her lame reply seemed to replace her hostility. "Maybe I'm a spirit."

"A spirit," he repeated, his curiosity tweaked. When she slapped him, he had expected her hand to pack a wallop. Yet her slaps had been more like caresses than retribution for insults. And when he carried her to safety behind the oak, she felt as light as the two inch fairy he'd seen in the blue room before she grew to human size. *Was Kacy a fairy?* Perhaps related to the one he'd seen? Or was she that fairy herself? But how could he feel such an attraction if she weren't human?

Displeased with his thoughts, Clay straightened his posture in the saddle. He didn't want to believe in spirits, fairies, angels, ghosts or other non-temporal beings. When Kacy didn't speak, he knew he should apologize, but he couldn't find the right words.

"Would you like to share my horse?" he asked in what he considered his best conciliatory tone.

With him towering above her from the top of his black stallion, Kacy felt intimidated but she replied with composure. "No."

"Let him."

She jerked her head from Thorne and stared up at Rey, who had risen to the top of the tree when Thorne arrived.

"Let him?" she echoed dumbly.

Rey nodded. *"Ask him to take you to visit the tenants and spend the day encouraging them with their work."*

"I don't want to spend the day with the earl."

"Then ask him to take you to your mare."

"Where is my mare, Rey?"

"Where you left her last night; at the other end of the woods, near the bailiff's cottage."

"Couldn't you bring her closer?"

"Of course. But perhaps you should use this time to gain the earl's trust."

"I have no idea how to convince him to trust me. He accused me of lying, spying and trying to seduce him. I shudder to think what he might accuse me of next."

Rey floated down from the high branch and dangled in midair, his feet a good foot off the ground. *"You allowed him to kiss you."*

Kacy's face flamed. "You're on his side. That's why you brought me here, isn't it? You don't really care what happens to me. You only want what's best for the earl."

"That isn't true," Rey chided gently. *"And in your heart you know it. I want what is best for both of you."*

"I'm sorry." She hung her head in contrition. "I shouldn't have said that. But I'm afraid this bizarre adventure is real and that scares the heck out of me."

"This adventure is as real as your life in the twenty-first century, Kacy."

She swallowed, rubbing her scar with her fingers. When she realized that was a nervous habit, she gathered her long hair and started to braid it in a single, thick braid. "If you won't make yourself visible to him," she said while she braided, "will you do something to prove I'm not talking to myself, Rey?"

"Perhaps your fairy godmother would lift you up here," Thorne suggested, his brow hiked in challenge.

Torn between asking Rey to comply and maintaining her distance, Kacy didn't think to ask Thorne why he referred to Rey as her fairy godmother.

"The earl wants to believe you're not here to add to his problems," Rey announced as Kacy finished her long braid and tied the end with a blue ribbon she'd stuck in her pocket earlier.

"Can't I convince him some other way?"

Before Rey answered another voice said, "You may not convince him at all."

That statement came from the direction of the stallion's rear end. Kacy turned to stare. And there on the curve of Blade's black tail stood the tiny two-inch fairy.

"Fey!" Kacy said in hushed wonderment. "I've missed you and if you weren't so tiny, I'd hug you till it hurt."

Laughter bubbled from Fey. "In due time, sweetling. However, not whilst we have an audience."

"How marvelous!" Kacy grinned. "I'm delighted to have both my guardian angel and fairy godmother here."

Fey smiled before she spread her wings, flew around Thorne and hovered in front of his nose.

"I see you have diminished," he remarked dryly.

Amazed, Kacy asked, "You can see her?"

Thorne regarded her with the first amusement she'd seen in his emerald eyes. "I possess a number of faults. However, I am not blind."

In spite of her irritation with him, Kacy laughed.

"It's about time you showed up," Rey said to Fey, drawing Kacy's attention to the two of them.

Fey plopped down between Blade's ears and folded her wings before she turned a condescending smile upon Rey, who escalated off the ground to dangle opposite Fey, near Blade's head.

"I resent your attitude, Rey."

He crossed his chubby arms across his chest, prepared to stare Fey down. Kacy saw Thorne glance from Fey to the spot she faced. He looked as perplexed by their one-sided conversation as he'd been by hers with Rey.

Kacy duly noted that as in the past, Fey was the first to cast her eyes down from Rey's startling gaze. Apparently satisfied, he said, *"I should have known you had returned when I saw Kacy dressed in that snug fitting habit."*

Kacy stared down at her satin-lined, royal blue riding habit. "I thought you left this for me, Rey."

"I did not."

"A riding habit's more suitable for today's outing than a gown," Fey said. "And I'll give credit where credit is due. You do need help with the earl. A more stubborn human I've rarely encountered."

She aimed her tiny hands at Thorne's forehead and sailed up to hover in front of his face again. "I saw you kiss Kacy." Fey glanced at Kacy. Without giving her time to recover from her mortification, Fey said, "You owe her an apology, Lord Banes. She didn't attempt to seduce you, and we all know that."

"I apologize."

Kacy didn't have time to acknowledge his words before Fey asked, "Have you guessed that I spooked his stallion when he considered kissing you again, sweetling?"

Fey somersaulted through the air, releasing a giggle before she perched on Rey's shoulder, folded her tiny wings behind her shoulders again and tweaked Rey's ear.

"Behave," he ordered without so much as a flinch.

"Who's going to make me?" She batted her eyes.

"Stop it, you two," Kacy blurted in frustration. She could imagine what Fey's antics looked like to Thorne who could only see her. "Shouldn't I get on with my mission?"

"Yes, of course." Fey smiled at Kacy with all the pride of a human guardian and Kacy's irritation dissolved.

"Good. Now, perhaps one of you should comply with the earl's suggestion to lift me up to his horse or bring..."

Before she even finished speaking, she found herself sitting sideways in front of Thorne, between his arms, while he held Blade's reins. Instead of looking surprised when she glanced at him, Thorne asked, "What do we do now?"

"Rey thinks we should visit your tenants together."

"What do you think?"

"That you're not worthy of being helped by an angel, a fairy, or me," she said coolly. "However, I'm fond of your tenants and if seeing us together will speed their work, I'm willing to endure your presence if you're willing to endure mine."

"I am willing."

Kacy didn't like his response. It came too quick. "I do have one requirement."

"Name it."

A trickle of annoyance slid through her at his superior, condescending tone. "You must promise not to kiss me again. Or touch me either, unless it's absolutely necessary. If you don't, I won't spend anymore time with you."

"You have my promise," he said dryly. "However, you must realize that not touching you is an impossibility with you sitting between me and Blade's reins."

Kacy didn't comment. She merely turned her head.

To her, the chaotic ride resembled an act in a three ring circus as they made their way through the thick, dense woods with tiny Fey perched on Blade's head while human size Rey floated near Kacy's booted feet in a horizontal position.

In spite of her irritation with Thorne, she enjoyed the early morning shadows and fresh dewy smells. Silvery cobwebs, spun by busy spiders, were all the more visible due to the light, misty fog that shrouded the entire woods. Although she hated to admit it, she admired Thorne's ability to maneuver his great black stallion with little effort through the nearly impenetrable trees. She wondered why there wasn't a bridle path and had a silent answer conveyed from Rey.

During the last years of the old earl's life, he'd been unable to ride and hadn't allowed anyone else that pleasure either. *What an awful man he must have been!*

Thorne interrupted her musing. "Presumably you rode the black mare I saw near my bailiff's cottage last evening."

Kacy spared him a brief glance, nodded, then wiggled as far away as she could get without falling off.

Thorne's indrawn breath hissed behind her before he said, "I thought people in the future drive cars to get where they wish to go."

"They do." She flipped her long braid. When it struck his chest, she felt as though she had scored an important victory. "Most people who ride horses do so for pleasure, or to win a race, not actually to get anywhere. I took riding lessons because Fey suggested it."

Although she tried not to look at Thorne, she couldn't keep her eyes off him very long. He rolled his eyes with droll humor. "The same Fey who is your fairy godmother?"

"The very same," Kacy said.

"Do all children in the future have fairy godmothers?"

"As far as I know, I'm the only one who did. I always thought Fey and Rey were imaginary." Her voice quivered. "Now I'm beginning to believe they're real."

Feeling oddly exposed; she stared ahead and pondered her unusual childhood. She'd never told anybody about Rey and Fey, except Jennifer, and she couldn't wait to see her again so she could tell her they were real.

A doe bounded gracefully across their path with two fawns at her heels. Moments later a stag, whose winter rack had been shed, joined them. Then Kacy caught a glimpse of a fox chasing a rabbit. Dismayed, she let out a wail.

Thorne's stallion veered left. Had she not been between his strong arms, the sudden change would likely have unseated her. *So much for holding herself away from him.*

With Rey now floating above them, Blade's canter speeded to a full gallop. Kacy realized they were chasing the fox and wondered why. A few moments later, they passed the fox and Thorne loosened his arms from around her, slid his right leg over his saddle and swooped down low to scoop up the hopping rabbit. After he swung his leg back over Blade, he plopped the frightened animal on Kacy's lap.

"Are you going to thank me for rescuing it from the clutches of death, my lady?"

She almost smiled. How easy it would be to forget she was miffed. "Yes," she said politely. "Thank you."

"What will you do with the rabbit?"

"Give her to one of your tenants, I suppose."

"To eat?"

"Of course not. That fate's no better than having the fox consume her. Maybe some children want a pet."

"My tenants hardly have food to feed themselves, let alone enough to share with a pet," he said dourly.

Tempted to remind him their lives were much improved, Kacy decided to wait and let that fact speak for itself. "Your tenants aren't starving. Besides, rabbits don't require much food."

"Are you an expert on what they require?"

"No, but my grandmother loves animals so she gave me pets for birthdays, Easter and other holidays. Once I had a rabbit. He ate leafy greens. If the children want a pet, they can gather greens in the woods."

"Most people think my woods are haunted."

"Are they?"

"Not unless that enormous tent is filled with spirits."

Kacy didn't comment and Thorne let the subject drop. "You might give the rabbit to my stable lads, Timothy and Thadius."

"That's a great suggestion." Pleased, Kacy petted the rabbit until it stopped shaking. Then she whispered, "I think the rabbit's asleep."

"Good." Thorne pulled her firmly against his chest.

Instead of resisting, she relaxed against him. No sense fighting something she enjoyed. And she might not be here much longer to enjoy it.

Eleven

Clay felt Kacy's warmth through her velvet riding habit. The lower half of his body went rigid. He searched for something to say to chase away the lustful vein his thoughts were taking. "The only ladies I have met with nails painted to match their lips were charlatans."

Kacy opened her mouth. And promptly closed it again.

Careful to keep his expression impassive, Clay teased, "What? No smart retort from my feisty vixen visitor?"

He felt her inhale and exhale before she asked, "Are you rude to all women or just to me?"

He bit back the curse forming in his throat. "I have not been honored by a visit from a lady of quality. In future I shall endeavor to be more genteel."

"If you think I'm gullible enough to believe that," she dismissed his apology with an inelegant snort, "you're not as smart as I assumed."

Amused, Clay fought a smile. His thoughts turned guiltily to the fact that Kacy had spent the night in a tent. The thieves could have harmed her. Clay cursed himself for not offering his protection sooner. Tonight she would stay at Havenhurst. They would sup together. He'd ply her with wine before they discussed her living arrangements. After that, he might kiss her again.

Those decisions made, his smile shone through. He turned his face aside so she wouldn't see it—and found the fairy staring at him with a suspicious gleam in her wee, green eyes.

"Does the fairy intend to spend every moment with us?"

Kacy shook her head. "Rey is waving goodbye now and I suspect Fey will soon be off as well."

"Where is Rey going?" Thorne spoiled his question by adding, "Good Lord, I cannot believe I asked about an invisible being who might well be nothing more than a figment of your imagination."

Kacy laughed. "Rey has others to watch over. He's also trying to arrange to return me to the future. In spite of what you might think, Lord Banes, I'm desperate to go home."

Concerned about her fixation with the future, Clay said, "You must not discuss the future with anyone else."

"I won't."

Startled by her quick reply, he glanced at her mouth.

"Whilst Rey and I are gone," Fey said, interrupting their absorption in each other, "we trust you to protect Kacy, Lord Banes. See that you do not disappoint us."

With that she waved her wand and vanished.

Kacy stared down at the rabbit in her lap. "I think Fey cast a spell to keep the rabbit subdued."

"Good." They rode in silence until Thorne rubbed his thumb along Kacy's backbone. She nearly jumped off the horse, but he tightened his arms and kept her close.

"Why did you do that?" she asked, her tone terse, brisk.

"To get your attention."

"Why do you want it?"

"I expected more chatter from you."

"I'm disappointed in you too, Thorne."

"I don't recall saying I'm disappointed."

Kacy blushed and couldn't think of a thing to say.

But Thorne had no such problem. "Why did you suggest I might be embarrassed if I peered inside the tent?"

She didn't want to tell him about Catharine. Neither did she want to withhold information that might later be misconstrued. Hoping Catharine would sleep all day and that Rey would watch over her, Kacy said, "Because a girl who hasn't slept much lately is asleep in there."

"Did she travel to England with you?"

"No."

"How did she come to be in the tent? She wasn't there when I took the thieves away."

"She was in the woods though."

"Do you know why?"

"I'd rather not say."

"Why the devil not?"

"Because it isn't any of our business. She'll leave soon and I may never see her again." To her relief, Thorne didn't pursue the issue and Kacy saw no reason to tell him they looked like identical twins.

At Bardsy's cottage, the changes in his bailiff shocked Clay. Bardsy looked years younger than his five and forty years. No longer hunch-shouldered, he stood erect and proud, and despite drooping eyelids, his gaze was alert as he greeted, "Good morning, good folk."

"Good morning," Kacy returned, her smile as bright as the sun now shining full upon them. Clay couldn't help wondering how it would feel to have that smile turned on him. Or what he'd have to do to earn a smile that warm.

"Good morning," Clay said. What magic had erased the wrinkles and creases from Bardsy's face? In an attempt to keep his shock to himself, Clay added, "We're off to visit the tenants and would have you join us."

"'Twould be me veriest pleasure, milord," Bardsy said. "I'll go git me horse and Miss Rose's mare."

Kacy waited for the two worthy looking steeds to round a corner of the cottage.

She saw Clay's eyes bulge in disbelief and sensed he came close to dropping his jaw as Bardsy said, "This be Pillow, milord." His horse neighed and Bardsy exposed a crooked grin.

"And that's my mare," Kacy said.

After Thorne helped her mount the black mare, they visited the fields where tenants toiled. Pleased with their progress, she enjoyed observing Thorne with his tenants. It was apparent they admired and respected him, but were also a bit in awe. When they thanked her for the feast, she again felt guilty for taking credit for Rey's miracles.

Around midday, the trio stopped by cottages where women too old to help with tilling minded children too young to work. A small group played *Farmer in the Dell*, a game Kacy had taught them last night. As they finished, Janey Sathers, a shy, lame-armed eight-year-old, who overcame her shyness around Kacy asked, "Will ya play wiff us, Miss Rose?"

Kacy didn't think Thorne would want to be delayed and wondered how to decline without hurting Janey's feelings.

Thorne surprised her by saying, "She might enjoy that."

He dismounted to help her off the mare. Kacy raised the dozing rabbit above her head. As her body slid down Thorne's, she was acutely aware of him—his scent, his warmth... his strength. He turned her on as no other man ever had. Unable to control her thoughts, she looked away and wondered what to do with the rabbit until Janey's mother, sitting in an old
rocker said, "Let me hold the rabbit."

Kacy smiled as she gave the sleeping rabbit to Sarah Sathers, who rested it on her swollen, pregnant tummy.

Still reeling from Thorne's touch, Kacy drew fresh air into her lungs and expelled it very slowly before she joined the children. Although self-conscious under his watchful gaze, she smiled while they played *Farmer in the Dell*. Afterwards, Sarah Sathers clapped as though she had been royally entertained.

"You be good with children," Sarah said.

Kacy smiled. "Maybe they're good with me."

"We likes ya, lots." Janey stood as close as she could get.

"Yeah," her little brother, Lamont added, "We likes the games an' songs ya teached us, too."

"Taught us," Kacy corrected gently.

Their father, Miles, arrived home from the fields just then. When he saw their visitors, he smiled. "Sarah and me would be honored to have you share our midday meal, milord."

Kacy knew earls didn't eat with their tenants, but she sent Thorne a pleading look. Yesterday and the day before, the Sathers' were the last tenants she had visited and she felt drawn to the family with two children and one on the way.

When Thorne said, "We would be pleased to share your repast, Miles," Kacy smiled. She didn't know what she would have done if he had spurned the Sathers' hospitality. And then she worried whether they had enough food to share.

Inside their small, battered cottage, Sarah set the sleeping rabbit in a corner before she washed her hands. Kacy saw Thorne's eyes widen in amazement. Outside, the cottage looked as though a strong wind might blow it away. Inside, though it had earthen floors and was sparsely furnished, Sarah kept it clean and tidy—cleaner and tidier than his huge elaborate mansion with its overabundance of servants.

Sarah spread a well-used cloth over the square table's scarred surface while Kacy washed her hands. After Thorne, Miles, Bardsy and the children washed, Miles led them to rickety pine chairs. Thorne sat beside Kacy. Flustered by the cozy closeness, she was aware of every move his lean, handsome body made, while Janey used her good hand and arm to help her mother set the table.

Sarah served a tasty meal. Miles broke apart one of two cobloafs, crusty bread with round lumps on top, upon which they spread gobs of freshly churned butter. The ragout stew, made of highly seasoned vegetables and venison, was thick and savory.

"This is delicious," Kacy complimented Sarah.

"Yes," Thorne agreed. "It tastes very good."

"Aye. It do," Bardsy added as he emptied his bowl. And to prove he and Thorne meant what they said, they both accepted second servings and more bread.

The men discussed sowing and planting while the
women and children listened. When they finished eating, Janey said,
"Miss Rose tol' us stories at the feast last night."

"An taught us games," little Lamont added.

"Will ya teach us more?" Janey asked.

Kacy smiled. "Of course." She hadn't had much experience with
children, but she adored the tenant's young ones.

"Now?" Janey quizzed, setting her spoon down and refolding her
well-used napkin with her good right hand.

About to suggest another time, Kacy was startled when Thorne
said, "My bailiff and I shall visit the other fields, Miss Rose. You may
stay here and play with the children."

Although she resented his autocratic tone, she reined in her
irritation and turned a smile to Janey. "Have you played *London
Bridge*?"

"Naw." Janey and Lamont both shook their heads.

And Lamont demanded, "How it be played, Miss Rose?"

"I think it will be easier to show you than tell you."

"Kin we play right now?"

"As soon as I help your mother with the dishes."

Sarah looked shocked. Miles, Thorne and Bardsy did as well. With
a rueful shake of her head, Kacy said, "Where I came from everyone
helps if there are no servants."

"Where'd ya come frum?" Miles asked, curiosity
evident in his gray eyes.

"America." Not willing to invent plausible answers to more
questions, because Denver wouldn't be settled until the next decade,
she stacked Lamont's chipped blue bowl along with Janey's on top
of hers and changed subjects. "Do you think the other children are
finished eating, Lamont?"

"I'll go see." He scrambled off his chair, his short legs wobbling as
he dashed out the door.

Clay stood and thanked Sarah for the meal. She looked as though
she could deliver the babe at any moment. For the first time in years,

he admitted he wanted children of his own. A mental picture of Kacy holding their baby formed as he walked to the low door which forced him to duck or grouse, as so many cottage and pub doors did.

Anticipating a frown aimed at him, he glanced back at Kacy. She was already busily helping his tenant's ungainly wife with the washing up. Clay told himself he'd been right to suggest she remain here. The tenant's progress was men's work. But disappointment knifed through him. He would have liked one of her smiles to speed him on his way.

The unseasonably warm day was perfect for plowing. In the east field, a few bold, full-grown lads had stripped to the waist. Black braces crisscrossed their bare backs to hold up trousers while they toiled. Their naked torsos drew titters from the ladies, young and old alike and Clay wondered if they would wind
up sunburned.

Seated atop the nag, Bardsy voiced Clay's other silent thought, "The tenant's numbers'll be considerably increased with new babes by next spring."

And I'll have more mouths to feed, Clay thought. He hadn't yet mentioned his idea of teaching the tenants to hunt. If necessary, he would, but it might prove difficult to convince them the woods weren't haunted. In any event, before more hunting occurred, that enormous tent must be taken down and Kacy convinced to stay in the mansion.

Dusk was in the offing by the time they returned to the Sathers' humble cottage. Little Lamont sat outdoors in the old rocker, minding the rabbit. A troubled expression haunted his eyes.

"Is something amiss, lad?" Clay asked.

"Janey fell an' hurt her arm. Miss Rose said it be broke and she be trying ta fix it."

"Keep the lad company," Clay instructed Bardsy.

In the cottage, Clay found Kacy on the floor, bent over Janey, wrapping long white strips of cotton fabric around her arm and twigs that had been placed near her skin.

He dropped to his knees beside her. "How can I help?"

Without glancing up, Kacy said, "Hold her arm."

"What happened?" he asked, while he did as instructed.

"She was playing tag and fell." Sarah wrung her hands.

"Are you certain 'tis broken?"

"Positive," Kacy said without looking at him.

"It's her lame arm," Sarah said, her worry evident. "The bone bent, lopsided. I feared it might break through her skin."

"I won't die, will I?" Janey whimpered, trying to be brave but unable to block her tears.

"No," Kacy said, adroitly winding the bandage and applying slight pressure to keep the makeshift splint she'd fashioned in place. "You're going to be fine, sweetheart. I set the bone. It will mend and in a few weeks you'll be good as new."

When she finished wrapping, she secured the ends, then sat back on her heels. "That should take care of it."

"Should we put her to bed?" Sarah asked anxiously.

Kacy nodded. "Rest will do her good."

"I cannot tell you how much I appreciate what you've done," Sarah said after Thorne carried Janey to the bed and she bent to cover her daughter with a frayed blanket.

"I'm sure you would have managed just fine," Kacy said.

"I might have gone to pieces." Sarah pressed her hands to her back as though to ease the burden of carrying her unborn child.

"Are ya sure I won't die?" Janey asked.

"Yes." Kacy touched Janey's arm gently, wishing she could heal her broken bone and lameness, too. And then she felt her strength drain as some miracle healed Janey.

"I be better." Janey's eyes opened wide and her cheeks flushed with excitement as she sat up.

Kacy smiled tiredly, but said nothing.

"I kin move me arm." And Janey did, bulky splinted bandage and all. "Look, mum. Look at me arm."

"Tis a miracle," Sarah said with awe-filled eyes. "However did you make it possible for her to move her lame arm, Miss Rose?"

Kacy shrugged and felt Thorne's eyes on her, but she didn't meet his gaze. How could she explain something she didn't understand herself?

Janey moved her arm, wiggling her fingers in continued disbelief. "Kin we take the bandage off?"

"I don't know," Sarah said. "What do you think, Miss Rose?"

"Perhaps we should leave it on overnight," Kacy said.

The excitement finally wore Janey out and she lay back down and fell asleep. Kacy covered her and straightened, feeling uncommonly weak as she bid Sarah goodbye.

Outside, Thorne took Kacy's arm. "You look all in."

"I'm fine." But when he slipped his arm about her waist, she leaned gratefully against him.

He frowned. "Are you sure you are all right?"

"Yes," she nodded, unable to believe how weak she felt. Did this mean she might not wake up from her coma? That she had lost too much strength and would die? It didn't matter. If she had the choice to make again, she'd wish Janey's broken bone healed and her lameness gone. This morning Rey had explained that in her spirit-state, she had the ability to wish others well, but he'd cautioned that the gift would drain her; endanger her mortality; make her vulnerable to death.

Looking at Lamont, Kacy asked, "Would you mind taking care of the rabbit for a while longer?"

"I wud like that lots. How long kin I keep 'er?"

"Would you like to have her as your pet?" Clay asked.

"Yeah," Lamont nodded his shaggy brown head vigorously.

"You'll have to ask your parents if it's all right."

"I will. I will."

Kacy took a step and faltered. Concerned, Clay started to lead her to the mare, but she collapsed against him. He cursed himself for not acting sooner as he slid his arm beneath her knees and lifted her close to his chest, then headed for his stallion. After he mounted behind her, Kacy's eyes fluttered open.

"I'm sorry. I don't seem to have any energy."

He cradled her close. "You're unwell."

She didn't reply. She merely closed her eyes again.

Clay bid Bardsy and Lamont goodbye, then urged Blade into a gallop and raced home. Instead of climbing another set of stairs, he carried

Kacy to his own chamber and lay her on his bed. After he removed her boots and loosened her clothes to make her more comfortable, he stood.

She reached out blindly. "Hold me Thorne... please. You're so warm and I'm so cold."

Unable to resist her plea, he lay down beside her, kicked off his boots, drew her close and closed his eyes. Clay didn't realize he'd fallen asleep until he dreamed. He knew was dreaming, and tried to wake up, but he couldn't, so he listened to the hushed voices.

"Rey," the fairy Fey whispered. "What's Kacy doing here? I took her trunk to the tent this morning."

"Claythorne brought her here," the masculine voice Clay assumed belonged to Rey, the angel, said. "She used up all her strength to heal Janey Sathers' lame and broken arm."

"Have you replaced Kacy's strength?"

"Claythorne replaced it."

"Have you given him the power to heal?"

"No. The bond they share makes it possible for him to replenish her strength."

How? Clay wondered sluggishly. *What bond do we share?*

"Does sharing his strength weaken him?"

"No."

"What will happen if Kacy overuses her gift to heal?"

"She may fade, Fey."

"Does she know that?"

"I explained that she possesses the gift to heal, but if she overuses the gift, it may leave her vulnerable."

Vulnerable to what? Clay wondered, still unable to open his eyes, or shake off the sluggish feeling or quiet the voices in the strange dream.

"That isn't fair," Fey said.

"Tis the best I could do under the circumstances."

"You didn't want to bring her here," the fairy said.

"But you coaxed until I agreed."

"Was I wrong? Would she be better off if I hadn't coaxed?"

"Only time will tell."

Displeased, Clay reminded himself he was dreaming, not eavesdropping on two otherworldly beings.

"What about my magic, Rey? Can I use it to give Kacy strength if she needs it?"

"No, Fey. Kacy needs more than fairy magic to survive. Hush now, so that the mortals may rest."

Clay managed to open his eyes. The orange glow of flames licked logs in the fireplace, indicating a servant had come in and started a fire. In the dim light, Clay studied Kacy's exquisite features and inhaled her delicate scent. Having her in his bed was enough to drive him mad.

This couldn't be a hallucination, not with Kacy in his arms, feeling as though she belonged here. Always had and always would. What in the blazes prompted those thoughts? And what in the devil was he going to do with her? The same sensation that had flooded him the first time he saw her returned with a vengeance. How could he possibly live the rest of his life without her?

Twelve

Morning of The Fourth Day

Kacy slept until somebody stirred beside her. Accustomed to sleeping alone, she thought she must be dreaming until warm breath fanned her face. As she inhaled Thorne's familiar masculine scent, her eyes flew open.

His intent gaze made her insides quiver. When she realized he had his arm wrapped around her waist and his legs entwined with hers, she felt awkward and tongue-tied.

"Good morning," he said.

Embarrassed, she ducked her head. Had she slept all night in his room? She remembered begging him to keep her warm. And they must have spent the whole night together because daylight filtered through a slit in the closed, dark green curtains. Too mortified to speak, she stared at the buttons on his rumpled pale blue shirt.

"Look at me," he commanded, his tone husky.

She did, reluctantly. The warmth she saw in his eyes made her heart pound. Did he feel the same attraction she felt? Or would he look at any woman the way he was looking at her after they spent a night together?

"How do you feel?" he asked.

She blinked as she recalled how tired she'd been after she wished she could heal Janey's arm. "Fine, thank you," she managed.

He shifted his legs. Excitement and awareness zipped through her and the intimacy beneath the goose down robbed her breath. How long would they lie here if she didn't pull away? She decided not to find out and wiggled until he loosened his arm, then she untangled their legs, tossed the covers aside and sat up.

The royal blue riding habit she'd slept in was wrinkled and soiled from kneeling on the Sather's earthen floor. "I need something clean to wear."

She heard Thorne's feet slap the carpet on the other side of the bed and made the mistake of looking at him again. The space between them charged with electric current. She had trouble thinking and was relieved when he said, "I sent someone to fetch your trunk at daybreak. If you wish to bathe, I shall instruct servants to bring a tub and hot water. Will you mind bathing in my chambers?"

"Do you intend to watch?" She could have bitten her tongue off.

He laughed. Actually laughed. His shoulders shook, his mouth quivered and old memories stirred inside Kacy. She'd seen him laugh like that before. Not often because they had lived in difficult times, but occasionally in prior lives he'd laughed with
wholehearted humor as he was laughing now.

When he finally stopped, she said, "If you'll excuse me, I'll go find some clean clothes." She started for the door, but he captured her elbow and turned her to face him.

"I shall send the maid, Maisy, to collect your things."

"That isn't necessary. I'm not used to having a maid."

"You shall have one whilst you share my home."

"I don't want to be waited on."

"I insist. I don't wish you to overtax yourself."

He lowered his head. She yearned for his kiss, but didn't dare let him. They might wind up back on the bed. And she didn't want to be accused of trying to seduce him again. She pushed against his chest, freed her arm and backed away. "Where will you be while I bathe?"

A flash of disappointment crossed his handsome features. "I shall collect clean clothes and change elsewhere."

"I don't want to impose."

"I divine you also don't wish to require the servants to carry buckets of water up another flight of stairs."

"That's right."

He grinned approval before he strode to the wardrobe where he selected a clean shirt and trousers, then opened a bureau drawer and collected more personal items. As she watched, Kacy felt as though they were sharing something intimate. In spite of the sexual revolution near the end of the twentieth century, she'd never spent a night with a man or shared a room with one. Doing so now made her blush. What must he think of her for showing up without any warning or a visible chaperone? It was a little late to worry about that now, but it bothered her that he'd accused her of attempting to seduce him, as well as another man.

At the bedroom door, Thorne paused long enough to say, "I shall wait until you join me to break my fast."

With nothing else to do, Kacy sat down until Maisy arrived. The curly-haired young maid carried a pale green gown and clean underclothes. A stream of servants soon followed, with a copper tub and dozens of kettles of water.

After the luxurious bath, which Kacy insisted on taking by herself, Maisy returned to style her hair. The maid chattered about the earl and Kacy decided she liked the easy camaraderie. In fact, she liked everybody she'd met and she liked Thorne too much for her own good.

When she strolled into the dining room, he wasn't there. The eggs looked undercooked, the gristled gammon overcooked, the burned toast and sugared jelly unappetizing.

"If Fey were here," Kacy mumbled, "I'd ask her to conjure something decent to eat."

"I am here, sweetling." A tiny light blinked on and off, then Fey appeared in its place. She fluttered her wings in midair, as though treading water to stay in place.

Kacy grinned as Fey twirled her wand and magically refinished the sideboard and dining table, then changed the food and vanished when Thorne arrived. He looked startled, yet pleased when he saw the refurbished sideboard covered with a new lace-edged linen runner and scrumptious food.

"Did the fairy help prepare this?"

"She did." Kacy winced, anticipating a rebuke.

Instead Thorne said, "It doesn't look half bad."

Relieved, Kacy smiled. In England half bad meant very good. If somebody described a girl as not half bad looking, it meant she was drop-dead gorgeous.

"If you wish," she offered, tentatively, "I could ask Fey to cast a spell over your cook which would make everything she prepares from now on taste wonderful."

Thorne looked doubtful. "Could you truly?"

"Consider it done."

"You must convey my appreciation." As he loaded his plate, he asked, "Could Fey cast the spell without Cook Edna Mae or anyone else knowing one has been cast?"

"I don't know. I'll have to ask Fey."

"Please do."

~ * ~

Hours later, Clay discovered Kacy had left the mansion before midday. Displeased that she hadn't told him, he stood before the tent flap in the woods. "Miss Rose, are you in there?"

After what he had already experienced during the days past, he didn't expect another surprise. He got one just the same. She opened the flap and looked at him with no recognition whatsoever in her lovely blue eyes. What's more, her dimple had disappeared. When? How? Why?

Startled, as well as a little disappointed because he adored her dimple, he asked, "Why did you leave the mansion? I thought it understood that you are welcome to stay there."

Her gaze shifted to a spot behind him. "I have no need to stay in a mansion, thank you very much."

"That, my dear Miss Rose, is a matter of opinion."

"I am not Miss Rose."

Impatient, he demanded, "Who are you then?"

"I would rather not say."

It occurred to him that her voice sounded different, her accent English, but he was in no mood to quibble. "Am I to assume you no longer wish to help me?"

Her eyes filled with incomprehension. "Whatever could I possibly do, sir?"

Infuriated that she pretended they hadn't met, but knowing he couldn't leave her here alone and unprotected, he said, "The tent must go. You may

stay in my home."

To his astonishment, a voice behind him asked, "Without benefit of a proper chaperon, Lord Banes? I'm surprised to hear you suggest a compromising situation to my friend."

He spun around. And felt as dumb as a dim-witted peacock. *Two Kacy Rose's?* He didn't like that one whit, but it solved the mystery of how she had managed to appear in his home time and again. It wasn't magic after all.

But as the second Kacy walked closer, he saw her dimple and knew she was the only one he'd seen during the previous days. Relieved, he resisted the sudden urge to touch her and glanced instead at the other young lady. They looked enough alike to be the same person. But he felt a marked attraction for the one dressed in pale green who held a small bouquet of wild yellow primroses, while he felt nothing at all for the one who clung to the tent flap as though it could protect her honor.

As another thought occurred, Clay frowned and demanded in a thundering scold, "Are there more than two of you?"

Kacy laughed. "Of course not."

Enchanted by the glow in her lively eyes, Clay watched her saunter past him and soothingly touch the arm of the other miss before she said, "This is Lord Banes, Earl of Havenhurst."

"You failed to introduce her," he said.

"The fewer people who know her name, the better off she'll be."

Didn't Kacy trust him? Stung, Clay realized how she must have felt by his accusations and distrust. "Your secret shall be safe with me," he vowed.

"Then it pleases me to introduce Miss Catharine Paice."

Catharine gasped. "Are you certain he can be trusted? That he will not tell a single soul he has seen me?"

Kacy nodded. "Lord Banes is a man of honor."

Catharine's eyes clouded with doubt. "How do you know?"

"I just do," Kacy said.

How *did* she know? Clay wondered. Never had he seen two people who looked so much alike. "Are you twins?"

"No," Kacy said. "Catharine's English. I'm American. And I didn't know anything about her until yesterday. However, Catharine thinks she could be my ancestor."

"Surely you haven't told her your tales of coming..."

"From the future?" Kacy finished when he stopped. "Of course I have. Catharine has dreamed about me for years, just as I've dreamed about you."

Clay resisted the temptation to ask how anyone could dream about someone they'd never met. Then a sudden distant memory flashed. Dressed as a Viking warrior, he charged through his enemies on a black stallion, rescued Kacy from her hiding place behind a huge boulder and galloped her to safety. After he kissed her, he promised to return, but by the time he did, she had perished from a fatal illness. Shocked by the memory, he told himself it must have been a dream, but he couldn't remember when he'd had it.

"If you discuss the future again," he cautioned, "someone might consider you mad and attempt to commit you to Bedlam."

The smile left Kacy's face and her demeanor turned somber as she inspected the yellow primroses she held. "I have no intention of talking about the future with anyone else, Lord Banes. However, Catharine believes me. I wish you could, too."

He didn't give her false hope. "It matters not where you came from. A tent is not a proper place for either of you to stay; therefore, you may both stay in my home, such as it is. Come, you may ride Blade. I shall walk."

To his relief, Kacy didn't disagree.

Stable lads and grooms crowded around when they arrived at Havenhurst. All eighteen lads stared in slack-jawed amazement at Kacy and Catharine while Clay helped them dismount.

"Ye look like the same person," Timothy ventured.

"Amazing, isn't it?" Kacy agreed with a cheery smile.

"Yeth," Thadius answered and the others nodded.

At the front portal, Montfort did a double take, then gaped. He recovered quickly and assumed his usual unflappable calm while he stood aside for them to enter the mansion.

"Be ye both Miss Rose?" he asked as he looked back and forth between them.

Catharine's features froze, but Kacy said, "No. We're not related. My friend is a British subject. I'm a foreigner. You may call her Miss Tracy."

As they strolled down the hall, Catharine whispered, "I appreciate your inventing a name that rhymes with your own."

"I didn't know what else to do." Kacy waved the primroses she still carried. "These need water before they wilt." She released Clay's arm and nodded at Catharine to follow her. As they headed toward the kitchen, Clay said, "We shall sup at eight."

"We'll be ready," Kacy promised and he heard her say to Catharine, "I think you should share my room. It's nicer than the others."

"I would like that," Catharine said.

Thirteen

Evening of The Fourth Day

At dusk, a knock sounded on the blue room door. As Kacy stood to answer it, she said, "I feel as close to you as I imagine sisters might feel, Catharine."

Catharine smiled. "I feel the same way."

They had talked almost non-stop while Kacy arranged the primroses and later while they sipped tea.

Curly-haired Maisy stood in the hall when Kacy opened the door. "Be ye ready to change fer supper, milady?"

Kacy nodded. After they selected gowns from her trunk, Maisy helped them both change. Then she restyled their hair. Afterwards, side by side, Kacy and Catharine stared at their reflections in a full-length, oval mirror.

"Our gowns are beautiful." Kacy admired hers of pink and Catharine's of pale yellow.

"Yes, they are," Catharine agreed.

"Ye look like twins," Maisy said again and they grinned at each other in the mirror before they left the room.

Thorne waited at the foot of the stairs. "You both look lovely," he said.

"Thank you," Kacy responded.

Her expression guarded, Catharine exposed a timid smile.

In the parlor, Thorne poured them each a glass of sherry. While they sipped, he asked, "Where is your home, Catharine?"

She looked upset, so Kacy said, "Please don't question her. She'll be leaving soon and the less anyone knows about her, the better off she'll be."

Although he looked doubtful, Thorne didn't press the issue and Kacy's heart silently thanked him when he turned the conversation to the earldom and its problems.

They went to supper. At Kacy's request, Fey had cast a spell over Cook Edna Mae without her knowledge and Kacy watched Catharine and Thorne sample each dish. Repeatedly they mentioned how flavorful everything tasted.

Thorne entertained them with tales of his travels, and Catharine lost some of her fear. Kacy could tell by the way her expression relaxed as the meal wore on.

At the end of the meal, Thorne bypassed an after dinner drink and escorted them up to the music room. "Would you play for us?" he asked Kacy.

"I'll do more than that." She led them to the pianoforte. "I'll teach you songs you've never heard before."

Both quick learners, their voices blended with Kacy's when they sang some of her grandparent's favorite old songs. *You Are My Sunshine; When it's Springtime in the Rockies; Home on the Range.* As her fingers pranced across the black and white keys, Kacy had her first real glimpse of what life could be like during this time—ladies dressed in fancy gowns, their hair arranged in elaborate styles; men who behaved as gentlemen and treated ladies with care, consideration and kindness. A great deal could be said for Victorian tradition, she decided.

After a couple of hours, she stopped and folded her hands in her lap. "I suppose we should retire."

Thorne pulled a small watch attached to a chain from his fob pocket. "Yes. 'Tis late. Thank you for a lovely evening."

"Thank you," Kacy said sincerely.

"I thank you as well." Catharine blushed when Thorne offered his arm, but she placed her hand near the crook of his dark blue jacket-covered elbow. As they stepped into the hall, a dozen or more servants scurried away.

"Maisy," Thorne called to halt the maid. "What were you and the others doing just now?"

Maisy turned, her face beet red, her hands fluttering nervously at her sides. "We been listenin' to ye, milord. Yer music an' singing. It be lovely."

When he scowled, Kacy sensed he intended to chastise. To avoid hurting Maisy's feelings, she said, "That's a lovely compliment, Maisy. Perhaps in the future, there will be more music for all of you to hear."

Instead of the rebuke she expected from Thorne, he said, "Perhaps we may convince Miss Rose to play for us again."

He nodded dismissal to Maisy and she scurried up the stairs.

After he led Kacy and Catharine up to the blue room and bid them good night, Maisy helped them prepare for bed. Too keyed up to sleep after she left, they climbed under the goose down and talked half the night.

~ * ~

The next morning after breakfast, Thorne said, "Work awaits me in the study. I must excuse myself."

"Let's go to the parlor," Kacy suggested to Catharine.

They barely settled on a settee when Montfort announced, "Ye have a visitor, Miss Rose. He calls himself Mr. Rey. Shall I show him in here?"

"Please do."

When Rey arrived, she asked, "Can the servants see you?"

"Of course. Unless they're blind," he replied.

Kacy smiled. That sounded more like the Rey of her childhood. "Will you go to the study so Thorne can see you?"

Rey shook his head. "There's no need for that just now." To Catharine he said, "Are you ready for that trip to Europe?"

She nodded, but tears flooded her eyes as she looked at Kacy. "It seems a shame to part when we have only just met."

"Yes," Kacy agreed. "I hope we see each other again."

Kacy hugged Catharine and felt her tremble. "I wish you Godspeed and good luck."

"I wish the same for you."

Rey allowed no more time for sorrow. "We must go." He clasped Catharine's hand and led her out to a carriage. Kacy watched from the window. She suspected that once they were out of sight, Rey would whisk Catharine to Dover to cross the Channel, unless he whisked her straight to their destination.

"What should we do now?" Kacy heard Fey ask. She glanced up and spied Fey circling the dirty chandelier, shooting fairy dust at the crystals and making them sparkle like new.

"Maybe you should do that to all the chandeliers."

"Here," Fey tossed her wand. "You do it."

"I'd love to, but Thorne hasn't given me permission to clean, so I'd better not."

"Did he object to the changes in the breakfast room?"

"No. He didn't even mention them."

"Then let's get rid of some dirt and grime and see the real shape this place is in."

Kacy grinned. "I guess if he doesn't like what we do, we could dirty it up again."

Fey laughed. "I suppose we could."

~ * ~

Clay worked until he heard a clamor in the corridor. Curious, he went to investigate. Kacy stood near the top rung of a wobbly ladder. A bucket teetered on top while a dozen servants watched her demonstrate how to clean each crystal of the chandelier that already sparkled.

"What's going on?"

Kacy turned and lost her balance. The ladder went one way, she the other. Clay dashed over to catch her. Warm sudsy water splashed on their heads before the bucket clattered to the floor. She had instinctively wrapped her arms around his neck and the soggy rag in her hand soaked his back before she dropped it and shoved a wet strand of hair off her face.

"I'm sorry." She loosened her tight grip to meet his gaze. "That was terribly clumsy." Laughter spoiled her apology. "Do I look as funny as you do with bubbles in your hair?"

Clay grinned. He couldn't help himself, even though water trickled down his neck and back while servants watched. "I imagine we are both a sorry sight."

Kacy reached up and pushed a wet lock of hair off his forehead. "You look fine, but I must look like a drowned rat."

He thought she looked adorable, but before he could say so, a knock sounded on the front door.

Montfort, ever efficient, opened it.

Without being invited in, a middle-aged portly man, who had a thick curlicue mustache, stepped inside. His glance took in the scene and his eyes hardened.

"I demand to know what is going on."

Clay disliked him on sight. "Who wants to know?"

"I am Wilbur Lugamon—Catharine's father. And I demand that you set her down this instant."

"Only one man makes demands in my home," Clay said, as bubbles slid from his head to his cheek. "And I am that man."

"Set my daughter down," Wilbur shouted.

"I'm not your daughter," Kacy said. "My father died when I was four."

"I am your stepfather. Your mother is my wife."

Kacy shook her head. Some of the bubbles in her hair popped and disappeared. "My mother died in the same accident that took my father's life. You must have mistaken me for someone else. My name is Kathryn Cassandra Rose. I'm an American and I don't know you. I've never seen you before."

"I am your stepfather," he insisted, "and I demand that you leave here. At once. With me."

"No way," Kacy disagreed. "You can't make me do anything I don't want to do. You have no control over me or my life."

"As your guardian," Wilbur said in a cold, harsh voice, "I will prove how much control I have when I get you home, Catharine."

"Enough," Clay thundered, enraged by the lust he saw in Wilbur Lugamon's eyes. A protective instinct rose within Clay as he realized Catharine must have run away from home. Now he understood why she didn't want anyone to know her whereabouts. Lugamon soured his stomach. He imagined he did the same to hers. "This is not the lady you seek."

Clay hoped Catharine kept out of sight until Lugamon left. "This young lady is, as she stated, Miss Rose, an American and my house guest."

He felt Kacy shudder as Wilbur eyed her with cold, calculating eyes.

Clay barely resisted the urge to set Kacy down and toss Wilbur out. He itched to beat that smirk off his fat face.

As Kacy touched her scar, Wilbur demanded, "How long have you been here?"

"That is none of your concern," Clay said coldly.

Wilbur turned his furious gaze on Clay. "If you have compromised her, I shall demand restitution."

Wilbur's greedy eyes glanced beyond him to the sitting room and settled on a solid gold statue Clay had purchased in Africa. "Catharine is betrothed to Mr. Albert Smytheton. He offered a large sum of money for her hand, but he may not want her if you have compromised her. If Smytheton withdraws his offer, I shall expect recompense for the sum I will lose if she does not marry him."

"Aren't brides expected to present a dowry to their grooms when they marry?" Kacy asked, looking confused.

"Yes," Clay said.

Wilbur's face turned mottled shades of purple. "Cease your prattle, Catharine and do not question me again."

"I'm not Catharine and this is a free country, therefore it gives me the right to free speech so I'll say what I want, when I want, and you can't stop me."

"Bravo," Clay whispered in her ear. Her smile shot straight to his heart.

"We shall see how brave you are when I bring a constable to force you to leave with me."

Wilbur's shouted words turned their eyes back to him. Clay set Kacy on her feet before he spoke. "Get out of my home, Lugamon, before I throw you out."

"I shall be back," he raged as Montfort opened the door.

Kacy and Clay turned and walked away.

"He made my insides cringe." Kacy shivered and folded her arms, as though she could protect herself, Clay thought, while he opened the door to his study and waited for her to enter.

"Is Catharine upstairs?" he asked after he closed the door.

Kacy shook her head. Droplets of water freckled her face. She swiped at them and moved closer to the fireplace. "Rey took her to Europe this morning." Kacy shivered again and rubbed her damp arms. "Wilbur can't make me go with him, can he? I mean he can't prove I'm Catharine. Can he?"

Clay shook his head. Water drops peppered his own face. "Don't worry. If Wilbur brings a constable, I shall explain you're not Catharine. As a Peer of the Realm, my word has more sway than Lugamon's and the servants and stable lads can vouch that there are two of you."

"Thanks. I appreciate that."

Kacy raised her fingers to her cheek and rubbed the tiny indentation Clay adored. And now he admitted another perplexing fact to himself. He could not think of anything about Kacy Rose that he did not adore.

Fourteen

Morning of The Fifth Day

Kacy wandered through the mansion. Thorne was in his study. Rey was with Catharine. But where had Fey gone?

Frightened by Wilbur Lugamon's visit, Kacy needed reassurance.

"You look worried," Fey said when Kacy entered the music room and saw Fey on the window ledge, swinging on a tiny silver swing she had apparently conjured to amuse herself.

"Catharine's stepfather was here late yesterday."

Fey flew out of the swing. "What did he want?"

"Catharine. He thinks I'm her and he threatened to come back with the constable and force me to go with him."

"I don't think the earl will let him take you."

"But he might," Kacy said.

"He never failed to protect you in other lives."

"Maybe not, but he always left me."

"Do not allow Wilbur's visit to upset you, Kacy. Worry drains your strength, just as healing someone does."

"But what if he comes back and Thorne isn't here and you or Rey aren't either?"

"One of us will always be nearby."

"I hope so," Kacy sighed. "Now I realize how helpless women were... are in the past."

"You're not helpless. Nor is Thorne. He's a Peer of the Realm and I'm confident he'll protect you now as he did in other lives."

"I wish I could believe that, but he might be glad to have Wilbur take me off his hands." Kacy swallowed to keep tears at bay. "Maybe I'll be gone before Wilbur returns."

"Maybe," Fey said and changed subjects. "Is there something you'd like to do this afternoon?"

Kacy nodded. "I'd like to go check on Janey."

"Then let us be off."

"I'll tell Maisy where I'm going, in case Thorne asks. He wasn't very happy when I left yesterday without telling him."

Fey flicked her wand. The swing disappeared. "I'll meet you by the front door."

When Kacy joined her a few minutes later, Fey was human size, without wings, but she couldn't be bothered with horses or a carriage. She looked around, made sure nobody watched, waved her wand again and they were at the Sather's cottage.

"I'll return in about an hour," Fey said. "I must go to fairyland."

"Thanks. That'll give me time to visit with Sarah."

After Fey disappeared, Kacy watched Janey play with her brother and the rabbit in front of their cottage. Janey's bandage had been removed and when she looked up she beamed a bright smile at Kacy.

"Miss Rose, me arm, it be all better." Janey raised her left hand and waved, something she couldn't do before.

"I'm very pleased for you."

"Do ya wanna pet my rabbit?" little Lamont asked.

"Yes." Kacy walked closer, stooped and petted the tame rabbit. "Have you named her?"

"Yeah. Me Da says she be a girl, so I named her Molly."

"That's a fine name."

Sarah came out of her cottage. She smiled, but walked slowly, her hand pressed against her lower back. "I didna have back pain with me first two," she said. "It worries me that something might be wrong."

"You shouldn't worry," Kacy said as she touched Sarah's back and wished the pain away before they sat down.

"It feels good to sit," Sarah said, but didn't comment on her back again.

About an hour later, Thorne arrived. "Maisy said I'd find you here."

"Is anything wrong?" Kacy asked, worried that Catharine's stepfather might have returned.

"No." Thorne's eyes roved over her and her heart gave a little jump. Did he feel it, too? The bond that created a feeling of oneness?

As they prepared to leave, some tenants carried a man, covered with blood, from the field.

"He fell on a plow point," one man explained.

Worried about the huge amount of blood he had lost, Kacy didn't hesitate to touch him and wish him healed. The act, combined with what she'd lost by wishing Sarah's back pain away, drained her.

"The bleeding has stopped," Thorne said.

Sarah had hurried into her cottage as soon as she saw them coming and she returned with clean rags and a kettle of water that she set next to Kacy.

A little startled to be in charge, Kacy cleaned the man's wound. As she did, more energy deserted her. When she finished, she tried to stand. And swooned instead.

Clay snatched her up in his arms. He found it difficult to believe she had healed the man's wound, but apparently she had. Did she truly possess the ability to heal others? How could he doubt it when she'd healed Janey Sathers' lame and broken arm? How could Kacy, or any human, possess such a gift?

Once again Blade galloped them home. This time Clay carried Kacy up to the blue room where he kicked the door shut. He told himself he didn't believe what the fairy Fey had said in his dream—that he and Kacy shared a bond which gave him the ability to renew her strength. But he didn't know any other way to help her, so he lay down and folded her close while she slept.

Her nap lasted about an hour.

His concern and lust lasted much longer.

Memories of other lives attacked Kacy the instant she awakened. Snuggled in Thorne's arms, sensual yearnings surged through her. Her strength had returned, but she couldn't look him in the eye. She wiggled away and sat on the edge of bed, her back to him while she wondered what to say. Finally she asked, "Would you consider inviting the tenants to a feast to celebrate planting the fields after they finish?"

Thorne slid off the bed and walked around to stand in front of her. "My home is not fit for a dog's funeral, let alone a feast."

She looked up and pleaded, "Your tenants live on your estate and they aren't used to splendor. They'll think the mansion lovely and be thrilled with an invitation."

Thorne scowled. "I shall consider it."

"Please do so quickly," Kacy pressed. "If a feast is to be prepared, a lot of work must be done."

"Would you oversee such work and the preparations?"

"I'd love to," she said without knowing if she'd be here long enough to finish what she started. "And if you had as much sense as your horse, you'd agree, if only to see me try to cope with everything."

Thorne bent down until his head was level with hers. "I shall give it my approval on one condition."

"What is it?"

"That you agree to do something I suggest."

"Do you have something in mind?"

His gaze roamed over her. "I shall tell you later."

"How much later?"

"After the feast."

"All right. I'll do whatever you want, if it isn't illegal or immoral and it's within my power to do."

His eyes all but devoured hers. "It will not be illegal, nor immoral and it will be within your power."

Kacy had trouble breathing even though he touched her only with his heated gaze. She forgot about the feast and all the things they ought to discuss. Her mind cried for his touch. Her body pleaded for it.

In one swift move, he scooped her off the bed and kissed her. Soundly. "That seals our agreement," he murmured against her forehead.

Lost in sheer pleasure, Kacy tilted her head, hoping for another kiss. Thorne didn't disappoint her. He claimed her lips like a starving man. She arched against him and put her heart and soul in the searing kiss that rocked her to the core of her very being. Dazed when it ended, she wondered how he felt. His eyes burned. Even so, he set her on her feet and stepped away. If he hadn't, she might have thrown herself back into his arms and kissed him again.

"Tis settled then. Now I must work."

Kacy licked her lips. She could still taste him. Smell him. It took all her control not to reach out and touch him. "I'll sort out what needs to be done before the feast."

Thorne walked to the door, then paused. "I shall instruct the housekeepers to follow your advice. Do me a favor. Do not overtax yourself."

"I appreciate your concern."

"Then heed it."

"I will."

"And do not go anywhere without consulting me. If I cannot accompany you, I will summon someone I trust to go with you."

"Thank you." She smiled, and wondered if he could read the love in her heart that she had vowed not to feel.

Alone, she made a mental list of all the things that needed attention before she met with the housekeepers. They organized the servants. Sent some to work in the ballroom; others to the attic to see if the furniture stored there was in better shape than what currently filled the rooms.

Periodically Kacy checked their progress. To her dismay they accomplished very little and all her efforts to inspire them seemed to be in vain. She wondered when Fey would return and imagined using her wand to spiff things up.

While she considered that, Thorne approached. "Bardsy approves of your suggestion to celebrate the planting. Therefore, I have instructed him to invite the tenants to a feast to be held Sunday next."

Kacy frowned. "The day after tomorrow?" When Thorne nodded, she dropped her jaw in surprise.

He touched her chin with his forefinger and gently eased her mouth closed. "It gives me enormous pleasure to know I have the capacity to render you speechless," he teased with an amused gleam in his potent green eyes.

That isn't the only capacity he possessed. If only he knew about their previous lives and the fact that they had always been drawn to each other, loved each other, but never fulfilled their love. Assaulted by more memories, Kacy wondered what it would be like to be loved by Thorne now. In previous lives, it had been marvelous.

When he dropped his hand to his side, she gave herself a mental shake. No matter how handsome or how gallant he was, she had no right to expect him to fall in love with her. He didn't believe she'd come from the future and she didn't know how to convince him.

"There's so much to do. Can we be ready by Sunday?"

"Concentrate on the ballroom. We'll eat in there. And tell Cook Edna Mae she may hire as much help as she needs to prepare the feast."

Another depressing thought occurred to Kacy. What if she went back to the future before the feast? Before Thorne recalled any of their shared memories? Shaken by the fear of losing him again, she said, "Are you going to the village to purchase seed?"

He nodded and Kacy smiled.

Dazzled by her smile, awareness waged a war inside him. Clay knew that if they had been behind closed doors, he would have taken her in his arms. He stuck his hands in his pockets to keep from reaching for her. What would it be like to have her in his home on a permanent basis? Not half bad, he decided.

Thoughts of Wilbur Lugamon intruded. If the man so much as touched her, Clay would maim him for life. He protected what belonged to him. And Kacy did belong to him. Part of him had known that the first moment he saw her in his library, and although he'd fought the attraction, he would fight it no more. In the future he intended to enjoy more than sharing meals and discussing the earldom—things of a much more personal nature—in the privacy of his bedchamber. "I must go. Bardsy awaits me."

"Have a safe trip," she said softly.

As he and Bardsy rode toward the village, Bardsy said, "Miss Rose gave 'er diamonds ta me the other eventide, milord. She thought I might need 'um fer a 'mergency. But I 'spect you kin get more by selling 'um than I kin."

Bardsy pulled the sparkling jewels from a pocket inside his coat. A shaft of warmth speared Clay. Speechless, he accepted them. Any other woman would have bragged, using her unselfish deed to impress him. But Kacy hadn't even mentioned it. He didn't know what to make of that... or her.

The diamonds were worth a small fortune and could conceivably go a long way toward restoring his mansion. Why then, had she suggested he give her money for such a purpose if, as she claimed, their guardian angel intended to provide food for his tenants?

The question weighed heavily in his thoughts and he allowed himself to consider the tales he had accused her of fabricating. Could she have come from the future? And, if so, would she return? He shook those questions away. Traveling through time was impossible and he shouldn't waste time considering such an implausible notion. By agreeing to host the feast, she had agreed to do something he wanted. And he knew exactly what that would be. He would bed Miss Kacy Rose and protect her. In return, she would satisfy and obey him.

After they purchased seed, he and Bardsy parted. As Blade galloped home, Clay convinced himself he'd be doing Kacy a favor by keeping her. If she repeated her preposterous claims of coming from the future, being brought to Havenhurst by a heavenly power and having an invisible guardian angel, she might find herself in a peck of trouble. Even if Wilbur Lugamon were not a threat, she needed someone to protect her. And as her keeper, he could and would insist that she cease her unthinkable tales.

Kacy would keep him from being lonely and unless he chose, neither of them need eat nor sleep alone again.

Fifteen

Evening of The Fifth Day

Clay sat in his study. A crystal snifter with imported brandy, which he hadn't yet sampled, dangled between two fingers. He had done the unthinkable. Placed his trust in a woman. One he'd known a mere few days. But he felt as though he'd always known her and could trust her as he'd never trusted another. Why?

He shook his head to clear it. The price of seed, as anticipated, had doubled since last year. Still, he had stuck to his part of the bargain and purchased it. Would Kacy keep her bargain when he told her what he expected?

Upon his return, he had inspected the ballroom. Servants had been instructed to ready it for the feast. The layers of grime had vanished. Clay suspected Fey's magic was responsible. Still, the room had been neglected for so many years it wasn't fit for a celebration. He didn't want to disappoint his tenants, who amazed him with all they had accomplished, but he shouldn't have agreed to host a feast in the mansion. Perhaps it could be held outdoors. Without tasting the excellent brandy, he set his snifter down,
intent on discussing the matter with Kacy.

She didn't answer his knock on the blue room door. Had she bitten off more than she could chew and abandoned him with no more warning than she had arrived five days past? As he descended the stairs, his thoughts reverted to the feel of her while she slept in his arms, two evenings past and again this morning. Why did she feel as though she belonged in his arms and bed? No other woman ever had. Not even Oraline. She had been a tease, a temptress, unworthy of his high regard. Odd, he hadn't realized until now that he hadn't loved Oraline. Her defection injured his pride, but it hadn't touched his heart. Neither had any other woman. Kacy alone owned that distinction.

He found her in the ballroom with Fey. In human size, Fey slumped on one of the shabby, silk-padded chairs scattered haphazardly around the room while Kacy paced the scarred, clean floor.

"We can't be ready by Sunday," he heard her say.

"Not with a host of slovenly servants," Fey agreed as she flicked a speck of dust off her dark green gown. "The only way to get this place in shape is with my wand."

"We used your magic to clean, but Rey doesn't want us to frighten the servants or let them know you're a fairy."

"Pish, posh." Fey wrinkled her Lilliputian nose. "Servants will soon forget magic. People always do. And I could cast a spell which would neither frighten
nor surprise them after I restored the mansion."

Kacy stopped pacing. "Really?"

Fey nodded.

Clay decided to make his presence known and cleared his throat.

They turned and Fey asked, "How much did you overhear?"

"That you fancy using magic to refurbish my home."

Kacy snapped her fingers. "We *can* use your magic, Fey."

"Without invoking Rey's wrath?" she asked dryly.

Excitement radiated in Kacy's eyes. "If we send the servants away while we use it, they can't be frightened."

"Splendid idea," Fey beamed. "But when they return, the shock might send some of them into hysterics, if not to their early graves."

Clay thwarted a grin at Fey's dire prediction.

Undaunted, Kacy asked, "Can't you cast a spell like you did over Cook Edna Mae to make them forget the condition it's in now? If they think the mansion has always been beautiful, we'll accomplish what we want without frightening a soul."

"I should have thought of that," Fey giggled. "Now, how do you propose we get rid of them?"

"We could send them to whitewash the tenant's cottages in the morning. If you can provide whitewash, that is."

"Yes. And tonight whilst the tenants sleep, I shall shore up their cottages and make them fit to live in."

Kacy smiled. "That would be wonderful." She looked at Clay. "Maybe the servants could take what isn't needed here and distribute it between the tenants."

Clay hiked a brow, but said nothing.

"What a clever plan," Fey gushed. "I don't know when I've been more proud of you." Although devoid of wings in human size, she flew around the room and waved the wand she slid from her pocket. A silvery mist floated through the entire room. When it disappeared, new paint covered the walls and ceiling, glitter replaced the tarnish on the gold plated chandelier, and the scars on the floor disappeared, turning into newly polished shiny smooth boards.

"The room looks brand new," Kacy said, a gleam of approval in her lovely eyes.

Fey clapped her hands. Her wand snapped with each clap. "Of course it does. I can't wait to release more fairy dust. In the morning, as soon as we send the servants away, first thing we do is paint every room."

"First thing we do," Kacy said as one rodent chased another across the shiny floor, "is get rid of the rats." She raised her fingers to the dimple on her cheek. "What do you think of our suggestions, Lord Banes?"

"That they sound too good to be true."

"You have nothing to lose and everything to gain," Fey said.

"Actually, I could give Kacy my wand and you could refurbish without me. Betwixt the two of you, you could make this place fit for a king."

"That would be marvelous," Kacy said.

When Clay didn't comment, Fey asked, "Do you like what I did to this room?"

"It is brilliant," he admitted. The crystals dangling from the chandelier sparkled so brightly they almost hurt his eyes. "How long will your magic last?"

"As long as a human restoration. And your servants can keep it clean all the days of your life, if you wish."

"If I agree to you casting spells?"

Fey nodded. "My spells will only make them do what they should have been doing if your uncle hadn't allowed them to rest on their laurels."

Not sure what problems her magic might create, Clay delayed his decision and pulled his watch from his pocket to note the hour. "Tis time to sup. Will you join me?"

"Oh dear," Kacy moaned. "I lost track of time. I must look a fright!"

Dressed in a yellow frock with blond curls framing her pretty face and strands escaping the yellow ribbon at her nape, Clay thought she looked adorable. It occurred to him that he would like to muss her up a bit more.

"I shall see to your appearance." Fey waved her wand.

Before Clay could blink, Kacy's soiled frock changed to a clean apricot gown and her hair hung loose and looked as though it had been brushed at least a hundred strokes.

Fey waved her wand again and replaced her own clothes and restyled her own silver-blond curls.

"You do great things with that wand Fey," Kacy said.

"Tomorrow *you* shall do great things with it," Fey said, grinning.

Kacy laughed. Clay enjoyed her easy laughter. He also enjoyed being near her. After the feast, she would grace his home, share his bed and satisfy his lust.

He caught Fey eyeing him with a speculative gleam. Had she cast a spell over him as she had over Cook Edna Mae? He wasn't about to ask. But he wondered if she was responsible for the vague feeling that he had known Kacy before, in some far and distant time.

He offered his arms, one to Fey, the other to Kacy. As they strolled toward the dining room, he said, "Perhaps you should remain in human size and pretend to be Kacy's aunt and chaperon, Fey."

"Tis an excellent suggestion," she beamed. "However, being this size taxes me and I must visit fairyland now and then to recharge myself."

"I find that acceptable. What do you think, Kacy?"

She smiled. "Works for me."

~ * ~

Dinner was exceptional and conversation pleasant. When it was over, Fey yawned. "If you'll excuse me, I shall go refurbish a room for my stay here. Do you have a preference for which room I use, Lord Banes?"

"Feel free to choose whichever one pleases you."

"Thank you." With a wave of her wand, she vanished.

Clay led Kacy to the library. She looked nervous when he closed the door. "Is something wrong?"

"No. I'm just concerned about your decision regarding Fey's magic. Have you made up your mind?"

He relaxed his stance. "Can she truly repair the cottages whilst the tenants sleep?"

Kacy nodded.

"What would I tell the solicitors if they accuse me of using my wealth to mend, repair and refurbish?"

"Your records will prove that your wealth hasn't been touched and neither Rey nor Fey will let you be blamed for going against the will."

"How will they manage that?"

Kacy smiled. "Through trust."

He hiked his brow. "Trust?"

She nodded. "Rey and Fey have assured me the solicitors will be dealt with when the time comes." Kacy folded her arms. "If we use Fey's wand, we could restore your home to its former glory, or to whatever you wish it to be."

Thorne folded his arms, too. "You may employ magic if you can assure me I shan't live to regret it."

"I can do that."

"Good." He lowered his head.

The anticipation of his kiss erased all other thoughts from Kacy's mind. She trembled, closed her eyes and felt her knees wobble.

He kissed her then. The sweet depth of it surpassed all she had known before. It knocked her off balance, into chaos. She threw caution to the wind and kissed him back with all the passion she had stored up for several disappointing lifetimes. The tension she felt in his body matched hers and she hugged him closer, feeding his hunger the only way she knew how—by fitting herself more intimately into the contours of his body and surrendering to the desire that threatened to burn her alive.

The consuming kiss ended slowly, first with an easing of pressure on her lips, then with the loosening of his embrace, followed by a soft groan from deep in his throat, then full release as he let her go and stepped back.

His eyes burned and his nostrils flared as they stared.

A sudden sadness filled her heart as a deep seated yearning to fulfill the love they had shared in past lives surfaced. She felt the yearning well up from the bottom of her heart and spill into every corner of her soul in an unstoppable flood.

She watched his gaze travel from her face to the tips of her black slippered toes peeking out from the hem of the apricot gown. Her throat clogged with an overload of emotion when he said in a husky voice, "That color suits you."

"Thank you."

Without another word, he placed her trembling hand on his arm, and walked her up two flights of stairs. He opened the blue room door, followed her inside and scanned the room. "Dare I hope we're alone?"

Kacy grinned to cover the sadness in her heart. She was beginning to fear that the next time she saw Rey, he'd be ready to take her back to the twenty-first century.

"I understand Rey's still in Europe with Catharine and I'm sure Fey won't disturb us."

"Do you mean your Aunt Fey?"

When Kacy nodded, Thorne grinned and without warning, he kissed her again. As before, passion erupted between them.

The way he kissed her, touched her and caressed her dashed the sadness from her soul. His hands roamed over her back and lower to press her closer and make her aware of his desire. Her heart lurched with indescribable joy as hope emerged and she knew with a sudden sureness that she had been brought to this time and place for one reason—to be reunited with him. Why hadn't she realized that before?

Vaguely, she wondered if Thorne might urge her to the bed where they could be more intimate. He didn't. But when he ended the kiss, he held her close, his chin resting atop her head. "I fancy you," he said, "as I have never fancied another."

His husky admission forged a shimmering thrill straight to her heart and she wondered if he knew how much she wanted him. But she realized, in her soul, if he tried to make love to her, she'd stop him. Not only because she'd been brought here by a guardian angel, but also because it wasn't in her nature to sleep with a man without the benefit of marriage. She'd never done it in other lives and couldn't change what she'd always been. She didn't want to change either.

Still, she was disappointed when Thorne withdrew and held her at arm's length. "My home is in your hands. I trust I will not live to regret it."

Kacy raised her eyes, expecting trepidation. Instead she saw a strange warmth, mingled with hope and something she couldn't interpret. She felt a slow blush creep over her face. The thought of pleasing him made her happier and stronger than she'd felt all day. Now she knew why she had never been drawn to other men. Why she hadn't been able to respond to one's kisses. She loved the man standing before her. And had for eons of mortal time.

Would she be allowed to stay here with him so they could fulfill the destiny that had always eluded them? Or would she be returned to her own time?

Sixteen

Morning of The Sixth Day

"The stable lads and grooms..." Fey said the instant Kacy woke up. In her two-inch size near the top of the four-poster canopy, Fey pointed her hands and swan-dived to Kacy's pillow. "What shall we do with them?"

Kacy rubbed her sleepy eyes. "We could have them drive the servants to the cottages and help with the whitewashing. Then we could redo the stables, too."

"Stupendous." Fey waved her wand and grew to human size before she urged Kacy out of bed.

But Kacy moved too fast and felt dizzy. When Maisy came to help her get ready for bed last night, she'd had a toothache. Kacy examined the tooth and swollen gum and decided Maisy had an infectious abscess that had festered a long time. In her reticule, Kacy had found some mints. As Maisy popped one in her mouth, Kacy touched her chin and wished her abscess away. Maisy glowed with appreciation. And she took the mints with her, in case the pain returned.

While Kacy recalled this, Fey waved her through a bath and garbed her in a simple, yet pretty beige gown. Grateful she didn't have to waste time dressing or waiting for Maisy to fix her hair, Kacy smiled. "Thanks Fey."

"My pleasure. Now, if you're to meet the Earl for breakfast, you mustn't dawdle. He's an early riser and is already in the breakfast room."

Fey soared off the bed. A trail of silver fairy dust floated behind her. "I cast my spells during the night. When the servants awakened, all thought that whitewashing cottages and taking discarded furniture and bed linens to the tenants is an annual occurrence. You and Thorne shall have the mansion all to yourselves."

"Did you repair the cottages?"

"Certainly. And everybody thinks they have always been in the condition they're now in."

"Thanks, Fey. You're wonderful."

"You're more than welcome. Now go. The Earl awaits."

"Aren't you going to join us?"

Fey shook her head. "I shall rummage through family history books, tomes and albums to determine how the mansion looked in its original and subsequent states."

"That's a great idea."

"Of course it is. Now off with you."

Kacy didn't have enough energy to hurry. Last night she had stumbled to bed, too weak to crawl under the covers. Sometime during the night she sensed Fey's presence when she covered her. This morning Kacy didn't feel much better than she had after she wished Maisy's abscess away.

When Kacy reached the breakfast room, she paused at the door to catch her breath.

Thorne smiled when he saw her. "Another breakfast fit for human consumption."

Kacy smiled back, hoping she'd feel better after she ate. Although the antique oak table struck her as cold, Thorne's presence warmed her heart. He walked close and offered his arm. For some odd reason, when she touched him, a ribbon of energy wound its way through her.

"I am indebted to Fey for the spell she cast over Cook."

"Fresh strawberries! I love strawberries."

Thorne exposed a curious look. "What else do you love?"

She blushed. "You might be surprised."

He must have sensed she didn't intend to elaborate because he said, "May I assume we shall not be graced with Fey's presence whilst we break our fast?"

Kacy laughed at his hopeful, yet doubtful, expression. "You may."

"I shall count that as a blessing rather than risk asking where she might be."

Would Fey's snooping in his library anger him? Kacy told herself not to worry about it as he led her to the sideboard. By the time they reached the stacked plates, more of her energy had returned. Did his strength replenish hers? If so, did it drain his?

"Are you all right?" she asked.

"I have never felt better," he replied.

Relieved, she picked up a pink-flowered plate trimmed with gold. "The china is beautiful," she said and Thorne treated her to another rare smile.

"Twas my mother's. One of her few possessions I managed to salvage after my uncle sold my parent's home and most of their possessions."

Kacy didn't comment. She could only think of unkind things to say about his uncle and her grandmother always said not to say anything if she couldn't say something nice.

They filled their plates and turned to the table. A freshly starched white linen tablecloth covered its smooth surface and a bouquet of pink roses created a cheerful atmosphere. Thorne pulled out a chair for Kacy.

"Thank you, Lord Banes."

"You may call me Thorne."

She stared up at him. "Are you sure?"

He nodded.

"Thorne isn't an insult. It suits you, as Thor would if your name were Thoren, or Theo if you were named Theopolus," she said, hoping to stir memories of past lives.

Apparently it didn't work, but his eyes twinkled as he sat beside her, so close their knees brushed under the table. Kacy savored the contact, happy to have him close rather than at the far end of the long, formal table.

As they sampled their savory selections, she wished she knew his thoughts. He probably didn't want her here. "I think after the mansion is refurbished and the feast is over, I should find some other place to stay."

"Nonsense."

Kacy's heart bounced against her rib cage as his knee brushed hers again. "Maybe I'll return to my own time."

"This is now your time and Havenhurst is your home."

Did he finally believe she had come from the future?

She decided to ask, but before she could, he said, "I do not believe you have told me any falsehoods."

That statement knocked her emotions out of kilter. *He believed her.* Shocked, she managed to ask, "What convinced you?"

"The songs."

"What?"

"The songs you taught Catharine and I. They were quite unusual. I do not think anything like them exists yet."

Kacy beamed. She couldn't help it. "Thank you for believing me. I feel as though I've won a victory of great worth."

"And I, as well."

Breathless, she asked, "What does that mean?"

"In due time, I shall tell you. Eat your food. You need your strength. We have much to accomplish today."

"All right." Kacy took a bite of her fluffy muffin.

When the meal ended, Thorne urged her to her feet, draped her hand over his arm and led her to the corridor. A family of rats scurried along the wall. He frowned and turned to face her. "If you rid my home of a few rodents with Fey's wand, I shall be grateful for almost as long as eternity."

A strange sensation pulsed through Kacy. *Almost as long as eternity.* She had heard those words before today. No, not those exactly, but similar words. *Almost eternity.* In her dream last night, Thorne said he had been searching for her for almost eternity. A wave of dizziness floated through her.

He squeezed her hand, ever so gently. Strength and vigor swirled through her, replacing the dizziness. Did his touch renew her energy? She felt stronger now than when they left the breakfast room after she ate a substantial breakfast.

"Do you think Fey has deserted us?"

"No. We'll see her soon, I'm sure."

"Shall we see the servants off?"

Kacy nodded. Another surge of energy flowed through her as they strolled, hand in hand, to the front door.

Outside, they witnessed the power of Fey's spell. Servants chatted and laughed as they crowded into the earl's carriages. Kacy waved goodbye and smiled when they waved back and set off with wagons full of old furniture behind them. As soon as they were gone, she and Thorne hurried to the ballroom.

Fey, still in human size, announced cheerily, "My search turned up daguerreotypes, sketches and inventories of every room as it was furnished throughout two centuries. These may help you decide
how to restore the mansion."

While Thorne stared at the information gathered in the center of the shiny new floor, Kacy saw three rats scurry across the far end of the room. Conjuring visions of people dying of the bubonic plague, she recoiled and whispered, "The rats. Fey, how can we get rid of the rats?"

Fey waved her wand and mumbled something unintelligible. "They're all gathered in a burlap bundle, hovering off the ground between the stable and the mansion. Where would you have me put them?"

"Could you dump them in a pond and drown them?"

"And pollute the pond?" Fey looked shocked. "Certainly not. Rats are the only animals I hate. I shall dump them in the middle of the Atlantic. They can't do much harm there."

"They won't harm the sea life, will they?" Kacy asked.

"Of course not." Fey waved her wand again. Then she giggled. "They're gone; every last rat. And to ensure the mansion remains free of them, I shall conjure a hungry cat or two."

"Splendid," Kacy approved and asked Thorne, "Do you object to cats?"

"No. Timothy and Thadius may treat them as pets."

"I must go now," Fey announced. "I need fairyland to replenish my strength." She extended her wand. "This contains all the magic you might wish for Kacy, but it will work only for you. I know you won't misuse it."

Without further ado, Fey waved and vanished.

~ * ~

Using the daguerreotypes, sketches and inventories from the past, Kacy and Thorne went from room to room. With a magical flick of the wand, she cleared each of its contents, cleaned and disinfected, painted and wallpapered according to Thorne's whim. Then she conjured carpets, window coverings, furniture, wall hangings, portraits, tapestries and accessories until each room was a masterpiece unto itself.

By noon every floor, including the servant's, was completed to their satisfaction and all the treasures, which had been broken, sold or misplaced, were restored, replaced or replicated.

To Kacy's delight, Thorne held her hand as they headed outdoors. She thought the gesture romantic and marveled again when her flagging energy strengthened.

They stood before the mansion. With a few words and waves of the wand, the outside of the mansion, grounds and gardens transformed, until they looked magnificent. After that they cleaned and refurbished the stable, supplanted old straw with new and topped the bins of oats until they overflowed. Then they refurbished the groom's and stable lad's quarters.

A short time later they sat on a blanket on the manicured front lawn, sharing a snack Kacy conjured of ham, cheese, grapes, bread and wine. They ate slowly, awareness growing between them.

To her delight, Thorne plucked a red grape from its small vine and extended it. Kacy opened her mouth. His finger touched her tongue for one brief instant. Her heart pounded as he released the grape and slowly pulled his hand away.

As she chewed the juicy red grape, he popped one into his own mouth. "There are no seeds." He looked surprised.

"In the future, most red grapes don't have seeds. I guess they've been cultivated out through scientific research."

He looked away, his expression inscrutable. She felt his withdrawal shutting her out, creating tension between them. She sighed quietly, wishing she could somehow pour her memories into his brain so he'd understand their shared past and realize how brief their time together now might be. If he understood and believed and trusted her, it wouldn't matter where she came from. Their love would fall into place and it would be strong enough to overcome anything.

She picked up the wand. "Have you eaten all you want?"

When he nodded, she waved the wand and the remaining food disappeared.

"The business of stocking the kitchen is next."

Thorne helped her to her feet, then followed her inside. Kacy flicked the wand, filling the larder with staples, replacing chipped dishes, tarnished silver, and battered kettles, jugs, paraffin lamps and the wobbly, ancient tea trolley.

"Now it's time to prepare for the feast." She smiled.

Thorne smiled, too. Some of the tension between them eased.

Kacy suggested a menu and he approved. "Sounds fit for the Queen."

In the ballroom, she waved the wand, feeling like she was in the middle of a beautiful dream as she made her requests and the wand conjured round tables, set with linen cloths, napkins, china, silverware, crystal goblets and small bouquets of spring flowers.

Staring at the vacant space beneath the chandelier, she said wistfully, "I wonder if it would be possible to hire musicians."

"With the feast tomorrow," Thorne said, "we haven't time to engage musicians from London. Make your request and wave the wand. Let us see what happens."

Kacy did. A heartbeat later, a host of tiny fairies appeared. With a nod at her, they assumed human size and conjured a variety of musical instruments, which they placed in a vacant corner of the ballroom. After promising to return the next day, they disappeared.

As she sat down to catch her breath, Kacy decided they had indeed, worked wonders. She was tired. Yet, oh so pleased! Thorne looked pleased as well.

"Will you be comfortable living here?" he asked.

"No one in her right mind would be uncomfortable here."

"Will you assume the duty of managing the housekeepers and instructing them in their daily duties?"

"I'd be glad to, for as long as I'm here, but you only need one housekeeper."

"Which one do you suggest we keep?"

Touched that he asked and had used the word 'we', Kacy said, "Bertha. She's been here the longest. Rey suggested that I talk to the vicar. He might know somebody who needs a housekeeper and other people who want servants."

"I cannot dismiss them."

"You won't. You'll donate them."

Thorne looked puzzled. "Donate servants?"

Kacy nodded, fingering her scar. "They'll work some place else, but they'll be employed by you, which means you'll pay their salary for a couple more years, like I suggested before. Hopefully, by then, the people they work for will want them to stay and will be happy to pay for their services."

"How do you think of such convoluted solutions?"

Kacy shrugged. "Maybe I have a convoluted mind."

Thorne startled her when he said, "You have enhanced not only the lives of my servants and tenants, you have enhanced mine as well."

As he stared, a sudden breathless sensuality gripped her. To calm the turbulence vibrating between them, she teased, "Guess I'm here to please."

"What more will you do to please me?"

Her lashes fluttered. Dizzily, she met the twin fires in his eyes. "I'm not going to answer that."

"Why the devil not?"

"Because if we play with fire, one or both of us might get burned."

Thorne reached out and cupped her chin. The sporadic beat of her heart made her reckless. She moved her hand from her own cheek to his shoulder.

Clay didn't need more encouragement. He looped her arms all the way around his neck, gathered her close and kissed her until he felt her shivering against his chest. Her responsive shivers made him tremble with need. Raw need. He moved his lips along her jaw line and whispered when he could speak again, "I've wanted to do that all day."

"Me, too," she murmured.

Delighted by her admission, he grinned. "Soon, Kacy Rose, we shall do more than kiss."

"You shouldn't say things like that." But she ran her hands through his hair and made him want more. Right now.

He settled his mouth on hers again, vaguely wondering when he would tire of her. At the moment he was content and wanted nothing more than to kiss and hold, and fondle. Her sweet rose and gardenia scent filled his nostrils and her warm, wet mouth welcomed his. To give her more pleasure, he caressed her back and discovered he wanted more, too. Much more. He slid his hand to her breast and swallowed her gasp of surprise. Then, like a conqueror, he devoured with his lips.

He wanted her to want him as much as he wanted her. With his mouth sealed against hers, he drew her to a chair, sat down and settled her on his lap. He heard a satisfied purr as she moved her hands over his back, up his neck, exploring his hair. An odd emotion stirred in his chest. Before he could identify it, she eased away. Disappointment knifed through him.

"I think—maybe—we'd better stop. Your servants could return at any time."

"As you wish," he said, far from ready to cease. But he attempted to squelch his desire. And found it demmed difficult.

Seventeen

Midmorning of The Seventh Day

Curious villagers gawked as Clay ushered Kacy and Fey over the threshold of the church, which had been refurbished by an endowment from him more than a year ago. He led them to his pew near the front of the chapel. In the next pew sat the Marquis of Rotherhile and his granddaughter, Valerie. Across from them sat the vicar's wife and only son, Lamont Crandon, also Sarah Sathers' brother, after whom her son had been named. Both nodded greetings. Noting the interest in Lamont's eyes, Clay scowled.

Whispered gossip flowed through the chapel. Some suggested the pretty young lady, Kacy, might be Clay's distant relative while others speculated she might be his intended. When her mouth curved in a smile, Clay knew she heard the hushed tones. She looked lovely. From the whispers echoing through the congregation, he knew the villagers agreed with his silent appraisal.

The service began with a song. The rich lilt of Kacy's voice blended with Clay's deep baritone, reminding him of the songs they'd sung in the music room a few nights past with Catharine. He hoped she was indeed with Kacy's guardian angel and had enough gumption to stay away from Wilbur Lugamon.

Vicar Crandon preached about patience and Job. Clay listened with half an ear. Worried about the restoration of his mansion and how the villagers would perceive it, he silently stewed. An answer from an unknown source flashed. The villagers, like his servants, grooms, stable lads and tenants, believed his home had always been grand. That perplexed him as much as everything else he had experienced during the week past.

After the service, villagers spilled out to the newly stoned courtyard, also due to Clay's generosity. Before he could offer his arm to Kacy and Fey, Lamont Crandon commandeered Kacy's attention.

"You do not remember me, do you?"

Kacy shook her head.

"For three years I have harbored the hope that you would."

Clay frowned. Had he mistaken her for Catharine? Lamont didn't give him a chance to ask.

"Although your stepfather refused to grant me a proper introduction, I have never forgotten how lovely you looked at the Crystal Palace Exhibition. I hoped you would attend one of the many balls so I could request a waltz. However, you left London without fully participating in The Season."

"I'm afraid you have mistaken me for someone else," Kacy said, smiling.

"You are not Catharine Paice?"

"No. I'm not."

"I should have known. You have an accent."

Kacy smiled. "Because I'm an American."

Clay had kept his jealousy under control, but it clawed at his insides. "Allow me to make the introductions."

After he did, he added, "Miss Rose is my intended."

He felt Kacy stiffen and saw Lamont's disappointment.

"When are you to be married?"

"Soon," Clay said, not surprised by the shock that froze on Kacy's face. He hadn't meant to announce they were betrothed, but he couldn't apologize until they were alone.

"My father is the vicar," Lamont said. "May I have the privilege of introducing you to him?"

"Please do," Kacy said.

Another jolt of jealousy attacked Clay as he followed, impatient and unwilling to let Kacy out of his sight. The cut and fabric of Lamont's suit spoke of good taste and he carried himself with an air that suggested he was accustomed to having beautiful ladies at his side. Clay glanced back to see what had become of Fey and saw her climb, or rather glide, into the carriage.

Vicar Crandon, a good parson who unselfishly served his flock, smiled at Kacy. "Welcome to our parish, Miss Rose."

"Yes," his plump, pleasant mannered wife, Louise added. "We would be honored to have you come for tea, Miss Rose."

"I would like that," Kacy said graciously.

"Would this afternoon be convenient?" Lamont queried.

"I'm afraid not. The earl is hosting a feast today," Kacy explained. "Perhaps I could call on you tomorrow or Tuesday, if that would be convenient."

"Call any time," Lamont urged.

New sparks of irritation slammed through Clay. Nearly as tall as he and handsome to a fault, Lamont didn't resemble his parent's one whit and Clay resented him monopolizing Kacy. He reached for her hand, placed it on his arm and covered it with his, a proprietary gesture, he knew. "Miss Rose's aunt awaits us."

As he ushered Kacy to his carriage, villagers closed around them. Not willing to spend time just now with more introductions, Clay handed Kacy inside. But good manners dictated he could not ignore the marquis, who approached with his granddaughter. "I say, Claythorne" the marquis greeted, "You have some lovely visitors."

Before Clay could comment, Valerie laid her lily-white hand possessively on his arm. Coyly batting her long, dark lashes, she smiled flirtatiously. "How long do you expect your guests to remain at Havenhurst, Claythorne?"

"Indefinitely," he replied, mentally comparing her uncommon beauty to Kacy's and finding it lacking, even though with her flawless skin and elegant features most people considered Valerie the loveliest young lady in all Surrey.

"You haven't forgotten your promise to dine with us on Friday next, have you?"

"No." He knew by the pout on her pretty lips that she disapproved of his short, clipped replies, but he was in no mood to placate her. He spoke briefly to the marquis, then excused himself and climbed in the carriage.

~ * ~

At Havenhurst Fey excused herself to see to the feast.

Clay handed Kacy out, gazing down at her while he pondered how to apologize. When she fiddled with her scar, or rather her adorable dimple, he wondered if she knew she did that. With her hand raised, her cloak gaped away from the front of her gown and he caught an enticing glimpse of pale, tempting cleavage. A surge of unbridled lust charged though him. Tempted to sample her luscious lips again, he forced himself to hold onto his control. If he did more than touch her, it would be his undoing. He dropped her trembling arm.

"Rest before the feast," he ordered. "I don't want you to faint before day's end." Spinning on his heel, he stalked off before he gave in to the desire threatening to embarrass him. In his haste, he failed to apologize for the curt announcement he'd made at the church.

A few hours later Kacy stood at Thorne's side in his large entry along with Fey, still in human size without her wings, to welcome tenants to his ancestral home. They arrived together, as though there was safety in numbers and less to fear than arriving a few at a time.

"The tenants enjoyed themselves at the feast at me cottage," Bardsy said. "But being 'vited to the mansion be more than they dared hope for. All are in awe, milord."

Thorne's reply was a noncommittal nod and Kacy smiled, hoping to offset his solemn countenance.

Servants had already gathered in the ballroom. To avoid any awkwardness which might occur, Thorne nodded at Bardsy, a silent command for him to take charge. Bardsy strode to the center of the room before he announced, "His lordship bid us partake of the punch an' ale whilst we mingle with one another."

Aware of the tight rein Thorne held over his emotions, Kacy stayed at his side while adults chatted and children played. He maintained his silence, but his gaze strayed to the door so often Kacy feared he wanted to escape.

Like a proper chaperon, Fey remained nearby. Even so, Kacy sensed her magic. The small wooden casks called firkins, filled with cider and fruit punch, never went dry and the well-mannered strangers who had come to serve did so under Fey's command, replenishing the trays of sweetmeats the tenants finally found the nerve to sample.

When word came from the kitchen that the meal was ready Bardsy called, "Seat yerselves, folks. It be time ta eat."

Thorne led Kacy to a table near the door where he seated her between him and Timothy and Thadius. Fey sat beside Bardsy. Across from them sat the four Sathers. One chair remained vacant, the one next to Thorne.

"Kin the cats the earl gave us fer pets 'ave babies?" Timothy asked Kacy.

Pleased that Thorne had told them they could have the cats for pets, she said, "If one of them is a female."

"We named one Gilly and the other one Bernard," Timothy said, "cuz we don' know what they be."

Kacy smiled, aware of the stranger's arrival only when Thorne stood. "Excuse me for a few moments, please."

She nearly gasped as she watched him approach the man standing at the door. He looked exactly like Dirk, the man Jennifer had loved and lost. Could he be Dirk? Had he died in the future and come back in time to live? Startled and chock full of questions, Kacy couldn't take her eyes off him.

Clay offered his hand to his best friend. "Thank you for coming on such short notice, Drake."

Drake shook his hand. "Thank you for inviting me. Your home looks grand, Clay. I knew you would find a way to overcome the absurd stipulations in your uncle's will."

"Come meet my guests."

"With pleasure."

Clay's temper nearly got the best of him when he saw Kacy staring at Drake with her heart in her eyes. That emotion Clay could only call jealousy reared its ugly head again. Before today he'd never been jealous of another man. And he wouldn't be jealous now, especially of his best friend. They had attended Oxford together, invested in business ventures together and no woman would come between them.

With her eyes glued on Drake, Kacy said, "Dirk?"

"His Christian name is Drake," Clay all but growled.

She arched her delicate brows without moving her gaze from his friend. "Drake?"

"He is a duke," Clay said, irritated by the wonderment, no the fascination, with which she stared.

"Duke Drake." She smiled. "I like the way that sounds. I'll bet Jennifer will, too."

"His title isn't Duke Drake," Clay said, wondering why she had mentioned someone named Jennifer, but not about to ask. "He is the Duke of Stonemeade."

To Clay's surprise, Kacy stood and curtsied, raising the hem of her lavender gown slightly as she dipped before him.

"It's a pleasure to meet you, Your Grace."

She hadn't shown him such pomp and ceremony, Clay thought grimly, before he recalled she had genuflected before she left his library that first day. He told himself annoyance was the emotion gnawing at him, not jealousy, but knew he deluded himself.

"You remind me of someone I once knew," she said to Drake, offering her hand.

He kissed her hand, smiling his infamous charming smile. "May I hope he was someone you were fond of?"

"Yes. He lived near my best friend Jennifer, and we shared some very enjoyable times together."

"If the two of you can take your eyes off each other," Clay interrupted, irritated that Drake hadn't let go of Kacy's hand, "We have things to discuss." To Drake he said, "May I have a few words with you in private?"

Drake nodded and released Kacy's hand.

Clay let out a breath he hadn't known he'd been holding. In a vacant corner of the ballroom, he asked, "Did you bring the items I requested?"

"Yes." Drake clapped Clay on the shoulder. "Miss Rose is lovely and I would be remiss if I didn't tell
you that I envy you."

In an attempt to change the discussion, Clay asked, "How is Prudence?"

"Still mourning her husband."

"And Miranda?"

"Being her usual spoiled self. Wreaking as much havoc as possible in school. The head mistress would have booted her out ages ago if not for my title and wealth."

The guardianship of the two young women Drake had inherited was almost as much a burden as Clay's uncle's cursed will. No one, it seemed, lived without problems, Clay thought as he and Drake returned to the table where Kacy chatted animatedly with Bardsy, Fey, Sarah and Miles.

But the moment they sat down, Kacy stared at Drake again. His resemblance to Dirk was remarkable. Because she loved Thorne, she didn't want to leave this time. Still she felt torn between staying here and going back so she could tell Jennifer about the blond-haired, mustached man she'd just met. *If reincarnation worked backward as well as forward, he might be the man Jennifer had married a week before he died.*

Drake turned his gaze to Fey when she summoned a server to fetch him a drink. While they conversed, Thorne leaned over and whispered to Kacy, "I see a number of questions in your eyes."

"How good a friend is he?"

"The best. We attended Oxford together."

"We have that in common."

"What?"

"Jennifer and I attended Oxford for part of a term."

When Thorne frowned, Kacy did, too. "I won't tell anybody else," she said before he could censure her.

"For that I shall be grateful."

She couldn't resist adding, "I know nobody in this time will ever believe that women will someday be as welcome in hallowed universities as men."

Thorne frowned. And Kacy grinned.

The efficient servers served Thorne's table first. As the meal progressed, Kacy enjoyed the men's conversation. They discussed business matters, reminisced about younger days, and asked Miles' opinion and treated him like an equal, which made Kacy proud.

After everybody had eaten his or her fill, Thorne nodded at Bardsy, again giving him control with the easy authority of an aristocrat.

With a grin on his jowly face, Bardsy stood and claimed attention once more. "There be games. All who wish to play follow me."

Tenants and servants rushed to participate.

Kacy remained seated with Fey, Thorne and Drake while the Sathers' moved near the center of the ballroom to watch Janey and little Lamont play.

After the Duke excused himself, explaining he'd return in a few moments, Kacy said, "It's sad that people in the twenty-first century don't play or learn the pleasure of simple games like these. If parents don't hire clowns or magicians, or spend huge sums at restaurants or movies theaters, parties aren't considered fun."

Although Fey nodded, Thorne frowned. "I don't wish you to speak of the future in public."

Kacy lowered her head, raised a finger to her scar, feeling chastised for no good reason. They were alone. If anybody else could have heard, she wouldn't have said what she did.

When the games ended, Bardsy announced in a voice that rang with confidence, "We have musicians." Deferring to Thorne, he asked, "Will ye dance for us milord, with the lovely Miss Rose and show yer tenants how talented the gentry be?"

In a corner of the ballroom the human-size fairy musicians, nattily dressed in clothes fit for London's symphony orchestra, picked up their instruments and played a slow waltz. Without a word, Thorne stood and offered his arm.

Kacy placed her shaky hand on his dove-gray sleeve. When he turned her into his arms, her mind emptied of every thought. For a few moments she forgot she was mad at Thorne and that she didn't belong here. "I wonder if any other earl has ever entertained his tenants and servants in his ballroom. That you're doing so makes me proud, Thorne."

He stared hypnotically into her eyes but made no comment. Pleasure rippled through her as memories of other lifetimes blended with the emotions Thorne evoked with just his stare. His strength, his graceful movements, the glint in his riveting green eyes, his left hand clasping her right and his right arm around her waist guiding her with expert skill—all had a devastating effect on her.

As they waltzed, tenants and servants swayed to the music, while children and stable boys gathered on the sides to watch. Kacy wished other couples would dance too, but she knew that wouldn't have been deemed proper. She saw the Duke return. Moments later he and Fey joined them on the dance floor.

After three glorious dances, Thorne nodded at the musicians to stop. He released Kacy near the children, his gaze on her as little Lamont said, "You wook wike Cinderella dancing wiff the Prince, Miss Rose."

"Wud ya tell us Cinderella again?" Janey begged, her previous bashfulness as forgotten as last year's rain now that she no longer had a lame arm.

"Yes, do!" Lamont pleaded.

Before Kacy could protest, Thorne motioned the children to sit on the polished floor and instructed servers to bring chairs for Kacy, himself, Fey and the Duke.

Faced with no other choice, Kacy repeated the fairytales she'd told before. Children, parents, tenants and servants appeared spellbound. Even Drake and Thorne, with Timothy and Thadius sitting at their feet, seemed to enjoy each tale.

Summoning her nerve Kacy dipped deep into her memories and created a tale of a young couple who loved so intensely neither time nor death, nor distance, could keep them apart. Like all fairytales it had a happy ending but she didn't think Thorne understood why she told it. Was her love for him as hopeless as it had been in past lives?

The vicar's arrival drew everybody's attention.

Thorne urged Kacy from her chair and escorted her from the crowd. When they reached the vicar, he asked, "When do you wish the ceremony to begin, my lord?"

Turning his gaze to Kacy, Thorne said, "As soon as my bride is ready."

Her heart began to pound. "Your bride? Who... where?"

"Please join the crowd," he told the vicar, then he led Kacy to a private corner before he said, "The vicar is here perform a wedding ceremony. Ours."

Stunned, Kacy stammered, "Ours?"

He nodded.

"But I'm not dressed for a wedding and... and we haven't discussed marriage at all. It's... its serious business!"

"Of course it is and the arrangements have all been made. The Duke brought a gown for you and wedding me is what I claim for the bargain we struck."

"What bargain?"

"Surely you haven't forgotten that you agreed to do something I requested when I agreed to the feast. I believe your exact words were, 'I will do whatever you suggest if it isn't illegal, immoral and if it is within my power to do.'"

"Well, yes. I did say that. But what about banns? Don't they have to be posted days... weeks ahead of time?"

"Drake arranged for a Special License."

Kacy's heart was beating so hard, fast and loud she wondered if Thorne could hear it thumping against her chest. "Why… why didn't you tell me before now?"

"Because I didn't wish you to worry overmuch."

"You might have given me some kind of warning."

"As you warned me of your arrival at Havenhurst on Monday past?"

He had a point. But she felt trapped. Did he feel trapped, too? Is that why he had decided to marry her? If so, it was a sorry reason. "Don't you think we should wait a little while? Get to know each other better before…"

"No. I expect you to honor our agreement. Now."

"Why?"

"I shall show you why after the ceremony."

Kacy's throat turned so dry she didn't know how she managed to croak, "Show me?"

He nodded, a wicked, sexy gleam in his eyes. "In the privacy of my bedchamber."

Lust, she thought, unable to swallow. He wanted her to satisfy his lust. That's all marriage meant to him.

She could have cried and might have if Fey hadn't approached and demanded, "What's going on, sweetling? Why is the vicar here?"

"To perform a ceremony," Thorne announced and to Kacy he said, "I shall summon Maisy to help you change. Drake said your gown is in the blue room."

Kacy's panic escalated. No words of love, or tenderness, or devotion. Just a hasty decision and the consequences be damned. Had any other bride ever felt this sad? This forlorn? She grabbed Thorne's arm and squeaked, "Fey can help me. Maisy should stay here and enjoy herself."

Kacy didn't wait for him to agree. She raced for the stairs. Her throat hurt so much, she doubted she could repeat her vows.

Eighteen

Evening of The Seventh Day

Just inside the blue room door, Kacy stopped, too stunned to move any further. Fey fluttered about, admiring the voluminous wedding gown draped over the dressing screen and the veil, edged with frail lace, gracing the back of a chair. White satin slippers sat side by side on the seat of the powder-blue chair. A lacy chemise, hooped petticoat and all the other paraphernalia women wore in this time had been spread across the bed.

"I couldn't have conjured better myself," Fey said as a knock sounded on the door. She opened it, saw Maisy and said, "Go enjoy yourself, my dear. I shall help the bride."

Maisy darted a hurt glance at Kacy before she ducked her head. "Have I displeased ye then, milady?"

Kacy came out of her stupor, giving Maisy a gentle, if wan smile. "No, you haven't displeased me." She sensed Maisy wanted to be needed. "I'd like some time alone with my aunt. Could you return in a few minutes and fix my hair?"

Maisy perked up. "Ten minutes, milady. I'll be back."

As Kacy closed the door Fey urged, "Come sweetling, have a look." She waved the wand she pulled from her sleeve and raised the wedding gown in the air for closer inspection. "Beautiful," she approved. "Absolutely beautiful and you'll fill it out nicely. I think your groom is in for a pleasant surprise."

"He certainly surprised me," Kacy pouted. "I can't believe he set this up without telling me."

Fey laughed. "I can."

Suspicious Kacy asked, "Did you know he planned this?"

"No. I didn't have a clue. However," she paused to grin, "I dare say you dealt him a number of surprises this week. Maybe he wanted to deal one of his own."

"Maybe," Kacy conceded and moaned, "but it's for all the wrong reasons."

"Is it?"

"He doesn't love me. He probably suggested marriage because of some macho idea that if he marries me that'll protect me from Wilbur Lugamon."

"I don't believe that's the only reason, nor do you," Fey said in a no nonsense tone.

Yesterday Thorne had said he fancied her and Kacy blushed at the memory. "He may desire me, but lust isn't love."

"If that's all he's willing to admit at the moment, you must let it be enough, sweetling. Surely in time he'll realize he loves you."

"But I might not be here long enough for him to realize it," Kacy reminded Fey. "And what will happen if I go back to my own time? Will somebody accuse him of doing me in?"

Fey tapped her wand thoughtfully against her own arm. "So what do you want to do? Refuse to marry him in front of his servants and tenants? Destroy his trust in you? Prove that he's right about women? That they're all alike?"

"What does that crack mean?"

"The earl has twice been disappointed by women he expected to wed. His first betrothed tossed him over for an older, titled man, without bothering to tell Clay. The second stood him up at the altar, having already conceived and borne a son without his knowledge. I suspect that's why he kept this wedding a secret."

Hearing that, Kacy hung her head as Maisy had done. "I guess I don't have a choice, do I?"

"It doesn't appear that you do," Fey agreed and said, "Has it occurred to you that you might be suffering normal bridal jitters? That numerous brides suffer them and grooms do as well?"

Tears clouded Kacy's eyes. "What would I do without you, Fey? You're like the mother I barely remember and one of the best friends I've ever had. Every time I had a nightmare while I was growing up, you came to help me through my terror. How can I ever thank you?"

"I don't want your thanks, but I wouldn't mind a hug."

Kacy flung her arms around Fey, savoring the feel of Fey's arms as they closed around her. She had missed this, she thought, as they pulled apart and Kacy saw tears sparkling in Fey's silvery green eyes. "Is something wrong?"

Fey shook her blond curls and blinked the tears away. "I love you and I want you to be happy. Always remember that, no matter what happens. Will you do that for me?"

"Of course." Kacy had never seen tears in Fey's eyes before and they were more than a bit unsettling. She swallowed, then asked, "Do you know where Rey is?"

Fey nodded. "He went to Kolob."

"Kolob?" Kacy asked, curious.

"To discuss your mortality with the powers that be."

"Do you have any idea when he might be back?"

"No."

"I wish he were here. I'd like to talk to him before I marry Thorne."

"I'm afraid that won't be possible. The one thing I do know is that he won't be back within hours. He could be gone days. Weeks. Months."

Fey's words gave birth to a small hope. Maybe this
is where she belonged. Shoving worry aside, she started to undress.

~ * ~

Downstairs, Clay waited in his luxurious refurbished parlor with Drake at his side. Most of his tenants and servants stood in groups whispering among themselves. A few had found places to sit. Many leaned against walls while others crowded near the door to be the first to glimpse his bride.

The sunny day and scrumptious feast had been a perfect prelude to their wedding, Clay decided. As he thought of Kacy as his wife, he was tempted to reconsider the lonely path he had chosen that did not include love. But the solicitors posed the threat of exposure. They knew about the murder accusation in France and a man with a dark secret had no right to consider love. Although he desired Kacy, he would not love her. That would lead to disappointment—for both of them.

With Wilbur's threats and her reputation at stake, Clay considered marriage the only proper solution. So he would wed her. Then he could bed her without feeling guilty. He would ease the need that had grown with each hour since he had first set eyes upon her seven days ago.

While he waited for her to join him, he recalled being depressed, on the verge of considering suicide before he found her in the library. But during the ensuing days he hadn't had a moment to spare for any such thoughts. Kacy had kept him too involved and thoroughly entertained.

He told himself he was doing her a favor. With no relatives alive in this time, she needed a place to live and someone to protect her. It might as well be him. God willing, she would produce an heir before he tired of her... if he ever did. At the moment that seemed highly unlikely. But he told himself that was only because he hadn't lain with a woman for so long.

Clay didn't realize he was frowning until Vicar Crandon scowled at him. Clay gave himself a mental shake, forcing the wrinkles from his brow. Twice before he had considered marriage. Both times resulted in disaster. Oraline had married a man three times her age without bothering to tell Clay. Timothy's mother had not shown up for the ceremony. Clay discovered why later. She was another man's mistress and had already borne him a secret son—Timothy.

Only a fool would open himself up to a third failure. Yet, here Clay stood, waiting for his intended and deeply affected by the fact that tonight his bed would be lonely no more. Unfortunately, he had no control over how long that might last. If Kacy came from the future as she claimed, she could conceivably leave as abruptly as she had arrived. Nothing was permanent, he reminded himself. Life came with no guarantees. All the more reason to proceed with the ceremony. To enjoy Kacy while he could.

The sudden change in the music from the harpsichord, played by one of Fey's human size fairy friends, turned Clay's eyes to the door. His breath threatened to quit when he saw Kacy. *His bride at last. Where had that thought come from?*

She looked exquisite. The double doorway framed her in the lovely hoop-skirted wedding gown and Clay wished he could capture the scene on canvas. Around her neck and on her earlobes she wore the diamonds she'd given to Bardsy, which Clay in turn had given to Fey for Kacy to wear this eve.

He had told Maisy to have Kacy wear her hair down and she had complied. Never had he seen hair as lovely or as long as hers. It fell below her waist, a cloud of blonde silk. And never had he wanted to capture strands in his hands as he did now. Her beauty humbled him.

Their eyes met through her veil. Her expression was serene as she started toward him, every step filled with poise and grace. Pride filled him. The closer she came, the more he relaxed. He told himself she wouldn't vanish, but he had deliberately kept the ceremony a secret. When she reached his side, he breathed easier, but he reminded himself she was only his bride because of a quirk of fate. One more reason love need not partner their marriage.

Kacy barely saw the vicar. Terrified that she might be doing Thorne a huge disfavor, she wanted to bolt. He reached for one of her hands, but she gripped her beautiful bouquet of orchids and roses so tightly, he almost had to pry it away. Thankfully, her shaking subsided once her hand settled in his. He smiled down at her. Some of her nervousness receded. But not all.

She summoned a smile as the crowd gathered around them. Thorne squeezed her hand gently. Something inside her fluttered. It reminded her of the thrilling sensations he aroused whenever he kissed her. Soon, he'd own the right to do whatever he wished.

Calm down, she admonished herself. *Don't think about the reason he suggested marriage or that women in this time are treated like possessions instead of humans.*

In spite of her self-admonitions, her voice quivered when she answered the vicar's questions. But she noticed that as soon as she agreed to be Thorne's wife, his grip on her hand relaxed. She looked up and found him smiling down at her. The expectant gleam in his green eyes made her already pounding heart pound harder. Without quite knowing how it happened, a gorgeous ring appeared on the fourth finger on her left hand and Vicar Crandon pronounced them man and wife.

Thorne lifted her veil and bent his head to seal their vows. The quick bold kiss did nothing to restore her composure. It dawned on her that the ceremony was over. But the panic remained worse than ever. While Maisy had brushed her hair, Kacy realized that from this night on, something more would be expected of her. But if she got zapped back to the future, what would happen to Thorne? Maybe she should have faked illness and gone to bed. She hadn't because that was a coward's way out. But what a dilemma she now faced! How in the world could she get through tonight with all this anxiety attacking her like the plague?

As tenants and servants congratulated them, Thorne placed his arm around her waist and pulled her against his side. Kacy felt as though she were in a fog, then realized why. Her frothy veil had fallen back over her face. As though sensing her dilemma, Thorne drew the veil over her head and eased it behind her shoulders. If only she could breathe more easily. She didn't know what was most responsible for that problem; nerves or the hated *suffocating* corset. Probably both.

Toasts were made. Kacy hardly heard them and feared she'd never remember a single one. She stole a glance at Thorne. Dear heaven, how he pleased her! Then why was she so terrified? Unable to swallow the lump in her throat, she forced herself to stop toying with her scar.

Her groom, no, *her husband*, bent his head and whispered in her ear, "Would you please stop acting as though you wish I'd disappear?"

"Is that what you think I'm doing?" she asked evasively.

Clay considered his reply. If ever a woman existed whom he could love, Kacy was the one. But she didn't belong here. Suddenly he knew that everything she'd told him was true. He had finally met a woman who could conceivably make him glad he had been born a man, but she belonged to another time. Their marriage wouldn't last. Thank God he lacked the capacity to love! "What would you have me think?" he whispered.

She gave an elegant shrug but didn't meet his gaze.

"Kacy," he said, his tone low and seductive. Her body jerked, dislodging his arm about her waist. Incredulity sped through him as she gave him a cautious glance. "You are nervous."

"Yes." She shook with such agitation he wanted to draw her close and comfort her. But he sensed she didn't want to be touched at the moment. And gathering her in his arms in front of a room full of guests would be most improper.

To ease her distress he whispered, "Would you mind if I excuse us for a few moments?"

"Please do."

He made their apologies, then led Kacy from the parlor, down the corridor, to his library. "Now then," he said after he closed the door, "Tell me what has frightened you."

"Tonight." She wrung her hands, then fiddled with her dimple again.

Clay cursed himself for expecting her to want to
share his bed as much as he wanted her there. She looked so bloody adorable with her cheeks flaming, her eyes flashing brilliant blue sparks of frustration, and her hands doing their best to be still and failing.

"You've nothing to fear, Kacy."

"Easy for you to say, sir."

Sir? Apparently this was more serious than he had anticipated. "I shan't do anything you do not wish me to do." He prayed she didn't abhor the idea of making love.

"And that," she said ruefully, "is the crux of the problem."

He wrinkled his brow, not following her thoughts one whit.

"What if I disgrace myself by doing something terribly gauche and turning you completely off?"

Turning him off? He'd never heard such an odd expression. Still, he felt like a thickheaded dunce. He should have discussed this earlier. "There's nothing you could do to turn me off," he said with absolute conviction.

"I'm used to sleeping alone. What if I take up more than my half of the bed? Or toss and turn and keep you awake? I might even belch at the wrong time."

"So might I. But we would merely have a good laugh." Clay reached for her trembling hands. He kissed one, then the other. His mother's wedding ring on Kacy's left hand sparkled at him. Seeing it there filled him with male conceit. Kacy belonged to him. She was his wife, his countess... his bedmate. A sudden wish to take care of her and protect her for the rest of their lives descended.

Knowing that might prove impossible, he said gently, "Why not let me worry about what is to occur when we go to bed? That way I assume your nervousness and you relax."

"How long do I have?" She looked as though she was about to be led to the guillotine.

"How long would you like?"

"A year would do nicely, I think."

For a moment he thought she was serious. Then he saw the impish lights dancing in her glorious blue eyes. "We shall bid our guests good evening. Then I'll take you upstairs and demonstrate your fears are groundless."

Her eyes turned to soft, mesmerizing pools. "Thorne," she said, so quietly he had to incline his head so he wouldn't miss what she said next. "You're wonderful. How may I thank you for being so patient and understanding?"

"You thanked me by becoming my countess."

He bent his head and kissed her, not once but several intoxicating times. By the time the kisses ended and they straightened their clothes and smoothed their hair, a good number of their guests had already departed.

After Clay and Kacy bid Drake good night, a servant led him up to a guestroom. As they bid the remaining tenant's goodbye, Fey wandered over. "Now that you're married, you don't need me."

"When will we see you again?" Kacy asked.

"In a few days. I'll come by to see how you are."

"We'd like that," Kacy said.

"Yes, we would," Clay agreed.

"Be happy." Fey waved a cheery goodbye before she breezed through the front portal, still in human size, but Clay suspected she wouldn't be for long.

Nineteen

Kacy looked tired. To conserve her strength, Clay carried her up the stairs. "Should I summon Maisy to help you out of your gown?"

"I prefer your help. If that's permitted."

Pleased by her reply, desire surged once more to life. The heated kisses in the library had raised his hunger to new heights. Doing his best to ignore the lust whirling through him, he said, "Anything is permitted, my dear. There are no rules."

"If there aren't, how can we break them?"

Impish teasing again lit her eyes and he sensed she jested to cover her nervousness. "We could make a few to break," he jested back.

She smiled and laid her head against his shoulder. "I think you're wonderful, Thorne."

A sense of contentment stole over him, momentarily easing his lustful craving. At the top of the stairs he headed for the master suite. "If it's not customary for a groom to kiss his bride as he carries her over the threshold, perhaps we should establish a new tradition." He lowered his head and kissed Kacy's sweet lips. Pleased with her response, he didn't want to stop. He finally did, although his body shook with the effort to restrain his pent-up passion as he eased the door shut with his foot.

With her arms looped around his neck, she looked dazed when she said, "I have a confession."

"Do you?"

"Yes."

When she said no more he asked, "Are you going to tell me or must I pry the information from you?"

"I think our souls have known each other for almost eternity."

Feeling as though he had known her far longer than a mere week, he sat on the bed with her on his lap and forced himself to act calm. "Would you care to explain?"

She nodded. "I think we lived before in other lifetimes and that we knew and loved each other many times. I also think the reason I traveled back in time was to give us a chance to fulfill our love because we never did before."

When he didn't comment, she startled him by saying, "I know you don't love me yet, but I hope you will someday." She looked away, then back at him, fiddling with her dimple again. "Maybe if I had a tranquilizer, I wouldn't feel so nervous."

"What is a tranquilizer?"

"A pill. It gives people courage. Like alcohol does."

Clay grinned, pleased that she hadn't pursued the subject of other lifetimes, love and time travel. He didn't want anything to intrude upon this special time. "Do you know how much you delight me?"

"No, but I'm glad I do. You delight me, too."

"I know I do," he said with a smug grin. "Your body tells me each time I touch you."

"Such arrogant self-confidence. What am I to do with you?" she asked in mock dismay.

"Surrender all your charms to me."

Kacy's breath froze in her throat. "All my charms?" she repeated slowly, hesitantly.

"Every single one. And I shall surrender mine to you as well," he promised quietly.

For a long moment they stared. Finally she asked, "Wh-what do you want to do now?"

"Disrobe you," he replied huskily.

Kacy couldn't think of a clever reply. In truth she had trouble hanging on to any thoughts because of the urgent emotions she saw in his eyes. And being on his lap, *in his room,* suddenly made her nervous all over again.

He reached for the buttons at the back of her gown.

"Do I get to help you undress, too?" she managed to ask over the new lump threatening to close her throat.

"It would please me if you did."

Her mouth went dry. She swallowed once, then again. The dryness remained. But excitement thrummed through her, mixing with her nervousness as he unfastened the top button at the back of her neck, then the next... and the next.

Although a fire burned brightly across the room, cool air kissed her back as her gown parted. Not knowing quite what to do, she wound her arms around him. He lowered his head and began to nibble on her mouth. His tongue traced her lips, sending shivers down her partially bared spine. She tightened her hold and leaned against him. When he deepened the kiss, her breasts rubbed into his chest. Pleasure flowed through her and she let out a broken sigh as his hands moved up and down her bare back, then to her shoulders to urge her gown down over her arms.

The heat of his body affected her like an aphrodisiac. "This is a fun way to undress," she whispered against his mouth.

"The best," he agreed, teasing her lips with his tongue.

His gentle torment made her impatient. She tugged on his head, telling him without words that she wanted more.

Clay's tongue eased inside to stroke hers. Slowly, deliberately, exerting only scant pressure, he probed the fires of passion that he somehow knew lived inside her. When her soft moan told him she liked what he did, he pulled back to see the desire in her dazed eyes and knew it mirrored his own.

He drew the bodice of her gown down, inch by slow inch, over her lush breasts, covered with white lacy undergarments. Tantalized by the soft flesh peeking above her chemise, he murmured, "Such beauty," and bent his head to place tender kisses in
the tempting valley.

"I like that," she whispered.

"No more than I," he returned, controlling his desire by sheer force of will. "Will you unfasten my shirt?"

"Yes. But first I must work on your cravat." Reaching for it, she unwound and slid it out from under the stiff fake collar of his new frilly-fronted white shirt. "My first wifely duty." She grinned with satisfaction. "I haven't told you how handsome you look, Thorne. I'm very proud you're my groom."

"Now I am your husband," he reminded.

"I'm glad," she replied dreamily.

"Are you?"

"Yes. I can't imagine doing this sort of thing with anyone else. Or even wanting to," she added, drawing another smile from him.

He held his desire in check while she unfastened his press-studs, loosened and removed his stiff collar and cuffs, then unbuttoned his shirt. When her hands went to his shoulders to ease his formal jacket off, he unwrapped his arms from her to aid her in her task.

"Where I came from there's a saying for the bride," she said.

"What is it?" he asked, preoccupied with the tempting curve of her full breasts.

"Something old, something new, something borrowed, something blue."

He realized she was nervous again. "Tell me more."

She blushed becomingly. "Most of my possessions are new but the diamonds are apparently quite old. Do you like them?"

"Yes. Are you ready to remove them?"

She nodded. While he did that for her, he asked, "What did you use for the new?"

"My gown and veil. I borrowed a handkerchief from Fey. And this is blue." She lifted her gown and hooped petticoat to expose a lacy blue-ribbon garter, treating him also to a peek of her shapely legs.

"Very nice," he complimented. Taking quick advantage, he slid the garter over her knee, slowly, sensuously, trailing his fingers down her silk stockinged leg. As he eased the pliable lacy item beyond her ankle and off her dainty foot, he watched her clear blue eyes change from smiling and teasing to dreamy and smoky.

Pleased with himself, he straightened and smugly slipped the garter onto his wrist, all the time watching her fluctuating expression. "Ah, the spoils of war."

She arched her brows in question. "Do you consider this warfare?"

He kissed the tip of her nose. "No. However, I feel very much like a victorious hero tonight."

"You are a hero, Thorne. You're my hero. You've
been my hero for a very long time, in all my dreams."

Unwilling to pursue her seriously spoken words, he suggested, "Let's get this out of our way." He tugged on her petticoat. But rather than budge it clung
to her slender waist.

"I can't imagine why ladies wear these," she complained about the bell-shaped hoop crinoline. "The bottom half of my body looks like it's hiding inside a small mountain and I'll bet all this garb weighs at least ten pounds."

Clay laughed. He couldn't help himself. The look on her face was absolutely precious. Unable to recall ever having such fun in a bedroom, he raised the satin and tulle gown cleaving to her petticoat and unfastened the waistband. Her petticoat fell, deflated, to a puddle at her feet. She stepped outside the three-ringed hoop.

He laughed again when she said, "Men get all the breaks. They don't have to posture and preen or bow to every newfangled fad that comes along. I hate this blasted corset!" she added as he started to loosen the stays. "Corsets make breathing dreadfully difficult. I can't imagine they're good for anybody's health. No wonder so many women in this time suffer from the vapors."

Clay disliked the tight binding as well and agreed with her. "It would suit me if you never wore a corset again."

"May I have your permission to stop wearing them?"

"Do you think you need my permission?"

"From the look in your eyes, I assume I don't, but I've no wish to do anything which might embarrass you, Thorne."

She arched up to kiss his cheek, but he turned his head and captured her mouth with his. Delighted with her for taking the initiative, he almost forgot everything except his fascination with her tempting, seductive lips. But his starving body remembered and made its demands known.

Still, he treated the process of disrobing as a sensuous journey. Soon they were down to his drawers and her chemise and pantalets. He sat on the bed and pulled her onto his lap again.

A becoming blush covered her face. "You look great wearing my garter as a bracelet."

Pleased and amused by the compliment, yet not in the mood to explore his reason for keeping it on, he lowered his head. "You're so sweet," he whispered against her mouth and commanded in a rough whisper, "Open up, love."

She complied, and his tongue thrust inside, then retreated and penetrated once more. Her responses made him forget to go slow. His hunger turned ravenous and he wasn't sure he could control his pace. His mouth firmed; his kisses demanded. Kacy twisted and wiggled on his lap, moving against him in restless abandon, her fingers spearing through his hair while his hunger stroked hers, kneading it, lapping at it.

Clay's barely held control almost snapped when she started to whimper and move enticingly against his loins. Their kisses turned carnal, greedy. Desire ignited into raw need as his mouth slanted over hers with primal ownership. He ended the kisses to pull back for air. Her mouth looked rosy and wet. The sweet taste of her lingered on his tongue. Her chest rose and fell with irregularity and her breathing sounded choppy.

Turning her in his arms, he gently placed her in the center of the bed. For a moment he simply gazed at her. Then he stripped his drawers off and eased his length beside her. Although she looked nervous, she opened her arms. He moved between them, gathered her close and started his tender assault all over again.

Moments later she gasped when he tossed her chemise on the floor and lowered his mouth to her glorious breasts. His dreams of doing this no longer tormented him. Reality was far better than fantasy. Her breasts were fuller than he had fantasized and he hadn't been able to capture the intensity of his reaction to having her trembling in his bed. He felt as close to heaven as he ever expected to be.

He leaned up on his elbows to look at her. Although he saw unfulfilled passion, worry also laced her eyes. But his heart sensed victory. He lowered his head and made her shiver with desire.

Overwhelmed by the fire spreading through her, Kacy couldn't think. She could only react. She hugged him closer, trying to draw more of his warmth into her. Her hands raced up and down his back, over his shoulders and through his hair. When he turned his attention to her throat, she raised her head to give him better access. His teeth gently tugged on her earlobe. Jolts of sheer pleasure cascaded all the way down to her toes. Without conscious thought, she moved with silent demand for more. He shifted his position and kissed a line down her shoulder, then lower to her breast.

"Yes..." she pleaded, "Oh, yes!"

A riptide of tormenting pleasure catapulted through her as he kissed, licked and teased, worshiping every inch of her breast before finally drawing her rigid nipple into his mouth and curling his tongue around it.

She couldn't seem to get close enough. Her body arched up off the bed and his name came out in a long, slow moan. "Thor.. ne."

He raised his head to look at her again. Gloriously aroused, she breathed raggedly. "You're driving me mad."

"Am I?" he whispered, a conquering, confident gleam in his beautiful green eyes.

"Am I giving too much?" she teased, enjoying playing the flirt. "Allowing too many liberties, my lord?"

"No," he groaned. "You're doing everything exactly right."

"You must be, too." She trembled again as she stared into his eyes with absolute trust. "I love you, Thorne. I've loved you for eternity."

"And I am going to love you over and over again," he promised, lowering his mouth to her other breast and taking the initiative just as she wanted him to take control. Finally he moved his mouth to hers again and before she realized what he was doing, he'd stripped off her pantalets.

Now they were both totally naked. Except for the garter he wore as though it were a coveted prize. That thought made her smile. He looked incredibly masculine, even more so with that scrap of lace and blue ribbon circling his sun bronzed wrist. The sight would be etched into her mind forevermore, making her memories of this night more special than she had ever dared to imagine.

He slid his hand into the soft curls shielding her virginity. Her body quivered. For one instant she clamped her legs together.

"Open for me," he whispered huskily. "You shan't be sorry. I promise, love. Trust me."

Kacy obeyed his soft, gentle command and he made love to her with his fingers. She thought she might erupt right then and there, like a gushing volcano. Closing her eyes, she let the ecstasy consume her.

Clay rubbed the very spot he knew would drive her wild. Her touches on his flesh were the most erotic caresses he had ever known. When she was mindless to everything but finding fulfillment, he pulled her beneath him and wrapped her arms around his neck.

Hoping she was ready, he parted her legs with his knees.

"Please," she pleaded, and he sensed she didn't understand what she pleaded for. He intended to give it though, and pressed the tip of his arousal against her opening. Her eyes flew open and she stared straight into his eyes.

His blood pounded through him with such force he wasn't sure how much longer he could wait.

"I'm ready," she whispered, surprising him.

"I don't wish to hurt you, love. Yet I may. But only this once," he promised.

"I'm not afraid of pain, Thorne. Please hurry. The wait is unbearable."

He sheathed himself partially inside her. When he encountered the barrier of her virginity, he tried to gently push past the obstacle. It wouldn't give. He clenched his jaw. His breathing turned ragged. The pressure inside him was so intense he could barely hold onto what little control he had left. He knew he was hurting her when she moaned against his shoulder but hugged him close just the same.

Lowering his mouth to hers, he kissed her senseless before he made the final thrust. Her cry of pain was swallowed by his kiss. He moved slowly, then paused to give her time to adjust to him and to recover from his invasion. She tilted her hips, indicating she was ready to continue. Out he slid, then back in, kissing her forehead, her cheek, her ear and murmuring soft words to soothe her. As he had anticipated, she fit him perfectly and for one arrogant moment he thought she had been created exclusively for him.

Suddenly her body thrashed beneath him, demanding release. The pressure inside him was excruciatingly beautiful. Never had he experienced anything like it! Kacy was a fire in his arms, and her wild, uninhibited responses shook him to his very core. She held nothing back and her selfless act forced him to do the same. No longer capable of controlling his passion, the hunger inside him raged. Mindless to everything but giving them both fulfillment, he thrust and thrust and thrust.

Release came upon them in a rush. Kacy found hers first and as soon as she did, Clay gave in to his own orgasm. Burying his face against her clean sweet-scented hair, he let out a raw groan. Instinctively she squeezed him tighter and his body jerked with spasms as he released his essence inside her.

The splendor caught Kacy by surprise. She clung to Thorne as waves of blissful surrender washed over and through her. It took a long while to come back to reality. But she was in no hurry. This was her wedding night. And it was perfect.

Clay eventually found the strength to roll onto his side. He took Kacy with him; his arms still wrapped around her. "Are you all right?"

"Yes," she murmured dreamily. "I'm wonderful. And so are you."

He tightened his arms possessively. She belonged to him now. The thought filled him with pride and arrogant male vanity. Hoping he hadn't hurt her too much, he asked, "How do you feel?"

"Like your wife." She watched him slide the lacy blue-ribboned garter off his arm and set it on the bedside table. Henceforth he would consider it as precious as a valued treasure.

A few peaceful moments later, Kacy said, "Next time I want to do all those fantastic things to you."

Although the heat of their lovemaking hadn't yet cooled, his insatiable hunger already clamored for fulfillment again. "What fantastic things?" he asked in a husky drawl.

The flames from the fire flickered shadows across her face, but he saw her eyes fill with promise. "I'd rather show you than try to explain."

"Feel free," he invited, "to do anything you desire."

She smiled, slipping the garter onto her own small wrist. It looked lovely against her pale flesh. Her only adornment other than her wedding ring.

Then she stunned him by rolling over on top of him and laving his hardened nipple before drawing the nub between her warm, moist lips. He hadn't married a slow learner.

It was his turn to gasp out loud. And her turn to drive him to depths heretofore unknown.

Twenty

Afternoon of The Eleventh Day

Kacy stood in the garden, trying to decide which roses to cut for fresh bouquets in the mansion. They had been married four days and she was supremely happy. Except for one thing. Thorne had compartmentalized their marriage. Polite strangers by day, intimate lovers by night.

She'd tried to talk to him about the way he treated her. She even tried again to convince him they had known each other in previous lives. When she brought it up the morning after their wedding, he said he was busy. It didn't take long to learn he would discuss household matters throughout the day. Personal matters must wait until dinner. After that he was too busy giving them both pleasure to talk.

In her heart Kacy had said her silent good-byes to all those she loved in the future. This is where she wanted to be... where she wanted to live out the rest of her life. Surely she'd be allowed to stay. *Fate or the Gods in Kolob couldn't be so cruel as to separate them now, could they?*

Kacy inhaled the fresh garden air and started to clip. As she placed each rose and rosebud in the basket at her feet, she tried not to worry about her marriage. Every blissful hour brought her closer, she hoped, to the moment when Thorne would say he loved her. Because their best discussions took place before dinner, while they sipped sherry in the privacy of the parlor, she chose then to explain her memories and the glimpses she'd had of other lives. So far Thorne had brushed aside every attempt to convince him they had loved each other time and again. She wanted to be patient, but a sense of urgency had seized her and grew stronger each day.

She finished cutting roses and headed for the mansion. Fey had been to visit once; Rey hadn't visited at all. Fey said he was still in Kolob.

Nobody had been ill or gotten hurt and Kacy had used her unusual gift to heal only once—to remove the cataracts in Montfort's filmy eyes and heal some of his arthritic aches and pains. Sleeping with Thorne and making love restored her strength, she'd discovered. Each day was busy but delightful, each night another glorious adventure.

~ * ~

Kacy was in the music room arranging a bouquet when Fey arrived in human size. "The solicitors are here." she announced without preamble. "We should join your husband."

Kacy smiled. "My husband. I like how that sounds."

As they descended the stairs, Fey whispered, "Let me handle the solicitors. The less you and Thorne are
involved, the better off you'll be."

Kacy agreed with a silent nod.

The diatribe in the study reached them as they approached the half-open door. A portly man strode across the room, gesturing like he was on stage. "Tis clear you disobeyed the terms of the will, Lord Banes and refurbished Havenhurst without regard for your deceased uncle's will."

Another man, tall, thin and beady-eyed, claimed the floor before the stout one could continue when he paused to catch his breath. "Tis our duty to uphold the terms and conditions of the will. As they have been broken, we shall seek an audience with the Queen and inform her the earldom is forfeit."

Greed clouded his eyes and Kacy suspected he was thinking about the wealth he could claim if the earldom reverted to the crown.

"Cut the dramatics." Fey pushed the door further open, boldly walked inside and closed it with a decided thump after Kacy entered.

While the three men stared at Fey, Thorne's gaze captured Kacy's. She gave him what she hoped he interpreted as a warning to let Fey deal with the solicitors before she smiled.

Clay returned her smile. Lord, how she pleased him! Too much, he thought each day and knew he should distance himself, but every night he couldn't wait to be alone with her in his bed chamber.

Though not surprised by Fey's presence, he was surprised by the determined look on her pixie-fairy face. She looked ready to defend a citadel. He wasn't worried. Havenhurst's accounts were in order and the solicitors couldn't prove the restrictions imposed by his uncle's will had been broken, any more than he could prove they had forged the will, a suspicion that had formed some time ago and grown since Kacy's arrival. Still, having understood her warning glance, he decided to listen to what Fey had to say.

"Who in the devil are you?" The oldest of the three solicitors pulled his quizzing glass from his breast pocket, held it up to his eye, looking Fey over before he turned to inspect Kacy.

"A friend of the earl's," Fey replied sweetly. "And who might you be?" She tilted her head to one side. "No, do not tell me. Let me guess. One of the scoundrels who prepared the wretched will which seeks to tie the current earl's hands and run the earldom into the ground."

"That isn't true," Bernard disagreed.

"'What isn't true?" Fey asked, but without giving him a chance to answer, she asked more questions. "You're not one of the scoundrels?" She raised her silver-blond eyebrows in scornful disbelief. "Or does the will not restrict what the earl may do?"

"Do not attempt to con-confuse us," the stout, round girthed man named Lunchey, who had been pontificating when Fey and Kacy came downstairs, sputtered.

Fey turned a superior smile on him. "Is it possible to confuse such learned men?"

"Certainly not." He pushed out his portly chest, interpreting Fey's words as a compliment, rather than the jibe they were meant to be. "We are men of the law—"

"Who twist it to suit their own greedy black hearts," Fey concluded.

"How dare you put words in my mouth?"

"Why would I want to put anything in that foul smelling orifice?" Fey mocked.

Clay covered his mouth to hide a grin and realized Kacy was having the same problem when she raised her eyes to the ceiling and stared at the intricate scrolls sculpted thereon.

Lunchey drew himself up to his full unimpressive height and pretended to ignore Fey's insult. "The former earl's will forbids improvements to the earldom unless they are paid for by profits from the estate. We know there have been no profits for three years. The will also states the current earl may not use his wealth to support or improve the earldom in any manner whatsoever, yet the mansion has been splendidly refurbished and servants and tenants alike have new clothes as well as improved cottages and who knows what else."

"The will also prohibits the current earl from accepting loans from friends," bald-headed Meldrum added for emphasis. "In addition to the improvements in the mansion and tenant's cottages, all four fields have been planted. That alone could not have been accomplished without expending a goodly sum. Surely the dear price of seed depleted the annual stipend. You shall, therefore, fail to live within the conditions in the will before the end of the year."

"No loans were made." Kacy uttered her first words. "The changes here were a gift."

Feeling like an observer, rather than a participant, Clay wondered if he should make the effort to introduce her and Fey. Although not one to allow ladies to fight his battles, there were times when strength lay in silence. He decided to let the drama unfold without interfering.

"A gift?" Lunchey squinted in disbelief. "Would you have us believe the seed as well as this magnificent refurbishing," he gestured with his flabby hands, "was done by someone other than the earl and that no one expects remuneration?"

"Perhaps, there has been no refurbishing," Fey said with a mischievous twinkle, "and everything you see is an illusion, or has always been as you now see it."

"Impossible!" Meldrum said in a near shout.

"We must insist upon an audit of the earl's books," Lunchey said. "Unless they are out of order, they will show what has been expended."

"The books are in order," Clay said flatly.

"And you may audit them forever," Kacy added, looking like a lioness ready to defend her cub, which sent a pleased thrill through Clay, "but you won't find a single shilling that was spent on the mansion or the tenant's cottages."

"Where then," Lunchey demanded, "did the money come from to pay for the restoration?"

"No money was expended," Clay said.

Meldrum wrinkled his craggy brows in doubt. "How is that possible?"

"Everything was gifted," Fey repeated.

"From whom?"

"A friend."

"We must have names. I insist upon it."

"The only name you'll get is mine." Fey stepped closer and as she did, her height altered until she stood a foot taller than anyone in the room. A look of determination, combined with absolute authority, covered her face. Staring down at Clay's foes from her intimidating height, she announced, "I am Fey. The Earl of Havenhurst calls me Fairy Fey. I am fairy godmother to Kacy Rose, his wife."

Clay suppressed a smile, inordinately pleased when Kacy stepped closer while Fey lectured the solicitors. "Any changes you perceive at Havenhurst may be attributed to me and I did not expend a single farthing."

"That remains to be seen," Lunchey said, refusing to back away.

"You buffoons," Fey plucked her wand from her sleeve and pointed it at each solicitor.

Guilt slashed across each man's face and Clay decided to voice his suspicion. "Each of you shall rue the day you entered into an alliance to cheat me out of my inheritance."

All eyes turned to him. "We did not," sputtered Lunchey, "enter into agreement to cheat you of anything."

"What do you call forging the will?" Clay asked.

"You have no proof that we did such a diabolical thing!" Meldrum shouted.

"You're wrong," Fey disagreed. "Others witnessed your dastardly deed."

"The only men present were the three of us," gray-haired Bernard said, apparently without realizing what he'd just admitted.

"There were others present," Fey disagreed. "A guardian angel for one, although you didn't see him because he was like this." She waved her wand and made herself invisible while she reprimanded, "Lies and greed are your mainstay, you poor wretched fools."

Lunchey raised his fist in the direction of her voice. "We will not suffer your insults nor be threatened by whatever magic tricks you have learned to perform."

"You foolish man. Don't you know you shall not only suffer insults, you shall suffer much more?" Without giving him time to refute her statement, Fey reappeared, first in human size, then she shrank to her normal two-inch size before she spread her wings and flew to Clay. While the solicitor's gaped in shock, she whispered for Clay and Kacy's ears alone, "These knaves are in for the shock of their lives."

Clay didn't doubt she meant that and although he would have handled things differently, he allowed her to proceed.

She flew back to the stunned, tongue-tied men and asked in an angelic tone, "Would you believe the changes here occurred through the use of fairy magic?"

"Certainly not." Although Lunchey answered, the other two shook their heads in ludicrous unison. "We do not believe in magic, fairy or otherwise."

"Perhaps a small demonstration is in order." At Fey's suggestion Clay found himself, along with Fey, Kacy and the solicitors outdoors in a clearing beyond the woods, some distance from the mansion and stables.

"How did you do that?" Lunchey demanded, his body as rigid as the other two whose expressions were frozen in a combination of terror and comic disbelief.

Without answering, Fey asked, "Do you see anything over there?" She motioned to their right with her wand.

As a collective unit, they glanced beyond her tiny hand. Then each answered angrily. "No."

"Of course not."

"What is the meaning of this outrage?"

"Might I suggest you take another look?" Fey offered smugly.

They did. And gaped in stupefaction. A carnival, similar to one Clay had seen in his travels, appeared.

"Are you prepared for an experience you will never forget?" Fey asked, her voice an ominous challenge.

"Do not toy with us!" Lunchey, who had lost some of his arrogance, shouted to cover his apparent shock.

"You have yelled for the last time, you black-hearted knave." Fey waved her wand and cast a spell that rendered him dumb. He opened his mouth to speak but no words came out. Panicked, he tried again but all he managed were a few gurgled god-awful sounds. His two companions stepped away as though to remain close might afflict them as well.

Kacy almost felt sorry for them. But if, as Thorne suggested, they had forged the cursed will, they deserved whatever Fey dished out.

"Haven't the two of you anything to say?" Fey needled.

Both men shook their frightened heads.

"Then perhaps you are ready for the carnival."

Before they could blink, Fey transported the threesome to a ride where they twirled with unmerciful speed. "That's called a Tilt-a-Whirl," Kacy explained to Thorne. "It's usually enjoyable, but Fey's making it spin fast so they'll think it's dangerous."

While the solicitors yelled in terror, Fey flew them up to the top of a Ferris wheel. Before they became accustomed to the alarming height, their chair descended so fast they upchucked. Kacy glanced away. The sight made her queasy.

Without giving them time to recover, Fey whipped them from the Ferris wheel to the front seat of a roller coaster. By the time she plucked them from there, all three had soiled their trousers. She then stuck them in the middle of the carnival. Toothless hawkers, bearded pirates and gypsies of all sizes and shapes pushed them from stall to stall, hawking their wares and demanding coins. Too dazed to understand what was happening, the stunned trio suddenly found themselves in the center of a huge crowd of jeering elves, who defiled them further by spitting on them.

"Have you had enough?" Fey hovered above them, fluttering her eyelids in time to her waving wings.

When they nodded, she snatched them from the center of the crowd and stood them before Thorne and Kacy where she promptly ordered, "Apologize to the earl."

The beady-eyed solicitor found the nerve to say, "Elves and fairies. Do not expect us to believe anything as illogical as all that nonsense. This is nothing short of witchcraft." He pointed at the carnival a few feet away. Fey waved her wand. His arm froze in mid-air. He tried desperately to move it, but couldn't.

"Your corpulent compatriot, Mr. Lunchey, will speak again, but never without a speech impediment," Fey explained the stout solicitor's fate. "You," she said to the beady-eyed man, "will eventually move your arm again, Mr. Meldrum, but it will be as useless as a lame horse. Your problem is due to certain muscles which are now longer than normal, although I doubt you understand that any more than you understand your human punishment is but a glimpse of what you will face after death."

She turned to the older, gray-haired man. "What do you think your punishment should be, Mister Bernard?" Obviously frightened that she knew his name, he stood as mute as a statue. "I shall give you a few moments to think about it." Her gaze passed slowly over each man. "Now you know the restoration of Havenhurst was indeed accomplished by fairy magic. If any of you ever return here or attempt to cause trouble again, you will rue the day you were born."

"I expect you to destroy the will you forged and never again attempt to speak to me," Clay added.

After giving the solicitors a moment to digest his words, Fey said to Bernard, "For your involvement in this crime you will be inflicted with strabismus."

"Strabismus?" he echoed, looking as dumbfounded as he must have felt.

"A defect in your eyes, which will render them incapable of looking in the same direction." As soon as Fey said the word, he started to squint. "The only way to correct your problem is through a strabotomy—a surgical eye operation. However, that procedure shan't be available until the next century. You'll be dead long before then."

Fey looked pleased when she turned to Clay. "Have you anything more to say?"

He eyed each man thoughtfully; his brow hiked is question. "I presume you prefer the fairy's punishment to being charged with fraud and being disbarred?"

All three nodded.

"I further presume my uncle's original will was destroyed?"

Unable to speak yet, Lunchey nodded and Bernard said, "Yes. I believe it was."

"No," Meldrum said, "The original will was prepared before your cousin's demise. Your uncle never saw fit to change it, as you were second in line to inherit."

"You will forward the will to me at once. Understood?"

Meldrum nodded.

"And the money my uncle left in your hands?"

Meldrum's shiny bald head turned red and Clay suspected that of the three, he alone had a conscience. "Your uncle and cousin squandered his wealth. The money left with us came from the sale of your parent's estate. I deposited it in Barings Bank and will release our claim against it."

Before Clay could comment, Fey said, "You're not the only man these black hearts have harmed. Had Rey not restricted me I would have done more to the rascals. Now, before I zap them back to London and obtain your uncle's original will, have you anything more to say?"

Clay had trouble keeping a grin off his face. "Your magic still amazes me, Fey. You are a wondrous friend and a terror as a foe. I count myself fortunate that you came to my aid."

"You were worthy." Her voice softened as a smile covered her tiny face.

"And thank you for your help in restoring my ancestral mansion," Clay added.

"You are most welcome."

"Is there anything I can do to repay you?"

"Actually, there is." Fey grinned. "Escort your wife back to the mansion whilst I tend to these blokes." With an impish grin she waved the carnival away. Then she vanished, along with Messrs. Lunchey, Bernard and Meldrum.

Clay offered his arm to Kacy. Instead of taking it, she asked, "Have you always known the will was forged?"

"No. However, I had my suspicions."

"Then why didn't you do something about it?"

"Because I had no proof." *And because I did not wish all England to know I was accused of murder in France.*

He thought he saw disappointment in Kacy's eyes. Did she think less of him for allowing Fey to deal with the solicitors? He would not ask. It mattered not. Why then did he brood as he escorted her back to the mansion? He didn't love her. He merely desired her. And he still didn't believe they had known each other in prior lives. Why then did he dream they had?

Twenty-one

Morning of The Twelfth Day

Seated in his saddle atop Blade, Clay galloped along the road from the village. His thoughts were on Kacy as they had been too often of late. He had hoped to tire of her once they wed. Instead he wanted her more each day. Not an hour passed when he did not think of her. And that must stop.

He had to force his mind to dwell on other matters. Last evening Fey had returned with his uncle's last will and testament. It had been signed a fortnight after the birth of his cousin and contained none of the restrictions Clay had lived with these three years past.

As he neared the halfway mark home, a rabbit raced across the road, reminding Clay of the rabbit he'd captured while Kacy rode with him. That memory brought her back to mind in full force. She slept in his chamber every night, but he left her before daybreak, thinking that might help him distance himself. All it had done was deprive him of an enjoyable early morning romp between the bed sheets.

His body reacted to that thought, making him want her now, this instant. He blew his breath out between his clamped teeth. Tonight they would make love in *her* chamber. Then he would leave. He might miss sleeping beside her, but that habit must be broken before it became ingrained.

The nagging sensation that they did indeed share some kind of bond persisted. Still, he refused to give credence to her belief that they had known each other in past lives. Nor would he name what they shared as love, although it pleased his vanity to hear Kacy say she loved him. She hadn't said it since their wedding night, but her claims of living before continued to invade his dreams. Another reason to distance himself.

To his surprise, she had accomplished a great deal since their wedding; all without the use of Fey's wand. Kacy's visits to Vicar Crandon and his wife had resulted in placing two-thirds of his servants with other families. Clay had agreed to pay their salaries for the next year. Only a dozen servants remained at Havenhurst—Montfort, his butler, Cook Edna May, Ellen, the serving maid, Bertha, his housekeeper, who supervised the two maids; Maisy, Kacy's lady maid, two gardeners, one groom, and two stable lads, Timothy and Thadius. Clay's man, Benton, remained in London to supervise his staff at his home in Belgrave. Now that the earldom was running smoothly, Clay planned to pen a message stating he would be in London in a fortnight.

Kacy would accompany him. Clay wanted her to meet his friends. However, it wouldn't do to entertain her every evening in London. He would spend time at White's; play cards with his friends and get caught up on the latest on-dits and wagers.

His plans to distance himself pleased him. Thus far, Kacy was a model wife and countess—gracious sweet smiles... the embodiment of femininity. Each day she made no important decisions without first consulting him and with seemingly little effort, she ensured his home ran as smooth as the new grandfather clock in the foyer. She placed vases of flowers in the rooms they frequented and after they supped each evening, she played chess or card games with him. Twice she entertained him in the music room. In bed, she satisfied him as no woman ever had and to his delight, she enjoyed their loving making as much as he.

He couldn't have chosen a more appropriate wife, even if she was an American and unacquainted with his duties of peerage and the unwritten rules which governed polite society. She would learn and he believed she would neither betray nor embarrass him. Still, it wouldn't do to become too enamored. Men of his class married to produce an heir. They didn't marry the woman they loved. Too bad he hadn't considered that before he proposed to Oraline.

Through the grapevine he had heard she was now a widow and didn't get on with her deceased husband's daughters, all older than she. When he thought about Oraline now, he no longer felt bitter, not even the vague sense of loss that had once been quite intense. *Was Kacy responsible?* He didn't like to think so, but a persistent thought nagged that she was.

Be that as it may, today he would begin to take his midday meal in his study, alone. And tomorrow night he'd dine with his neighbors. Kacy would stay home. The Marquis and Valerie had not been formally told of his marriage. Guilt nagged him for not telling them sooner and he felt obligated to inform Valerie without Kacy's presence.

Clay arrived home and lived by his decisions. For the first time since their wedding, five days ago, he ate the midday meal by himself. And instead of inviting Kacy to share afternoon tea with him, he rode to the local pub and caught up on gossip.

That night as they supped, she asked, "Do men go to the pub to get away from their wives?"

Startled by her bold question, Clay answered, "No. They go there to discuss news and politics."

"And to stare at the pretty serving girls?"

"What makes you think the wenches are pretty?"

"Should I have said buxom?"

"You should not have begun this discussion."

"Is it off-limits?"

"It is inappropriate."

"I see." But from her expression, he didn't think she did and he wasn't pleased with himself for chiding her.

"I shall repair to the study. I have work to do." He saw her hurt, and cursed himself for treating her badly, but he needed to distance himself while he still could. "Why don't you select a book from the library and go to your room? I shall join you at bedtime."

Without a nod or even a word, she stood and left. He followed, watching her, a preoccupation he never seemed to tire of engaging in. When she reached the library and disappeared from view, he felt as though she were the one trying to distance herself. It was for the best, but it bothered him just the same.

When Clay joined her in her bedchamber, he expected her to be ready for bed. Instead she had apparently borrowed clothes from one of the maids. His eyes bulged as he took in the comely sight. "Why are you dressed like that?"

Instead of answering, she asked, "Do I look like a serving wench?"

"You look..." he nearly said foolish, but realized that wasn't true. She looked adorable. The white off-the-shoulder blouse exposed a good amount of cleavage; the shortened hem allowed a comely view of her shapely ankles and her blond locks cascaded from the lace-trimmed cap, making her appeal all the more fascinating.

"How do I look?" she prompted.

"Good enough to kiss." And he did.

When that kiss ended, he kissed her throat, then moved lower to sample the soft fleshy mounds peeking above her neckline. She drew in a sharp breath. He thought she was as ready to disrobe as he was.

"Your hair smells like smoke."

Startled, he raised his head to stare at her.

"Do you like the smell?"

"No. It stinks."

He thought he'd been seducing her and she couldn't bear the wait. Instead she'd been thinking about smoke, not making love. Did it repel her? The thought jolted him. No woman had ever turned him away.

"Has it ever occurred to you that inhaling second-hand smoke might be unhealthy?" she asked.

Clay had never heard anything more ridiculous. "How so?"

"It can damage your nose, throat and lungs and lead to cancer. I knew somebody who died of throat cancer. Watching the disease deteriorate him wasn't pleasant."

"Our home is heated with fireplaces," Clay said, "therefore, smoke isn't something either of us can avoid."

"Fireplace smoke and bonfires don't contain nicotine or tobacco. Cigarettes, cigars and pipes do. In the future, it's a proven fact that they can be extremely hazardous to people's health."

Clay thought she might be saying that because she didn't wish him to frequent the pub. He didn't intend to stop just to please her. Neither did he intend to give credence to facts she claimed occurred in the future. "Would you refuse to kiss me if I were to take up smoking?"

"I don't know." She shrugged and her breasts swayed in a seductive dance. "I've been kissed by men who smoke. It was like licking an ashtray."

Clay didn't know whether to be pleased or angry. How many men had kissed her? He told himself he didn't care and would be a damn fool to ask.

When she walked away and looked at something on top of her bureau, he had the feeling she didn't want to make love. He considered leaving, then decided he would make that decision, not her. Whether she liked the way he smelled or not. He strode over and pulled her into his arms.

She stared up at him. "Are we going to make love in here?"

"What do you think?" His gaze bore into hers while his hands busied themselves with the fastenings on her borrowed clothes.

Every touch, every kiss, every caress seemed to be their first and he paced each and every one with deliberate slowness, teasing and tormenting until he had her begging. Only then did he allow himself to give her the climax they both wanted and needed. And when they finished, he wondered again when he would tire of her. He had begun to fear he might not. Although displeased with that thought, he rolled onto his side and held her close until she asked, "Do you still love Oraline?"

He freed his arms and rolled to a sitting position. "What do you know about her?"

"Not much. Only that you asked her to marry you and she accepted your betrothal ring, then married a man old enough to be her grandfather because he had a title and old wealth."

"Never mention her name to me again."

Angry, he stood and strode from the room as naked as the day he was born. Alone in his chamber, he went to bed, where he dreamed the same dream over and over again. From a distance, he saw a beautiful woman he had loved and lost repeatedly. He tried to catch her each time she came near, but she floated out of his reach time and time again.

He broke out in a sweat as tormenting images taunted him and they grew worse when he awakened and realized Kacy was the woman he had loved and lost recurrently in his dream. For some odd reason, it made him feel as old as time. He told himself dreams had no meaning.

And he believed that most of the time.

Twenty-two

Morning of The Thirteenth Day

Today was her birthday. Kacy hadn't told Thorne. She didn't want him to think she expected a birthday gift. But she planned to celebrate tonight.

With money Fey provided, Kacy had gone to the village and purchased gifts for her guests, including all the household servants and stable workers. She'd bought something for everyone, except Thorne. She wanted something special for him. Something from the future. And Fey had produced what she wanted—two books. One of poetry by Elizabeth Barrett Browning, the other about reincarnation, *The Missing Link in Christianity.*

Thorne didn't join her for breakfast. Nor did he send for her to share morning tea. She hadn't yet asked if he'd mind if she invited the Sathers and the vicar's family to join Bardsy, Timothy and Thadius for supper. Disturbed by last night's dream, a dream of the future, she tried to understand it. Thorne had been in church with his wife and first-born, a son. He gazed at his wife with love-filled eyes, but Kacy wasn't his wife, although they looked alike. His wife had no scar; her skin was as flawless as Catharine's, like the skin Kacy coveted. As she thought about the dream now, her heart plunged, even as a sense of urgency descended. Would she be taken from this time? Would Catharine replace her as Thorne's wife?

Feeling doomed to live forever without him and his love, Kacy gathered her composure as best she could and approached his study.

"Come in," Thorne called after she knocked.

She opened the door and walked in.

He stood and stretched while he waited for her to speak.

Although she disliked breaking his rule about waiting until dinner to discuss personal matters, today she felt driven by an urgency she couldn't explain. "I have something I think I should tell you."

Curiosity filled his green eyes. "What is it?"

"I just realized I might have come here to help bring you and your true love together."

He hiked a black, dubious eyebrow but didn't comment.

Desperate to know if he had any memories of past lives and encouraged by his silence, Kacy said, "Suppose you and your lady love lived and loved each other long ago, say in the eleventh century. Suppose further that you went off to fight in the Crusades and didn't return, therefore, your love never had a chance to be fulfilled. If that occurred, could you conceive of the possibility that the two of you might now have the chance to be reunited in this life?"

His eyes bored into hers. "What are you suggesting?"

She had already mentioned reincarnation and insinuated they had known each other in previous lives, but he didn't believe that any more than he grasped the memories she so desperately wished he'd recall. With a shrug, she silently admitted defeat. "I have no right to suggest anything. However, I feel I should urge you not to send Catharine away if I leave and she returns to Havenhurst."

For half a second she thought she saw regret, but then Thorne asked, "Do you have plans to leave?"

Kacy had to force her next words out. "No, but I suspect Catharine might have been your love in a past life because I dreamed about the two of you last night. I know it was her because she didn't have a scar on her cheek." Kacy fingered her own. "In any event, you were in church with your first-born. A son."

Shaken by her dream, Kacy shuddered. "I think that may be why I met Catharine and why I was brought here. We might have been twins at one time and maybe I came to help reunite you because I understand the love in her heart."

"Love is for fools," Thorne growled.

"I think you're wrong."

"And I think you meddle in matters which are not your concern."

"Perhaps you're right," Kacy conceded. "None of this is clear." In actuality, she was confused, puzzled and bewildered.

"Why would you think Miss Paice and I loved in another time. What about yourself?"

Kacy knew she and Thorne had loved before, but he refused to believe it, so she saw no reason to mention that again. "I don't belong in this time. But Catharine does."

"Miss Paice," Thorne thundered, "holds no appeal for me whatsoever and I forbid you to discuss her with me again. Is that clear?"

"Crystal," Kacy said.

"What?"

"It's as clear as crystal," Kacy clarified.

But nothing was really clear, except that she was more confused than ever now. Turning, she left the study, forgetting to mention her desire to invite the Sathers' and the vicar's family to the mansion for supper.

To deal with the doom that settled on her shoulders, Kacy focused on her celebration. Let Thorne be surprised. It would serve him right. She conferred with Bertha, the stout, good-natured housekeeper and Edna Mae, Thorne's plump cook, then asked Timothy and Thadius to accompany her to the Sathers' cottage so she could invite them.

~ * ~

Sarah Sathers smiled. "We would be ever so happy to come."

"I thought we might eat early. At seven." Kacy wanted ample time for her guests to open their gifts afterwards and for the Sathers' to get home early. Sarah's delivery date was nearly here and Kacy thought she should get as much rest at night as possible before the baby came.

"Are you sure you want us to bring Janey and Lamont?"

"Yes. Timothy and Thadius will be there, so Janey and Lamont won't be the only young ones."

"Miles and I appreciate your invitation. Our lives have improved vastly since you came. And everyone, except perhaps my brother, is so happy you married the earl."

Kacy smiled. "I doubt anyone is as happy as I am."

From the Sathers' cottage she and the boys rode to the vicar's home to invite him, his wife, Louise and Lamont.

Back at the mansion, Kacy learned Thorne had ordered his midday meal to be served in his study. Because he was mad? Or because he feared he was getting too close to her? She knew why he held himself away during the day. He feared that if he spent too much time with her, he might discover he loved her. *The coward.*

Thorne sent word for her to join him for afternoon tea in his study. As soon as she poured, he said, "I shan't sup with you this evening. I'm dining out."

"Alone?"

"With the Marquis of Rotherhile and his granddaughter. The invitation was extended some time ago. I meant to tell you last evening. It slipped my mind."

"You needn't explain," Kacy said, glad that he had, yet hurt, too. *He'll be with the beautiful Valerie.* Unable to get that out of her mind, Kacy's heart pounded in trepidation as she sipped her tea. Maisy said Valerie had set her cap for Thorne and she wasn't merely lovely, she was as beautiful as a delicate Dresden doll. *You deserve to worry,* Kacy chastised herself, *for listening to Maisy's gossip.*

"I suppose I could cancel," Thorne said, but Kacy had the distinct feeling he said that only to be polite.

'Yes, do!' she wanted to shout, but forced herself to speak with calm. "That isn't necessary. I don't expect you to entertain me every evening."

He leaned closer and shook his head, a slow movement which emphasized the candor of his gaze. "Are you feeling all right?"

In spite of the heaviness in her heart, she made herself smile. "I feel stronger than I've felt in ages." She also felt a multitude of other emotions. Jealousy. Resentment. Fear. And the awful sensation that her time with him would soon end unless he admitted he loved her and wanted her to stay. Why did she have such thoughts?

It took a lot of nerve to work up the courage to ask; "Do you think you'll ever love me?"

He controlled his expression and she couldn't decipher his thoughts or mood when he said, "We share a mutual admiration. That should be enough."

"What if it isn't?"

"It must be."

For the second time that day her heart plunged. *How could he treat her like this? How could she let him?*

Emotionally he was as accessible as a log in the fire after it burned to ashes. She stood to leave. At the door she paused to venture another question. "Will you always be terminally repressed where love is concerned?"

She left before he could comment, but not before she saw anger darken his green eyes.

Alone in the library a few minutes later, doubt assaulted her like salt applied to raw wounds. Would Thorne ever love her? Maybe he didn't and therefore, couldn't say the words. More fear crowded in. Did he care for Valerie? Would he enjoy being with her tonight more than he enjoyed being home with his wife?

Feeling guilty for nagging at him, Kacy wandered up to the music room and played every love song she knew by heart. The disturbing premonition that she might leave this time soon and that Thorne might end up with Catharine made her heart ache, but she didn't know what to do about it. Her life was out of control. So was her future. Now she understood how Thorne must have felt with her arrival and the hurried up wedding ceremony. Did he regret it? Had she worn out her welcome? If so, how could he make such beautiful love to her every night?

At dusk, Kacy gathered her dignity as best she could after she changed her gown and went down to the parlor. Thorne came down the stairs a short time later and waved goodbye from the doorway.

"I hope you have a nice evening," she said, wishing he'd come in and kiss her goodbye.

But all he did was nod before he strode away.

Tears of self-pity scalded her eyes, threatening to overflow as she stood by the window and watched him climb in his carriage and ride away. Hurt that he hadn't kissed her, spoken a word, or invited her to go with him, Kacy recalled what they had shared. For the last four evenings they had dined by candlelight. Afterwards, she played the pianoforte to entertain him. Twice they played chess. Kacy almost beat him the second night. But he put her in check so she lost every game. Last night, in an attempt to best him at something, she taught him gin rummy. She won the first two hands. After that he beat her soundly and undercut her three times. She hoped to teach him cribbage, which should give her an advantage, at least in the beginning. She had asked Fey to provide a cribbage board and Fey had complied. To Kacy's amusement, the board was pink. Maybe that would distract Thorne's sharp mind.

Last night still puzzled her. In her room, he had made such sweet, slow love that she thought he might tell her he loved her. Instead he had left angry and they'd slept apart for the first time, something she feared might begin to be the norm.

More doubts crowded in. Last night's dream had truly shaken her. Would Thorne fall in love with Catharine after she left? Kacy swallowed another threat of tears. It hadn't occurred to her that he wouldn't celebrate her birthday with her tonight. Yesterday she'd considered telling him about it and might have if he hadn't avoided her most of the day and left her to sleep alone last night. This morning she considered it again, but he'd shut her out of his activities. At tea she'd considered telling him, but didn't for the same reason she hadn't told him earlier. She didn't want him to think she expected a gift. But she had told Timothy and Thadius and she smiled as she recalled their enthusiasm.

Ellen, the serving maid, interrupted Kacy's thoughts when she rapped on the parlor door. "Cook Edna Mae wishes to know when supper should be served."

"As soon as my guests arrive. I asked them to be here before seven."

"Very good." Ellen smiled. "Cook made birthday cake for pudding, Countess."

Kacy smiled, too. Modern Brits still called dessert pudding and Timothy and Thadius must have told Edna Mae they were celebrating Kacy's birthday. Pleased that she wouldn't be alone, she spied the two boys at the door.

"May we come in, Countess?"

Kacy smiled. "Please do."

Dressed in the new suits and white frilly fronted shirts that Fey's wand had conjured for them to wear to the feast and wedding, they looked like miniature men.

"We told Cook it be your birthday an' she made a big cake fer you," Thadius whistled through his missing front teeth.

"And this be yur present." Bashful Timothy presented an odd-shaped offering wrapped in the blanket from his cot behind the stable. "We made it," he announced as Kacy uncovered a wreath. Woven out of new straw with dried flowers and pinecones twined throughout, Kacy thought it beautiful.

"It's lovely. Thank you."

"Ya likes it, don't ya?" Thadius asked anxiously.

"Yes. It's one of the nicest gifts I've ever received."

Both boys beamed. "The earl's been trying ta teach us how ta make a wreath, but we never got it quite right, till now," Timothy said.

"I love it," she said and meant it. She was delighted Thorne spent time with them and that they were learning how to read and do their sums.

Although Kacy missed Thorne tremendously, she welcomed her guests with enthusiasm. Janey and Lamont took right up with Timothy and Thadius, and Kacy enjoyed visiting with Sarah and the vicar's wife, while the men discussed politics.

Relaxed in her role as hostess, Kacy enjoyed her celebration until the vicar asked, "Why isn't the earl here?"

Kacy explained, "He had a previous engagement he felt compelled to keep."

After dinner, Ellen carried Kacy's birthday cake in on a shiny silver tray and all twelve servants crowded inside the dining room to wish her a happy birthday. On an impulse, Kacy decided to teach everybody the popular American birthday song. After that she made a wish and blew out the single candle Edna Mae had put in the center of the cake. Then she insisted everyone have a piece of cake, including all the servants.

Later, up in the music room, Kacy played the pianoforte and taught her guests and the servants more songs. She learned a few from them, too. Then she surprised them with the gifts she had bought and wrapped. She even had a gift for Sarah Sathers' unborn baby.

It was, Kacy decided as the celebration broke up, a very special birthday. One she would never forget, even if Thorne had spent it with Valerie.

About five minutes after Kacy said goodbye to her guests, Miles rushed back in with Sarah cradled in his arms. "Countess, me wife needs ye. The babe be coming and she wants ye ta help deliver it."

"Carry her upstairs. We'll put her in a guest room."

Servants, plus the vicar and his wife trailed them as Miles carried Sarah up the stairs. "Put her in here." Kacy opened a door across the hall from hers.

While Miles placed Sarah gently on the bed, Kacy issued instructions. "Bertha, gather clean sheets and towels. Ellen, go down to the kitchen and heat water. Montfort, send somebody for the doctor. Maisy, you look after Janey and Lamont. Pick out a room, put them to bed and tell them some stories."

~ * ~

"O-o-o-o-h," Sarah groaned sometime later. Her labor pains had gone from short and mild to long and hard in a matter of minutes.

Her mother, Louise Crandon said, "I fear the babe be turned the wrong way. If only the doctor would hurry."

And Kacy thought, *If only Thorne were here, I wouldn't feel so alone.* "Everything's going to be all right," she told Sarah, while Miles wiped perspiration from her brow and Louise shooed the vicar and Lamont out of the room.

"This is no place for you. Go downstairs and find someplace else to wait."

Both men looked relieved.

"You're doing fine," Kacy repeated after they left.

"I'm sure you're right," Sarah managed through gritted teeth and harshly drawn breaths.

But Kacy sensed her doubt. And knew it matched her own.

Miles wiped more perspiration from Sarah's brow. "Is there anything I can do?"

"Hold my hand. I feel another pain coming."

Contraction, Kacy thought, but didn't say it. Sarah tried to breathe the way Kacy suggested, but nothing helped as the baby tried to work its way through the birth canal and apparently didn't succeed. Kacy's worry increased. She'd never seen a live birth and wished the doctor, or Fey or Rey were here to assist.

After another difficult hour, Louise sent Miles away.

Finally the baby came, feet first. With blue-tinged skin, he didn't make a sound. Louise picked him up by the feet and swatted him on the bottom. Still he didn't breathe or move, or utter a sound.

"Is something wrong?" Sarah asked in panic.

"I think he be stillborn," her mother said.

Kacy didn't say anything. Although she hadn't done it before, she knew what had to happen. She opened the baby's mouth and cleaned out mucous. Then, she started CPR, breathing in and out and pressing gently on the tiny chest. When that didn't work, she touched the exhausted Sarah and the tiny, stiff baby and wished them both healthy and well.

As Kacy's energy drained, the baby let out a wail. Relieved, Kacy sat down before she passed out.

Suddenly wide awake, alert and grateful, Sarah said, "You made him breathe."

"You made him breathe," Louise echoed.

"It's called CPR," Kacy said, not wanting to admit she possessed a wonderful gift that also drained her.

Bertha came in with a maid. They changed the sheets and cleaned up after the birthing, while Kacy watched Louise sponge bathe the baby. When he and Sarah were settled, Miles, the vicar and Lamont were allowed in.

"You look exhausted, Countess," Lamont said.

"Please do us a favor and go to bed before you fall down," Louise added.

Kacy exposed a tired smile. "Good night, then."

"Good night, and thank you for everything," Sarah said.

Kacy used the last of her strength to walk the short distance to her room. Beyond exhaustion, she wondered if she might lay down and never get up again. She certainly felt tired enough to die. Is this what Rey meant when he said the gift could be dangerous because it could make her vulnerable? That if she misused it, she might die?

Had she misused it? Had she usurped a higher authority by wishing life to a stillborn? But if she hadn't, knowing she possessed the capacity, she couldn't have lived with herself.

In her room she dragged herself across the floor and fell on the bed. Her feet dangled over the edge and her last conscious thoughts were questions. *Was her time with Thorne at an end? Where was he right now? What was he doing? Would he come to her when he arrived home? Would she have enough strength to wake up if he did?*

Twenty-three

Morning of The Fourteenth Day

Although Clay had returned in the wee hours of the morning, it wasn't his custom to sleep late and he arose early. Before he dressed for the day, the temptation to visit Kacy's chamber and slake his passion arose. Still irritated with her and with himself for wanting her so damn much, he fought the desire. And won—which felt like a major victory.

Downstairs, he instructed Montfort to inform Cook to serve his breakfast in the study. Clay hadn't enjoyed his evening away from home. He missed Kacy and lost patience with Valerie. When he announced his marriage, she seized his arm like a clinging vine and complained in a whiny tone, which put him in bad temper. To compensate, he stayed longer than he intended. He would not do so again.

The mansion had been dark and quiet when he arrived home. Only Montfort, his loyal butler, stayed up for his return. The desire to visit Kacy's bedchamber nearly overwhelmed him, but Clay decided not to disturb her. Leaving her alone might teach her to cease her prattle of other lives, love and questions about how he felt about Oraline. He no longer had to consider that. She meant nothing to him. How could she when Kacy meant so much? Startled by that admission, it took a few seconds to realize Montfort had twice tapped on the open door.

Clay looked up. "What is it?"

"Ye have a visitor."

"Who is calling at this early hour?"

Montfort's thin shoulders swayed with the semblance of a shrug. "He didna give his name, milord, but he claims to be the countess's guardian. He be the same man what took the other miss away."

Thinking Montfort must be mistaken and Wilbur Lugamon was the early morning caller, Clay mentally prepared himself for an unpleasant ordeal. "Show him in."

He stood up behind his desk as Montfort ushered in the visitor. Instead of Wilbur Lugamon, a short, eccentric-looking man with fluffy white hair and beard entered. Clay had never seen a man dressed entirely in white before and he eyed him with open curiosity. His visitor eyed him too, but without much curiosity.

"I have come for Kacy."

Clay frowned. "Who are you?"

"My name is Rey."

"You're an angel?" Clay asked in disbelief. He looked like an ordinary man, except for his startling blue eyes, more brilliant than the sky on a clear, cloudless day.

The stranger nodded. "I must take her home."

A cold chill shivered up Clay's spine. "This is her home now. She's my wife."

The stocky man rocked back on the heels of his white shoes and stayed in that curious posture as he said, "Kacy explained she came from the future. Also that you have known and loved each other before. However, you chose not to believe her, nor to be receptive to the memories that lie within you. Now the matter is out of my hands. The powers in Kolob decreed she must return to her own time or die."

Clay straightened his shoulders. Kacy belonged to him. He couldn't let her go. She was his wife. And then the last two words the stranger uttered penetrated. *Or die.* "Or die?" he echoed, his voice a strangled, choked groan.

A look Clay could only interpret as pity covered his round cherubic face as Rey flattened his feet back on the imported carpet and nodded. Clay didn't need his pity. He needed him gone, along with his unpleasant announcements.

Rey folded his arms across his white waistcoated chest. "When did you last see her?"

"Why do you ask?"

Each word Rey spoke pierced Clay like a separate, razor sharp accusation. "You were given knowledge of her gift to heal and your ability to replenish her strength when she uses the gift. Last evening, you failed to look in on her. You failed again this morn. There is no kind way to say this. Kacy lies near death."

"No-o-o-o!" The savage denial tore from Clay's throat and he leapt toward the door in an attempt to reach her as quickly as possible.

The angel raised his hand.

Clay came to an abrupt stop. Startled by the invisible power that held him still, he said, "Kacy has been healthy all week, with energy to spare."

"Until last evening," Rey explained. "She attended the delivery of Sarah Sathers son. The babe came stillborn and Kacy could not resist wishing her strength to him as well as to Sarah."

"Kacy went to the Sathers' cottage last evening?"

Rey shook his white-haired head. "She invited them here along with the vicar, his wife and son to celebrate her birthday. Sarah's labor began as they started home."

Remorse flooded Clay. He had missed Kacy's soiree. Why hadn't she told him it was her birthday? Because she knew he wanted to distance himself?

With Rey standing solemnly beside him, Clay could barely think, but he asked, "Why was Kacy brought here, if she doesn't belong?"

"That is not for me to say."

"Then who will tell me?"

"Consider her time here as a gift."

"When are gifts given," Clay scoffed, still unable to move, "then taken away?"

"Had you recognized her as your soul mate and admitted your love, she could have stayed. However, you do not love her…"

"Yes, I do," Clay interrupted. "I do love her."

"Then I am truly sorry. For both of you. You failed to declare your love. Now it's too late. If she is to live, the powers that be have decreed there must be a unification of her body and soul in the twenty-first century. If you love her as you say, I urge you not to detain me further, nor to hinder her recovery by attempting to touch her, but to bid me return her without delay."

Panicked, Clay couldn't speak. He didn't want to lose her. Not again. A memory flashed; a memory of them together in another time, another place and he knew then that everything she said was true. They had known and loved each other before.

Filled with regret, remorse, self-disgust and recriminations he croaked, "Will I ever see her again?"

"I cannot say." Rey turned and Clay discovered he could move so he followed Rey up the grand staircase.

Was Kacy lost to him for all eternity? That thought shocked him as much as anything. In one blinding glimpse he knew their souls had faced similar situations before. And then, like now, the wrong endings had occurred. The insight rattled his insides and turned his life upside down.

In Kacy's bedchamber, Clay saw that she did indeed look deathly ill. Rey gathered her in his arms as though she weighed no more than a feather. When Clay reached out to touch her, Rey shook his white head. "She's vulnerable. If you touch her now, it may hamper her recovery."

Feeling helpless, Clay dropped his hands to his sides and watched Rey carry her from the room.

"How am to I explain her disappearance?" he asked at the top of the staircase.

"That is not for me to say. For the sake of those who are awake, I shall carry Kacy out to a carriage. Once we are inside, I shall return her to the future without delay."

Alone by the front portal a few moments later, Clay watched Rey climb into the carriage. One moment he saw them inside. The next they were gone... vanished into thin air.

Clay's head screamed denial. A blast of unreality followed. Perhaps this was a hallucination. Perhaps when he went upstairs, Kacy would be there, waiting for him. But he knew he deluded himself. She was gone. And without her he didn't fancy facing the future.

His anger focused on Rey. Would an angel take a man's wife from him? Rey had no wings or anything else to indicate he was an other-worldly-being. Fey at least had wings some of the time. Could Rey be the devil? But if he were, how would he treat Kacy? And who had given her the power to heal? Why had she been given a gift that put her in grave danger?

Clay's fury gave way to sorrow. Long, dull years stretched out before him. The coldness of winter pressed down upon his soul. Would he ever again feel warm? Or see the sunshine without thinking of Kacy's smile?

The one woman who was exactly right for him—perfect in fact—didn't belong in his time. But, dear God, how many times in how many lifetimes had they met, fallen in love and lost each other? The answer revealed itself in a series of tormenting memories.

He had loved her *for almost eternity.* That's what she'd said on their wedding night, but he had disregarded the importance, nay, the significance of the wondrous miracle that had occurred. He blinked and swore the moisture in his eyes wasn't tears. Everybody knew grown men did not cry.

~ * ~

Kacy opened her eyes slowly, cautiously. Even before she saw her surroundings, she knew she was no longer at Havenhurst. The light above her bed, along with the mechanical whir of air from the heating system announced she had left the past. She looked around the small room, so like a hospital in the States and yet so different.

When she saw Jennifer sitting in a chair reading a book, Kacy cleared her throat. "Hi, Jen."

Jennifer jumped up. Her paperback fell on the floor.

"Kacy. Thank God, you're awake! How do you feel?"

"I'm not sure. How long have I been in here?"

"Two weeks."

Time in both centuries must run pretty parallel, Kacy decided, before fear slammed through her with all the weight of an avalanche. Two weeks was all she and Thorne had had together. Two weeks out of whole lifetimes. It wasn't enough.

Turmoil churned inside her. Would she ever see him again? Please, her soul begged, let me go back. Why had she left his time? The answer came with the next swift breath. *Because he didn't love her.* Fighting the sobs that threatened to consume her, she turned her gaze up to the ceiling.

"Kacy, what's wrong?" Jennifer asked.

"I met him," she managed to croak, as tears puddled in her eyes.

"Who?"

"The man..." A sob gurgled up her throat. "In... my dreams."

"What was he like?"

"Wonderful!" She swiped at the tears pouring down her cheeks. "He... married... me."

"Kacy, you must have dreamed—"

"No." She pulled her left hand from under the covers so Jennifer could see her ring. "I married Thorne."

"Thorne? Is that his name?"

"No. It's Claythorne."

"Isn't calling him Thorne sort of disrespectful?"

"I guess it is. He... Clay's in the past, clear back in 1854 and I'm afraid I might never see him again."

"I'm sorry," Jennifer said and spread her arms.

Kacy flung herself into Jen's arms and cried until there were only dry, soul-wracking sobs left.

By the time a nurse came in, Kacy had calmed down a bit.

"It's lucky you are…" the nurse with an Irish accent said, after she took Kacy's temperature, blood pressure and pulse, "… to be alive, lass. How do you feel?"

"Pretty good," Kacy lied. She ached all over, not only in her heart. Every bone and muscle felt as though they had been rolled over by a steam engine.

"I must ring doctor and tell him our good news."

As soon as she left, Kacy forced her heartache under control and asked, "My grandparents? How are they, Jen?"

"About as you might imagine. Anxious. Worried. Heart-sick."

"Where are they?"

"At the hotel. They flew over right after I called and they've spent as many hours here as I have."

"I'm so sorry I worried them… and you."

"You saved my life, Kacy."

"I didn't do anything you wouldn't have done. But I had the most awesome adventure. I flew in the sky, then a time tunnel and after I met Thorne—I mean Clay," she amended, because Thorne did sound quite disrespectful, "I had memories of knowing him before in other lives. That's why I've dreamed about him."

"Tell me everything that happened."

"Pull your chair closer and I will."

And she did.

Twenty-four

Evening of The Sixtieth Day
Denver, Colorado—The Present

Perched on top of the TV in the living room of the small house Kacy and Jennifer shared, Rey and Fey observed the two friends without them being aware of their presence.

"Give her and Thorne another chance," Fey pleaded with Rey. "Please. I'll never ask you for another favor."

"You said that once before. So I arranged to take her to meet him."

Fey lowered her head and blinked away silver teardrops. "Rey, you must help them because nobody else can. She's so miserable I cannot bear it. Every night she cries herself to sleep."

"She does not cry herself to sleep," Rey stoutly disagreed. "That is unhealthy and she has better sense."

"Her heart is crying," Fey differed. "She and Thorne are both unutterably miserable."

"I thought you didn't approve of him," Rey said.

"I do. He took such good care of Kacy. And he married her. Besides, she loves him so. I think he loves her, too. He's just too stubborn to admit it."

"What makes you think his stubbornness wouldn't be a problem if she were to go back?"

"I'm sure their love would prevail in the end."

"It never has before."

"But this time, Kacy knows about past lives and…"

"Give me a smile, Fairy Fey," Rey interrupted, "and fret no more. Let us be quiet and listen to the mortals." He patted his shoulder in invitation and Fey flew up to perch on it before she turned her attention to Kacy and Jennifer.

"Are you sure you want to stay in tonight?" Jennifer asked. "Now that you're recovered, maybe we should go out and celebrate."

Kacy glanced around the small two-bedroom house they had rented near Denver University when they started college almost two years ago. Because they signed annual leases, they hadn't given it up when they went to England for a semester at Oxford.

"I don't feel up to going out, Jen. I'm sorry. I know I'm not much fun. Maybe you should get a new roommate and I should move back home with Gram and Granddad."

"I don't want a new roommate. And you know that." Jennifer glanced at Kacy's tummy. "How are you going to explain your pregnancy to your grandparents?"

"I haven't decided." She plopped on the second-hand, rose-colored couch and patted her still flat stomach. "It's hard to believe a baby is growing inside me." When she missed her first period, she blamed the accident. Her second wasn't quite due, but she'd felt queasy so she'd taken a home pregnancy test and been shocked at the positive result.

They had left England a month ago. She still had trouble believing she had conceived in the past. In spite of the complications that would create, she was delighted she carried a part of Clay inside her, even if she might never see him again. Whenever she thought about that, raw pain reverberated all the way through her. If he loved her, she might have been able to stay with him. Fey said that's why Rey had been instructed to bring her back. At least her fairy godmother and guardian angel were still in her life, but so far they hadn't given her any news about Clay.

Her thoughts returned to her baby. She worried he or she might not be all right because of her accident, but reminded herself she hadn't conceived until after it happened. Had traveling through the time tunnel harmed her baby? Or the drugs they pumped into her while she lay unconscious? She'd ask Rey the next time she saw him.

"I wish I had some way of communicating with Clay. He has a right to know about the baby."

She didn't realize she said her thought out-loud until Jennifer said, "I wish I could meet him."

"I wish you could, too. And his best friend Drake, as well. He reminds me so much of Dirk."

The mention of Dirk made Jennifer wince. Kacy knew why. They'd been very much in love before a freak accident claimed his life and killed their chance of happiness.

"How often have you seen Rey and Fey since your return?"

"They visited me in the London Bridge Hospital, and I've seen them a couple of times since we came home. Not in dreams or fantasies either. I'm always wide awake."

The doorbell rang and Jennifer stood. "Somebody probably wants to sell us some encyclopedias."

She gaped when she opened the door and from the couch Kacy gasped, "Catharine! Is it really you?"

Catharine nodded. "May I come in?"

"Yes. Of course." Kacy dashed across the room.

"You look exactly alike," Jennifer said, looking from one to the other. "I know you told me you did, Kacy, but it's one thing to hear and quite another to see."

"How did you get here?" Kacy asked Catharine.

"Rey brought me," Catharine said, "and he provided these clothes." She glanced down at her skirt. "I feel indecent with my limbs exposed, but I couldn't bring myself to wear men's trousers." She looked at Jennifer and Kacy's jeans and turned red. "I am sorry. I did not mean to insult."

"It's all right," Kacy said. "Why did Rey bring you?"

"To show you this." Catharine extended a newspaper.

Kacy stared at the London Times dated June 8, 1854. Then she staggered to a chair and dropped on it.

"What's wrong?" Jennifer asked.

"Clay's been charged with murder," Kacy choked out. "Charged with murdering me. Is that right, Catharine?"

She nodded. "I am afraid it is."

Kacy slumped back and closed her eyes.

Fey flew down to ensure she hadn't fainted, then flew straight at Rey in her two-inch size and punched him on the chest, which didn't faze him because her fist was so small and in any event, he was immune to attacks of any sort.

"You brought Catharine here," Fey hissed. "Why didn't you tell me?"

Rey's smile was his only answer, but Fey sensed it was all part of a plan as he extended his hand so she could perch on his wrist while they viewed the scene taking place below them. She didn't want to miss a single word.

"What will happen to Clay?" Kacy asked when she recovered from part of her shock.

"I will go back to try to facilitate his release," Catharine said, "unless you wish to go in my place."

"Would you stay here, Catharine?" Kacy asked.

"Yes. However, I understand there are conditions which you and I must both agree to if that is to occur."

"What are they?"

"We must swap places. Perhaps identities as well."

Hope blossomed like a bright new flame and Kacy grinned. "When can I leave?"

"Soon." Rey floated to the floor and made himself visible. "There are a few other conditions you should be aware of before you make up your mind to go."

Her heart pounding, Kacy asked, "What are they?"

"The scar on your cheek must be removed because you may decide to assume Catharine's identity and she yours."

"No problem." Kacy raised her hand to finger her scar one last time. It disappeared even as she touched it and all she felt was the smooth skin she'd always craved. "What other conditions are there?"

"If you return to the nineteenth century, you must live out the rest of your natural life in that time."

"That's exactly what I want. Are there more conditions?"

"Catharine must stay here."

"I have already said that I would."

"Thanks." Kacy smiled. "This must be what I meant when I said you were on the brink of discovering a whole new life, Catharine."

"That may be true."

Rey turned to Jennifer. "As Kacy's best friend, would you help Catharine adjust to this century?"

Jennifer gulped audibly. "I'll help any way I can, but Kacy..." her eyes watered, "... I'll miss you so!"

"I'll miss you too, but I'll keep a diary and try to find a way to get it to you so you'll know how things turn out." She looked at Rey. "Is that okay?"

He nodded, then said, "Wilbur Lugamon is the
man who accused Lord Banes of murder. He claims the earl married Catharine, who assumed a fictitious name. Wilbur also discovered what the solicitors knew—that Claythorne was accused of Timothy's mother's death in France before he became an earl."

"But he didn't kill her," Kacy said. "You told me Timothy's mother is alive, at least in their time," she added, "unless she died within the last six weeks."

"She did not. Yvette is in London as we speak. Now then," he said, his manner solemn, "Catharine gathered information, which will arm you with enough knowledge to have Wilbur imprisoned or deported. Do you feel up to dealing with that?"

Kacy nodded. "And I'll be eternally grateful to you for taking me back, and to you Catharine, for agreeing to stay here—and to you Jen, for agreeing to help her adjust to this time." Tears clouded Kacy's eyes.

Fey winked and Kacy tried to smile as she asked Catharine, "Will you watch out for my grandparents? I hate to leave them, but I have to go."

"I know you do and I shall do my best to ensure they are all right. Will you visit my mum and comfort her if she needs comforting?"

"Yes, of course. I'm so excited. Can we go now, Rey?"

He nodded and extended his hand as Fey grabbed hold of his white collar. "You're a fantastic angel, Rey. You've exasperated and delighted me for eons of mortal time."

Twenty-five

Afternoon of The Sixty-First Day
London, England 1854

After Rey explained Clay was being tried before his peers, a house full of lords, Fey waved her wand and garbed Kacy in clothes fit for a countess, arranged her hair in an elaborate style and conjured a bonnet. Then Rey whisked her to the wide oak door of the chamber where the trial was under way. She squared her shoulders and took a deep breath before she pushed the door open and walked inside.

Ignoring the stares and whispers, Kacy made her way regally up the aisle between the rows of spectators.

"Who are you?" The white-bewigged, red-robed judge frowned at the disturbance and at Kacy in particular.

"The Countess of Havenhurst," she calmly replied.

Pandemonium erupted. Screams and shouts vied for her attention, but she had eyes only for Clay, standing stiff and silent before the bar.

Memory hadn't exaggerated his physical attributes. He looked more handsome than ever. Faint surprise stirred in his green eyes, but she saw no welcoming warmth in their depths. She had envisioned his wrists in shackles and his ankles bound with manacles. Perhaps being a Peer of the Realm had kept him from that awful fate. Still her heart ached for him and she yearned to be near him. Instead she stood in the center of the aisle until the judge quieted the chamber with the repeated pounding of his gavel.

"As you can see," she said, "I'm very much alive and I respectfully request that the charges against my husband, Claythorne Banes, Earl of Havenhurst, be dropped at once."

"Your request will be taken under consideration."

Her hope that the charges would be dismissed immediately dashed to the floor as the judge said, "Please approach the bench, Countess."

Kacy did as bidden, glancing briefly at Clay, then at the lords in wigs and robes, who sat like stern jurors near the front of the chamber.

Two barristers from opposite sides of the bench hastened forward to confer with the judge. After a heated discussion, the judge announced, "I shall direct all questions to the countess." He started with, "Where have you been, My Lady?"

"Out of the country." Kacy replied and although she knew Theodore Roosevelt crossed the Atlantic as a child in nine days during 1869, so she'd had ample time for two crossings, she hurriedly added, "In a place where there is no means of easy communication with this part of the civilized world."

While murmured whispers raced through the spectators and filled the galleries, Kacy's eyes were drawn to Clay's accuser, Wilbur Lugamon. Having seen him only once before, she nearly choked at his barbaric glare. Although she despised him for the fear he had instilled in Catharine and his accusation that Clay had murdered her, Kacy didn't relish making an enemy of him.

She returned her attention to the judge as the chamber quieted. "Pray forgive me for my misconduct, your honor. When I left England, I had no idea that a man as good and honorable as my husband would be charged with so vile a crime as murder. And to charge him without evidence is unconscionable."

Wondering if she'd just said a word that wasn't used in the nineteenth century, she folded her hands together while she looked back at Wilbur Lugamon. "By what right do you accuse anyone, you who have twice broken the law with your acts of bigamy?"

"How dare you accuse me of such a crime?"

Startled gasps once more erupted in the chamber.

Kacy waited until the judge pounded his gavel and quiet reigned once more before she spoke again. "For the official record I wish to state that my hasty departure from Havenhurst was due to an emergency. Someone very dear to me suffered an accident and I was anxious to rush to her unconscious side. I also wish to state, I didn't leave because my marriage to the Earl of Havenhurst was unhappy. Quite the contrary. If he is guilty of any crime, it is only that of being a kind, considerate husband who allowed his wife to go to her friend in all due haste."

The accusing barrister spoke up. "The earl has also been accused of murdering a woman in France."

"That's another preposterous lie," Kacy said. "The French woman is not only alive and well, she's here in this very chamber."

The barrister's eyes bulged is disbelief. "I do not believe you."

Kacy looked at the judge. "Would you ask the honorable barrister if he knows the French woman's name?"

The judge nodded and inclined his head at the barrister. "Do you?"

"Yes. Yvette Boudine."

"She's sitting in the tenth row, second seat, left of the center aisle," Kacy said.

"May I presume you know why she is here?" the judge asked.

"You may. I understand the earl gave her money a few years ago when he offered to save her son from a life of begging in the streets of Paris. She promised to see her son often. Instead she went to the Riviera. Her disappearance prompted the vile murder accusation but in truth, she sold her son and she came to England recently to attempt to extort more money from the earl."

The judge ordered Yvette Boudine to the bench. She stood, but didn't move and the judge sent a man to escort her. She looked frightened and ready to bolt.

"She doesn't speak English," Kacy explained. "You may wish to have someone interpret."

The judge did, questioning Yvette until satisfied that everything Kacy said was true.

Aching for Clay's quick release, Kacy drew in a breath after Yvette was dismissed and led from the chamber.

"As you can plainly see, my husband isn't guilty of the crime for which he has been accused and I ask that you release him now."

Quiet murmurs of approval spread through the chamber. But to Kacy's dismay the questioning continued for almost half an hour more. Instead of pretending to be Catharine, she opted for the truth.

"Although Catharine and I look very much alike, to my knowledge we're not related. I'm an American while she's a British subject. Well, I guess I am now too, since I married the earl. In any event, the earl's stable boys and servants saw both of us together. They can corroborate what I have said."

"That be true." Montfort stood, along with Bertha, Edna Mae, Maisy, Timothy and Thadius in the upper gallery. "We did see the two of 'um together, Yer Honor," Montfort called down.

"Where is Catharine?" Wilbur Lugamon shouted.

The judge slammed his gavel down hard. "You are out of order, Mr. Lugamon. Sit down, lest I have you restrained."

"I'll answer that if I may," Kacy said after Wilbur obeyed, his eyes ablaze with hostility.

"Please do," the judge invited.

"Catharine is in America with my family and friends. I understand she likes it there and does not plan to return to England."

"That's a lie," Wilbur yelled. "You are Catharine."

Kacy shook her head. The bonnet on top wobbled and she raised her hand to steady it. Armed with Catharine's research, Kacy gathered her courage and faced her other task with tense composure.

"Your honor, Wilbur Lugamon, married two women, one in Germany, the other in Paris and without divorcing or annulling either of those marriages, he came to England and married Eliza Paice. When he arrived in England, he discarded his last name Knudson. He has committed heinous crimes against the Crown of England and a British subject. Marriage is a sacred state and he desecrated it with his greed to gain access to the widowed Eliza Paice's wealth. But he has no legal right to her or her money."

Kacy pulled folded parchments from her reticule and gave them to the white bewigged, red-robed judge. "Catharine collected this information. It confirms what I have said."

Not a sound could be heard from the packed galleries while the judge inspected the parchments. A few moments later spectators leaned forward, eager to hear as the judge turned his attention to Clay's accuser.

"The evidence against you is conclusive."

Faced with imprisonment in England or deportment, Wilbur chose the latter. Thankfully when that was finally agreed upon, Kacy's impassioned plea had the desired effect and Clay was released amidst jubilant cries from the packed galleries.

Clay approached Kacy, his face expressionless when he offered his arm. She placed her hand on it. His arm felt stiff and unbending like his tense, rigid body, while they walked down the center aisle together. He didn't smile. He didn't even look at her. And Kacy felt as though they were still miles and years apart.

Curious spectators shouted questions. Clay ignored them. And Kacy tried to.

Outside, eager newspaper reporters swarmed around them. After one intimidating frown from Clay, all backed away and left them alone. One lone woman whom Kacy somehow knew to be Oraline approached.

"I knew you were not guilty, Claythorne."

Clay didn't even acknowledge her. Turning his back on her, he handed Kacy into the carriage she had acquired with Rey's help before she entered the trial chamber. He closed the door in Oraline's face before he sat across from Kacy, instead of at her side.

"What now?" He hiked a black eyebrow.

"I thought we might stay in London tonight, if you don't mind. I'm tired and tomorrow's soon enough to go home to Havenhurst, isn't it?"

"You seem to be in charge," Clay said with dry candor.

Oraline grabbed the door while he instructed the groom to drive them to his home in Belgrave

"Talk to me Claythorne," Oraline pleaded. "Please! I have so many things I want to tell you."

Clay tried to ease the door from her.

"You loved me," Oraline wailed. "I think you still do. Please do not shut me out. I need you, desperately!"

Beyond Oraline, Kacy saw a woman who looked very familiar. While they stared at each other, Kacy clapped a hand over her heart. Although she hadn't seen her mother since she was four years old, she'd always kept a framed photograph of her and her parents in her bedroom.

"Mother," she mouthed, too shocked to hear whatever else Oraline said before Clay wrested the door free and closed it on her again. Kacy tried to convince herself she must have hallucinated, or conjured the image of her mother. *She couldn't possibly be here, could she?*

After the groom pulled away from the curb, Kacy allowed herself to breathe a sigh of relief. "Thank heaven that's behind us." When Clay made no comment, she was quiet for a while. Then nervous, she babbled, "The look on Wilbur's face when he realized he was to be given a choice for his punishment but he'd surfeit all claim to Eliza Paice and her wealth was priceless."

Because Clay still didn't offer a comment of any kind, Kacy was quiet during the remainder of the drive. But dread started to build inside. Wasn't he pleased to see her? Glad she'd come back?

Along with a trunk full of things Rey had provided for Kacy, she had a satchel with a change of clothing for Clay and whatever else he might need for an overnight stay in London. But when they stopped at his home, she realized he must have clothes and whatever else he needed here.

Inside, he introduced her to his servants and his man, Benton. When Kacy suggested having tea, Clay complied to her request with a negligent shrug.

Tea wasn't the pleasant affair she'd envisioned. Clay barely looked at her. He spoke only when she asked a question. Each answer was short. Clipped. He wasn't in a good mood. She thought she understood. After all, she'd be disgruntled, too, if she'd been accused of a crime that hadn't even been committed.

Clay excused himself after tea and closeted himself in his study with his man, Benton. Kacy wandered through the house to acquaint herself with each room, while she wondered how often Clay stayed here.

Time dragged. When she found the courage to approach Clay to ask about supper, he instructed Benton to tell her he did not wish to be disturbed, not even to eat. At bedtime Kacy climbed the stairs. In the master bedroom, she stood before the square mirror on the wall behind a bulky cherry wood bureau. She had recovered completely from the accident during the twenty-first century, but the absence of the scar on her cheek made her look and feel like an entirely different person.

Exhausted by the swirling journey back to the nineteenth century as well as the day's harrowing events, Kacy removed the hair grips that held her long hair in the elaborate style Fey had fashioned, then shook her head. Closing her eyes, Kacy sighed. It felt good to be free of the hairgrips. She changed to a nightgown and slid between the sheets. In a matter of minutes, she fell asleep.

But she awakened when Clay came in. He carried a lamp and his face was a mask of cold, dark fury. "What are you doing in my bed?"

Disoriented, Kacy had trouble finding an answer, so all she did was stare.

He glared back, then without another word; he strode from the room.

Kacy turned over and tried to sleep. The task was beyond her ability. Clay returned a short time later, but he didn't get in bed. Instead he sat in a chair. Kacy suspected he slept no more than she did, which was no more than a few patchy winks.

Twenty-six

Morning of The Sixty-Second Day

At daylight Kacy opened her eyes and stared at Clay's black shoes, still on his feet, polished to a gleaming shine. She rolled onto her side to see the rest of him. He still wore the clothes he'd worn at his trial—brown trousers, white shirt and tweed jacket. They looked unrumpled, but his eyes looked tired.

As she lay there, nausea descended. She hadn't had morning sickness yet and she sat up, hoping it would go away. Instead the bitter taste of bile rose in her throat. By sheer will she forced it back down, then gingerly slid out of bed and fumbled in her reticule until she found the Tums she'd brought from the twenty-first century. Her hands shook as she popped one in her mouth and chewed before she dragged herself back to bed, taking the Tums with her.

To her horror, she gagged, then gagged again. Thankfully all she suffered were dry heaves, but they left her weak, so she lay back down, willing her stomach to settle.

She knew Clay watched her with his sharp green gaze. "Bloody hell!" he cursed before he stood and stalked out of the room.

When she felt well enough to get up, Kacy selected a clean yellow gown from her trunk. After she dressed, she brushed her hair and tied it at her nape with a yellow ribbon. Her queasiness gone, she felt hungry. But she didn't know whether to ask for a tray or go downstairs. A knock saved her from having to make a decision.

She opened the door to a servant dressed in black trousers, jacket and white shirt. He held a tray. "Your breakfast," he said, entering the room when she stepped aside. He set the tray on a small table, then extended a folded parchment.

"The Earl bid me deliver this."

Kacy unfolded the parchment and read,

> *Meet me downstairs at half past the hour. I pray you do not keep me waiting.*
>
> *Claythorne.*

The aroma of food turned her stomach and all she managed to get down was a small piece of dry toast and a few sips of sweetened, cream tea. Caffeine affected her nerves, but she'd heard it helped queasiness.

Shortly after she gave up trying to eat, two servants arrived for her trunk. Kacy followed them. Clay waited at the bottom of the stairs. Without speaking, he led her outside and handed her inside a large, comfortable carriage. Climbing in behind her, he sat in the opposite corner, as far from her, it seemed, as he could get.

Kacy knew the ride to Havenhurst would take most of the day. To her dismay, the atmosphere was as uncomfortable as last night had been. Clay greeted every attempt she made at conversation with a cool impersonal stare. She finally gave up and closed her eyes. Time travel, along with yesterday's tension and an almost sleepless night, had taken their toll. She leaned back and let exhaustion have its way.

Clay watched Catharine through slatted lids. She was every bit as beautiful as Kacy. Exquisite, in fact. But he missed the dimple on her cheek. It irritated him that she thought she could fool him by pretending to be his wife. Perhaps she had trained for the stage. She mimicked Kacy almost to a fault. But when she wasn't mimicking

Kacy, she reverted to that lost-little-girl look which made him want to shake her and protect her at the same time.

She couldn't always hide that timid, frightened look, which was the first thing he'd noticed when he saw Catharine in his woods in April, two months past. Now she was increasing. Did the vixen think she could pass the babe off as his?

"Bloody hell!" he cursed under his breath when her head nodded and her body swayed as the carriage made a turn. Afraid she might topple over he slid across the aisle and caught her before she did. Tempted to gather her in his arms, he resisted. But he stayed beside her so she could rest without falling off the seat.

He knew that if she'd said she was Catharine Paice at the trial, but not his wife, he would have been faced with the problem of producing Kacy. But that was impossible. She had left because he'd been too much of a dunce to admit he loved her. Now he feared he'd never see her again.

Wilbur had been unable to convince the constable to return with him to Havenhurst. The earl's business was the earl's business, he'd maintained, having known Clay all his life. But when Kacy left, Wilbur had pounced on the opportunity to accuse him of marrying his stepdaughter under an assumed name and murdering her. What a fiasco the month past had been!

Thank God his tenants hadn't suffered. As Kacy had predicted, the crops were flourishing. Without undue rain the seeds had sprouted into sturdy plants, their roots firmly entrenched in the soil. The yield would be plentiful.

Everybody missed Kacy—him, his tenants, servants, the stable lads and grooms. Even people in the village. She'd only been here a short time, but she always said something kind or offered suggestions to improve people's lives. During the brief days of their marriage she'd taken to cutting flowers from the garden and decorating the graves located at the edge of the east lawn. Lord, how he missed her! He was deeply indebted to her.

He might also be indebted to Catharine, but he wasn't obligated. Although he was attracted to her, he intended to remain faithful to his marriage vows. After all, his precious wife might be returned to him... though he didn't truly believe that would happen. Not now... after six long, interminable weeks. At first he hadn't given up hope. In truth, even now, a part of him clung to the belief that she would return someday. Surely there was a reason they had been reunited in this time? Perhaps one day it would happen again. God willing, he wouldn't be an old man, too old to appreciate the miracle he prayed for with each hour that passed.

~ * ~

By the time Kacy woke up, they had reached Havenhurst. Clay sat beside her. She wasn't in his beloved arms but the closeness of his body had kept her propped up while she slept. She breathed in a silent sigh of relief. His essence filled her senses, creating a yearning deep inside her. Maybe now things would return to normal.

While Clay handed her out of the carriage, Thadius and Timothy came running. When they saw her, their faces broke into big grins and they shouted, not quite in unison, "Welcome home, Countess! Welcome home!"

"It's nice to be here," she said, opening her arms.

Both boys rushed at her. She stooped to embrace them at the same time. "Our Gilly cat had lots of babies," Timothy said. "Surprised us, cuz we though she be a boy."

Kacy smiled. "How many kittens did Gilly cat have?"

"A whole slewth," Thadius said while Clay looked on, his expression cold and remote.

The dread building inside Kacy doubled. So much for getting back to normal. Heaven help her, she didn't even know what normal should be!

A few hours later, Clay ate supper in his study—Alone. Kacy ate in the dining room—also alone. This certainly wasn't anything like what she had envisioned or hoped to have happen. Finally, unable to bear the enforced separation from Clay any longer, she went to his study and knocked.

"Come in," he said, in the low voice she knew and loved so well.

Kacy stepped inside and closed the door. "I know you didn't sleep much last night, Clay. Don't you think you should go to bed early?"

Waves of cold anger radiated from him. He'd lost weight and torment dominated his eyes. Guilt pressed down upon her for the part she'd played in his trial.

"I'll go to bed when I am damn good and ready," he growled. "You may sleep wherever you please, except in the master chamber or the chamber next to it. Do you understand?"

Kacy blinked. Not only was he not glad she'd returned; he acted like a hostile stranger. And she didn't know how to break through the invisible wall he'd erected. Didn't even know why he'd erected one. Maybe if they spent some time apart, he'd come to his senses. Since she had promised to go see Catharine's mother, Kacy said, "May I impose upon your good will for the use of a carriage tomorrow? I'd like to go to Kent."

"To visit your mother?"

"To visit Catharine's mother. Where else would I go, Clay?"

"To your lover?"

"I have no lover other than you. I... Catharine and I switched identities. I'm your wife." she stammered, belatedly realizing she should have explained sooner.

"You certainly are not."

Fear spread through Kacy like a forest fire fueled by gusty wind. "You obtained a divorce in six weeks? I didn't know that was possible in this time."

"You need not concern yourself with the status of my marriage."

Was he joking because he was angry? Although she knew better than to argue, she couldn't leave the subject alone. "If you obtained a divorce, why were you accused of murdering your wife? It doesn't make sense. And if you hadn't been accused, I wouldn't have had to save you from the gallows, Clay."

"Do not call me Clay," he snarled. "You have no right to address me with such familiarity and you did not save me from the gallows. My peers would not have convicted me of a crime I did not commit; a crime that did not occur."

Kacy backed up a step. She'd never seen him look so cold, or sound so remote. "I never meant to imply that I... saved your life," she said with all the dignity she could muster, but she was fighting the urge to cry.

His glare turned to a furious scowl. "Do you think I don't know you have gotten yourself with child and think to pass it off as mine, Miss Paice?"

Kacy blinked. She'd told him they'd switched identities. Why didn't he believe her?

"You are mad," he bit out with cold contempt, "even to consider it. I shall name the child a bastard."

Kacy swallowed, even though she didn't believe him. He'd taken Timothy in and he loved both him and Thadius. Still she didn't challenge Clay. No good would be served by doing that. He was too angry to be reasonable. And suddenly she felt too weary to try. "I'm not going to fight with you. If you're too blind to see the truth when it's staring you in the face..."

"We are not fighting," he interrupted.

"Then why are you shouting at me?"

"I am not shouting!"

But he was and Kacy wanted to, too. For two cents, or two pence, she'd punch that snarl off his handsome face. In one last defiant and daring attempt, she blurted, "If you'd take me in your arms and kiss me instead of glaring at me like a stubborn idiot, you'd know who I am."

His eyes glittered like shards of green ice.

"Why would I lie about who I am?"

When he didn't reply, she knew he didn't believe anything she'd said and she decided in that selfsame instant to give up trying to convince him. He hadn't wanted her before and he didn't want her now. Coming back was a huge mistake but there was nothing she could about that. She was stuck here. But she wouldn't open herself up for any more hurt, or humiliation, or rejection.

Lifting her chin, she said with forced calm, "I hope you enjoy your vinegary disposition, Lord Banes, for I do not."

Without bidding him good night, she turned and made her way up two flights of stairs to the blue room. Minutes later, with Maisy's help, she undressed and went to bed.

~ * ~

Because she didn't take time to close the curtains, sunshine spilled through the windows early the next morning. When nausea surfaced, she popped two Tums in her mouth. As soon as her stomach settled, she got dressed and after a quick breakfast, she decided to confront Clay again before she left for Kent.

She found him in his study, pacing the floor.

"I'm not Catharine," she said. "I know everything there is to know about our marriage. And I know how kind and tender you can be, when we're making love, when your so deep…"

"Stop!" he thundered, his stance rigid, his face a mask of cold fury.

"How would I know the things I do if I'm not your wife?" she persisted, desperate to reach him, afraid she never would.

"You may have seen her and questioned her, or made up what you claim to know. What kind of fool do you take me for, Miss Paice?"

"A flipping stubborn one," she retorted. "What makes you think I'm her and not Kacy?"

"My wife never called me Clay."

Exasperated, she asked, "Is that all I did wrong? I thought calling you Thorne sounded disrespectful."

He shook his head. "The dimple on your cheek is gone."

"Of course it is." Kacy resisted the urge to touch her cheek. "Rey removed it in case I felt a need to assume Catharine's identity, but I think honesty is the best policy, don't you?"

"For another thing…" Clay continued as though she hadn't spoken, "… Kacy would not risk traveling a great distance if she were with child. And she walks with confidence. You walk with hesitancy." He paused, then added with malice; "You almost gagged on fear when you first looked at Wilbur. Kacy saw him only once and has no reason to fear him. And…" Clay added in a tone that chilled her blood, "You and I both saw your mother in the crowd outside the trial chamber. Although you never spoke, I saw the recognition you couldn't hide."

Kacy couldn't believe he'd been so observant and yet arrived at such wrong conclusions. "I can explain—"

"No, you cannot."

"It isn't fair for you to judge me without a trial. I'm certain if you'd step back and assume the role of an impartial judge, you'd come up with more evidence to prove I'm Kacy than to prove I'm not."

"You have overplayed your role, Miss Paice."

"I have?" Kacy asked, startled. "How? In what way?"

"Yesterday you babbled. Kacy does not."

"I was nervous yesterday."

"A trait I do not attribute to her." His hostile green eyes said he'd proven his point.

"I don't talk like Catharine. I have an American accent," she objected.

"Accents can be faked." He turned his back on her and Kacy felt like her heart was cracking in two.

"My wife befriended you. However, that does not give you the right to assume her place in my life. I hold her in high regard and I resent your attempt to convince me you are her."

"High regard? Don't you love her?"

"The state of my emotions is not open for discussion." He turned his head and eyed her coldly. "Have I made myself clear, Miss Paice?"

"Perfectly," Kacy said.

He gave her a curt nod. "A carriage waits to take you to Kent."

He can't wait to get rid of me. Hurt, she raised her chin, unwilling to let him know how much it cost her to say, "At the risk of further raising your ire, I need to know whether you expect me to return to Havenhurst or stay away."

"Since we're not married, living together would be breaking the law as much as Wilbur broke it by committing bigamy."

"There's a very big difference between our situation and his. Wilbur deliberately married three different women. You needn't marry anyone else. All you have to do—"

"Stop!" he thundered, his temper exploding again. "I do not know you. I saw you only briefly before you showed up at the trial. You spent one night in my home, but that doesn't give you the right to expect anything from me. However..." he said, pausing for breath and lowering his voice but still speaking stiffly, "... Inasmuch as your intervention speeded my release, you may live at Havenhurst if that is your heart's desire. I'm considering joining her majesty's army and going to the Crimea."

"No!" Kacy shouted, unable to bear the thought of Clay fighting in a war where so many men died because of the lack of proper medical care, endangering his life on the battlefield or catching the fever so many, including Florence Nightingale, had caught during the Crimean war. "I wouldn't dream of depriving you of your home, Lord Banes."

"Perhaps we could, after all, live here together," he suggested a compromise. "To the world we would present ourselves as husband and wife. But let there be no mistake, Miss Paice, we would live our own separate lives."

Kacy started to raise her finger to rub her scar, then remembered she didn't have it anymore. "I don't think that would work," she said, her nerves taut and stretched, her heart crying out with pain.

"Would you like me to set you up in a home of your own?"

He asked that with such pomposity she was tempted to treat him to a swift kick. Then she decided she wouldn't give him the satisfaction of seeing her lose her barely held together composure. She might be reduced to the status of a beggar, but she wouldn't beg him. "That won't be necessary."

She had her pride, although he'd done his best to trample all over it. "I don't need your assistance, Lord Banes. I'm perfectly capable of taking care of myself and my unborn child. We'll find a place to live where we're wanted."

Squaring her shoulders, she left his life. Emotion clogged her throat. Tears burned her eyes. And a terrible pain stabbed her heart. She didn't want to see him again. It hurt too much. But what would she do if she gave birth to a son? His heir?

She made it outside to the waiting carriage before she broke down.

Twenty-seven

Clay lifted two books from his desk drawer. Kacy had wrapped and left them for him the night of her birthday. He still regretted missing her soiree. Timothy, Thadius, Montfort, Bertha, Edna Mae and Maisy had all taken great delight in relating the celebration and displaying the gifts she'd given them.

He fingered his books with reverence. Both were from the future and he kept them under lock and key most of the time. Before his arrest, he'd read them twice. One book was titled *Reincarnation, The Missing Link in Christianity*. The other was a compilation of poems by Elizabeth Barrett Browning.

With the books in hand, he turned to the window to watch Catharine board his carriage. Only by rigid, self-imposed detachment had he managed to let her go. She was so bloody much like Kacy, he wanted to chain her to his side and never set her free. That thought made him feel as guilty of infidelity as if he had actually committed the sin. Out of whole lifetimes he and Kacy had shared less than a week as husband and wife. What had he done to deserve losing her so many times? No liquor was strong enough to allow him to sleep without her haunting memories. How much longer must he suffer before the pain would dull? It was profoundly disturbing to know that even in death he might find no balm to ease his agony. Why had he denied the memories for so bloody long?

Still gazing outside, he watched his groom close the carriage door. Too keyed up to stand still, Clay was about to force his tormented gaze from the window, when he saw Catharine raise her hand to her left cheek, *to the dimple that wasn't there.*

How could that simple act render such shock? How could that one gesture convince him when nothing she'd said had?

A blinding flash of pain broad-fisted him in the chest. The truth didn't merely sink in. It hit him with the force of a full gale wind on the open sea. Her dimple *had* been removed. Everything she'd said was true. She was Kacy. His wife. The lady he loved. The only lady he would ever love. He had loved her in a dozen lives or more. And his noble attempt to ignore the attraction between them had been for naught.

He felt like such a fool. Hurriedly dumping the books back in the drawer, he fumbled in his trouser pocket for his keys to lock them away. Then he dashed outside.

The carriage had already driven away. He raced to the stable. "Saddle Blade." he ordered Timothy, who wasted no time obeying the command.

~ * ~

While Clay urged Blade to a full gallop, racing after the carriage, his mind traveled a mile a minute. He hadn't been attracted to Catharine in April, but he felt an overwhelming desire for the lady riding off in his carriage. She was persistent. Brave. Desirable. Independent. Beautiful... and concerned. The bold way she'd dared him to kiss her was something Kacy might do. She even smelled like Kacy. And her shout when he mentioned going to the Crimea was downright flattering. But the way she touched her cheek was the most telling of all. Kacy always fingered her dimple when she was nervous or upset.

It dawned on him that the child she carried was his. Joy mixed with a devastating sense of horror. Would she forgive him? *We'll find a place to live where we are wanted.*

Haunted by the last words she'd said he kicked Blade to a faster gallop. Some reunion he had offered... a royal top-notch job of botching it.

After a few miles, when he failed to catch the carriage, he turned Blade toward the woods. He would take a shortcut. It wouldn't surprise him if Kacy were already in Kent. Not when she had both a guardian angel and a fairy godmother.

~ * ~

As she journeyed to Kent, Kacy wiped the tears from her cheeks. Tears wouldn't solve a thing, but she couldn't stop them. She had no idea where she could live. Maybe she could ask Rey to set up the huge pink and white tent in Clay's woods again. It would serve him right to know she was camped out practically under his nose. The thought of seeing him again brought another deluge of tears to her eyes and a lump in her throat.

For a few seconds she considered trying to book passage on a ship to the U.S. and make her way west before her baby came. Before the Civil War started in the next decade. She didn't know how she'd make a living. Her marketable skills were limited to computers, piano and sewing, but she only knew how to operate electric sewing machines. She'd intended to become a reporter, hopefully a foreign correspondent, after she graduated from college so her classes had been geared for a degree in journalism. With a baby on the way, that career was out of the question, even if nineteenth century society allowed such a thing. Women were expected to marry, stay home and overlook their husband's indiscretions.

Kacy twisted her hands in her lap. The future looked gloomy. Full of doom. Her heart hurt so much, she wished she could talk to Rey or Fey. As though he sensed her need, Rey appeared beside her.

"I feared your reunion might disappoint you," he said.

Kacy swallowed the lump in her throat. "I couldn't convince Clay I'm his wife."

"Fret not. Kent may be more to your liking."

"Will I have to pretend I'm Catharine?"

Rey shook his white-haired head. "Not if you don't wish to do so. Would you like me to shorten your journey?"

"Yes. Please."

Rey blinked. And the carriage stopped before a thatch-roofed house that looked warm, cozy and inviting.

"Is this where Catharine's mother lives?"

"It is. I shall go now, before the groom opens the door. He doesn't know I shortened the journey."

Ray vanished and Kacy swallowed again. Her dry throat hurt and her eyes were probably red. She swallowed, patted her cheeks and was surprised to find them dry. Had Rey, bless him, done that?

The carriage door opened. After Clay's groom assisted her from the carriage, he said, "I'll take the horses round back Countess, an' see they git water a'fore we travel agin."

"Thank you," Kacy said, not knowing what else to say. She couldn't send him back to Havenhurst until she knew if she'd need him to drive her someplace else. But where? She didn't have a clue.

A young, dark-haired, good-looking butler with pretty even white teeth answered her knock. "Why'd ye knock, Miss Catherine?" he asked, puzzled.

"I thought I should," she said, too weary to explain she wasn't Catharine. "Is your mistress in?"

The butler nodded. "Allow me to show ye to the parlor, then I'll summon 'er."

Catharine's mother smiled when she saw Kacy seated on the settee.

Kacy gasped, too startled to return her smile. "I saw you after the trial," she blurted. "You remind me of my own mother."

"I am your mother."

"No. You're not. I'm not Catharine."

"I know that Kacy and I'm not Catharine's mother."

Stunned, Kacy licked her lips, trying to think, trying to sort her thoughts. "Where is she?"

"I don't know. Your guardian angel arranged for me to take her place, but he said he's not at liberty to satisfy my curiosity."

Though her heart was heavy, Kacy smiled. "Rey's miracles never cease to amaze me."

Her mother reached for her hand and squeezed it gently. Kacy's emotions took hold. She threw herself into her mother's arms. "Oh, Mom, I'm so glad you're here."

"I'm glad too, Kacy."

When they broke apart, her mother said, "You're upset. Tell me what's wrong, darling."

Tears got the best of her and Kacy blubbered, "I'm going to have a baby and Clay doesn't believe it's his. He thinks I'm Catharine and I don't know what I'm going to do."

"Don't cry," her mother soothed, drawing Kacy close again. "You must be exhausted. Let me show you upstairs so you can rest. Then we'll have a cup of mint tea and decide what to do. I have money and title to Eliza Paice's home. If I sell it, we'll have more and we can live anywhere you wish."

"Thanks, Mom," Kacy sniffed through her tears. "I've been so afraid."

"Now you have me to share your fears, dear."

Kacy smiled through her tears. Upstairs she took her shoes off and climbed on the bed. She felt safe and secure. Before she fell asleep, she uttered a silent prayer to thank her guardian angel.

~ * ~

"I am Lord Banes," Clay announced when the lady of the house joined him in the parlor. "My wife is on her way here and I must see her as soon as she arrives."

"She is already here. However, she is travel weary, so I put her to bed until tea time."

"To bed?" he echoed, not surprised Kacy had already arrived, but a little surprised that the attractive, intelligent looking, middle-aged lady hadn't attempted to speak to Kacy yesterday after the trial. Eliza Paice looked like a lady who commanded and inspired respect. A lady who would be concerned about her daughter's welfare. She didn't look like a lady who would put up with Wilbur Lugamon.

"If you wish to wait until she wakes up, you may do so here or in the library. It's two doors down the hall."

Clay was annoyed Catharine's mother left without even introducing herself. But his concern was for Kacy. Taking his hostess's suggestion, he strolled to the library where he stared at the shelves filled with books. But he made no move to examine them. Instead he walked over and stared out the window, willing Kacy to wake up. Soon.

Would she forgive him? Hell, if he had to apologize every day for the rest of his life, he would, but he wouldn't spend another day without her. He started to pace the floor. The small room compelled him to take tiny steps, but he was in no mood to sit down.

Sometime later, when he heard voices in the corridor, he heaved a sigh and walked out. He saw Catharine's mother embrace Kacy when she finished her descent down the stairs.

"Did you rest?" she asked.

"Yes." Kacy nodded, then apparently sensed Clay's presence because she turned her head and stiffened when she saw him. "What is he doing here?" she asked Eliza.

"I must talk to you," Clay said.

"No way," Kacy disagreed. "I'd sooner talk to a rattler."

"A what?"

"A gorilla," she changed her mind. "Anything from the animal kingdom would be preferable to you."

"I know you're upset and you have a right to—"

"Upset?" Kacy turned and climbed a step to get away from him. Then she turned back to face him. "Why should I be upset? Just because I gave up everything to be near you... that doesn't mean I can't change my mind. That's a woman's prerogative." She turned again and climbed another step. When she turned back around, Clay had closed all the distance between them. Their heads were almost on the same level. So were their eyes.

With forced calm she said, "In the event you have suffered a momentary loss of memory, Lord Banes, I shall repeat what I told you at Havenhurst. I don't need you or your wealth. I can take care of myself and my child."

"Damn it," he cursed. "I want to apologize. Will you listen and give me a chance, Kacy?"

"I've heard all I care to hear." Standing eye to eye bolstered her courage. "I accept your apology. Now, please go away. I don't wish to see you anymore."

With that she stormed up the stairs, not knowing she left behind a befuddled, repentant man.

Twenty-eight

Kacy didn't expect Clay to storm up behind her. But he did. Halfway up the stairs, he snatched her in his arms.

"What I have to say requires privacy," he growled, his expression fierce.

She twisted and squirmed, trying to get free, but knew she didn't stand a chance. Her strength could never match his. She doubted anybody's could. Then it occurred to her that they might harm their unborn child if Clay lost his balance and they tumbled down the stairs. That fear stilled her. She'd fight her battle with words.

When they reached the door to the room where she'd rested she ordered, "Put me down."

"In due time." He peered inside, saw the rumpled bed, walked in and kicked the door shut. Then he strode over to the bed where he sat down with her trapped between his strong arms and forced to sit on his lap.

Kacy glared. "You said you wouldn't allow me to foist my child off on you, so what are you doing here?"

"I apologize for being a thick-headed, callous idiot."

He looked harried and full of remorse. But she didn't intend to forgive him. He'd hurt her too much.

"I don't know what more to say, except that I was afraid to believe you had actually returned, Kacy. Is that so difficult to understand?"

"I'm not sure," she admitted, albeit begrudgingly. He looked repentant, but she didn't want to trust him. He might hurt her again.

Behind her, the door opened and an angry voice snarled, "So the bitch canna keep her hands off you even in broad daylight."

Cold chills slithered down Kacy's spine. Wilbur Lugamon stood in the doorway. Rage twisted his face and distorted his fleshy features. No man had ever frightened her more. Thank heaven she wasn't alone. She flicked her eyes back to Clay. Wilbur's interruption had put more fury in his green eyes than she had ever seen. Yet even as she watched, Clay's expression changed to deadly calm. And was all the more dangerous because of it.

In one fluid motion he shifted her off his lap and stood up, his relaxed stance misleading. Kacy knew it could be lethal. She almost pitied Wilbur. But from Catharine, Kacy had learned how truly evil Wilbur was, so he deserved whatever Clay did.

"Apologize to my wife," he ordered with deceptive calm.

Wilbur's incredulous expression was almost comical. "Me, apologize to a slut?"

Clay vaulted across the room, flattening Wilbur so fast Kacy couldn't believe her eyes. To her further astonishment, Clay leaned over, seized Wilbur's feet and dragged him out into the hall. She dashed after them.

Clay hauled Wilbur, feet first, down the stairs. His grunts and outraged shouts reverberated through the three-story house as his big behind thumped every step.

Kacy met her mother and the butler at the bottom of the stairs. All three followed Clay, still dragging Wilbur, outside. Clay pulled him off the stoop, dropped Wilbur's feet and ordered coldly, "Get up."

Wilbur reminded Kacy of an overfed ox as he lumbered slowly to his big feet. Taller than Wilbur, Clay's body was also more lean and fit. He grabbed Wilbur by the collar and lifted him off the ground.

"How did you escape your escort out of the country?"

"I didna try," Wilbur bragged. "I let 'um put me on the ferry, but I caught the first one back."

"You will regret it," Clay warned.

"I will not," Wilbur disagreed. "This is my home. She's my stepdaughter. Eliza's my wife. And nobody can force me to give them up."

Kacy glanced at her mother. She didn't look the least bit upset. Kacy wished she had some of her calm. As though sensing how upset she was, her mother put her arm around her waist, then reached to hold one hand as Clay dropped Wilbur on his feet.

Holding him at arm's length, he said, " You have no claim here, bastard. My wife isn't your stepdaughter and her mother isn't your wife."

Wilbur's face turned a dark, mottled purple. He started to swing his fists. They missed their target.

A master at avoiding punches while launching his own, Clay had the edge in strength, agility and age. Kacy knew no man, not even the huge Wilbur, was a match for Clay or his exceptional skill. Even so, she hated to see him in a fight. He might get hurt. She didn't trust Wilbur. *He probably fought dirty.*

Clay punched with regular recurrence and avoided Wilbur's fists with little effort. His mind wasn't on the fight. It dwelled on Kacy. She'd been insulted. Incense gave him the strength of two men. But he didn't allow fury to blind him. He intended to avenge the insults. He didn't intend to maim Wilbur, although he thought that would serve justice. The authorities could mete out his punishment, but first Clay would teach him a lesson he wouldn't soon forget.

Fists continued to fly until Clay tired of the cat and mouse game. He launched one fierce backhanded blow. Wilbur fell, slumped on the ground, unable to get back up. Clay had suffered no more than a few light punches. But besting Wilbur didn't vent Clay's frustration. After he aimed a disgusted frown at Wilbur, Clay turned to look at Kacy. Her hands were clenched at her sides. Raw fear and concern filled her pretty blue eyes.

Kacy knew Clay might not be aware of the hatred in Wilbur's black evil heart. But she was and she didn't take her eyes off him. His hand snaked down to his boot.

"Clay, look out!" she screamed as Wilbur withdrew a knife. The flash of a silver blade slashed through the air. "He has a knife!" Kacy warned too late. Wilbur had already lunged for Clay's back.

But Clay reacted to what he saw in Kacy's eyes. Before the scream left her mouth, he spun around, out of Wilbur's reach. And then, with amazing speed, he stomped on Wilbur's wrist, heard the crunch of bones as the knife popped out of his fat hand. With a yelp of pain and rage Wilbur lunged for the knife with his other hand. Clay raised his foot to kick the knife out of Wilbur's reach. Wilbur lunged again. His head smashed into Clay's swift, black-booted kick.

Clay whipped back around and did his best to shield the smashed, bloody skull from Kacy. "Don't look. 'Tis not a pretty sight."

Her voice trembled when she asked, "Is he—dead?"

"One would assume so," the butler said, his gaze riveted on Wilbur.

Kacy started to shake visibly. Clay picked her up. "He's evil," she said weakly, shakily.

"Yes." Clay agreed, "Evil." To the gawking butler, he ordered, "Send for the undertaker."

Inside Eliza's home, Kacy remembered she was still mad at Clay. "Put me down. I can walk. I'm not an invalid." Her legs wobbled when he set her on her feet. "I'm perfectly capable of taking care of myself." She took one step. And promptly fainted.

"Bloody hell," Clay grumbled, catching her as she crumpled. He carried her to the parlor where he laid her gently on the blue settee.

Eliza rushed close. Both she and Clay breathed sighs of relief when Kacy's eyelids fluttered open.

"Kacy," Eliza said, "do you know who I am?"

Kacy smiled. "Of course I do."

Eliza smiled, too.

Behind them Clay cleared his throat. "Leave us."

Kacy countermanded his request. "Stay."

But Clay's intimidating glare sent her mother scurrying from the room.

Kacy tried to sit up. Wooziness stopped her. She closed her eyes until she regained her equilibrium. Clay had knelt beside the settee, his gaze level with hers.

"Go away," she mumbled.

"No."

She closed her eyes again. "And stay away."

"Impossible."

When she didn't open her eyes again, he said, "You promised to obey when you married me. Have you forgotten?"

"Yes."

He leaned close. She inhaled his spicy scent and felt the heat emanating from his body. "Liar." he whispered so quietly her eyes flipped open in surprise. His were filled with tender warmth. Unable to bear looking at them, she snapped her eyes shut again.

"Look at me Countess."

She wouldn't give him that satisfaction. "I'm not a countess."

"Do you deny that you married me?"

In spite of her better judgement, Kacy opened her eyes. The look on his handsome, arrogant face was so smug, she wanted to smack him clear across the room. She spoke with what she considered decent restraint. "Please go away. I don't wish to be near you any more because…"

"Because?" he prompted, taking her trembling hands in his, which so unnerved her she blurted the truth.

"Because when I'm near you I can't think straight."

Again he looked smug and pleased. She decided to shove him away. He let her move her hands to his chest, but his rigid, unyielding body felt like the Rock of Gibraltar so she didn't budge him an inch.

"I'll go away if you go with me," he said, his voice grave, his gaze somber.

"I'm not going anywhere with you. And if you don't let go of me, I'll kick you right where it'll hurt most. Do you understand?"

A glimmer of surprised respect flashed in his green eyes before he tightened his hold, silently daring her to try. A vision of Wilbur with the knife sliced through her anger and she fought tears. "I've grown weary of asking you but I'll do so one more time." Slowly she enunciated each word. "Please go away."

He cupped her chin. "Why?"

"Because I think I might cry," she admitted in a quivery voice. Then she burst into tears.

Clay gathered her close. "Tell me why you are crying, love."

Her arms crawled around him. "Wilbur could have hurt you."

Clay shifted to his feet, then sat beside her without letting her go. "Any other reasons?" he asked tenderly.

"And because you don't love me. I don't want to love you either. Cripes, now I'm soiling your shirt and I don't want to do that either. Please go away and leave me alone. I hate having you see me like this." But even as she spoke she tightened her arms around his neck.

"You can stop crying, Kacy. Because I do love you."

"No, you don't. You're just saying that because you feel obligated."

"I'm your husband, therefore, I am obligated."

His rebuttal wasn't at all what she wanted to hear. "I sound like a blithering idiot."

"No, you don't."

"Don't contradict me. I know how I sound," she said contrarily.

"Very well. You sound like a blithering idiot."

"You didn't have to agree."

In spite of the gravity of the situation, Clay smiled. "I'm only trying to be agreeable, love."

Love? "It doesn't matter how agreeable you are, I'm not going back to Havenhurst with you."

"Oh yes, my dear, you are. You and our babies growing inside you are going with me."

"Why? So you can send us away again? Hasn't it occurred to you that I'm tired of being sent away?"

"I only sent you away when you first arrived in April," he said gently.

"That isn't true. You sent me back to my old life six weeks ago."

"I didn't send you. Rey took you. He said you must return; that it was necessary for a unification of your body and spirit and he asked me not to make it difficult."

"You don't want me. You just feel sorry for me. And what makes you think I have more than one baby growing inside me?" she finally remembered to ask.

He tightened his arms around her, glaring with exasperation. "I just killed a man who insulted you. Would I do that for a woman I did not want?"

Kacy was going to forgive him; had in fact, already forgiven him. But she wasn't going to tell him yet. He deserved to stew a bit first.

"I love you," Clay said, softening his voice.

The words thrilled Kacy but she wasn't about to let him know that until she'd said a few more choice things.

"Didn't you hear me?"

"I heard you."

His perfect black brows arched in a puzzled frown. "You don't believe me?"

"I believe you."

"But you do not love me?"

He looked so disheartened, she nearly gave in to the temptation to assure him she most assuredly did love him. "As long as we're fighting we may as well clear the air of all our grievances."

"We're not fighting."

"What is this if it isn't verbal combat?" She had him there. And she knew it, too.

"Do you love me, Kacy?"

"Yes, but saying we love each other won't solve our problems."

"Why not?" He sat up straighter. Once again he was the arrogant, powerful earl, his head towering above hers. But he still held her in his arms. She liked that immensely.

"Because our problem is that I don't trust you."

"Why the devil not? I've been faithful to you and our vows." He paused and drew in a breath to add emphasis to his next statement. "Tell me what you don't trust."

"In our other lifetimes, you always left me. And in this one you either send me away or let me go. How can I trust you when I expect that to happen again?"

"I shan't leave you, nor let you go, ever again. I promise."

At her doubtful look, he said with determined calm, "I sent you away this morning because I didn't think you were you."

"All you had to do was kiss me and you'd have known."

"That, my dear, is the crux of the problem," he borrowed her words from their wedding night.

"I'm afraid I don't follow."

"I wanted to kiss you so bloody much I feared I would disgrace myself."

"Disgrace yourself?"

Clay drew in another deep breath. "My mind insisted I be loyal to my marriage vows while my deprived body shouted I be unfaithful with a young woman I believed to be Catharine Paice." He raised one hand, shoved his fingers through his thick, black hair. "Damnation! You looked so bloody much like my wife, even acted like her most of the time. However, I couldn't believe you would actually come back. You'd been gone six awful weeks. How was I to know you'd suddenly return? And how did you manage it anyway? I thought Rey gave up on me."

"He didn't give up. He brought me back. But I'm afraid we won't see much of him anymore." Kacy felt the loss of Rey keenly, but she consoled herself with the fact that he, like Fey, had promised to visit when their baby was born. *And to bring novocaine to help deaden the labor pain.* "In any event, I came back as soon as Catharine showed me the London newspaper dated June 8, 1854."

"Where is Catharine?"

"In the future with my friends and family. She and I can't switch places again. I must stay here for the rest of my natural life and Catharine must live in the future."

"I miss your dimple."

"I don't." Kacy smiled, unaware her cheek dimpled.

Clay smiled. "You still have it when you smile."

She looked puzzled. "I do?"

"Yes, love... you do."

Her smile deepened and she touched his cheek.

"You've forgiven me," he said with both wonder and awe.

"There was never anything to forgive," she said quietly. "I just wanted to make sure you knew how I felt. And I don't want you shutting me out of your life again. Strangers by day and lovers by night isn't my idea of a happy marriage."

"Nor is it mine. And I will do whatever it takes to make you happy."

Kacy smiled.

"Do you trust me?" Clay asked.

She nodded. "As much as I love you. And if you could bring yourself to say those three words to me again, I promise my response will be much improved."

He smiled. "I love you, Kacy. I have loved you forever. When I told Rey I loved you six weeks ago, I suddenly recalled all those past lives you mentioned."

Kacy's brow furrowed. "You did?"

He nodded. "You reminded me of someone the moment I first saw you. Someone important. Now I know why. Because you're the most important person I have ever known."

A new lump formed in her throat. "Oh Clay," she breathed raggedly, "that's the nicest thing you've ever said to me, in any of our lives."

"Will you come home with me?"

"You know I will."

"Do I?" he asked huskily.

"Of course. I love you, Clay... and all I want from you is to be wanted."

A few minutes later, after she was drugged with his kisses, he mumbled in the low husky voice she loved so darn much, "I assure you, Kacy, my beloved, that I shall do all in my power to prove how much I want you."

To her delight and his, he did.

Twenty-nine

Ninth Month of Their Marriage
January-1855

Kacy awakened in the middle of the night. Because her delivery was so close, she and Clay hadn't made love for a month. Their baby was due any time. She hoped for a boy so Clay would have an heir. But a daughter would be nice, too. Clay maintained they would have twins. Kacy hoped he wouldn't be disappointed if she only had a single birth.

The last seven months had been the happiest of any of their lives. Although she no longer possessed the gift to heal, Clay remembered all their previous lives and they had discussed and rehashed them a number of times. In addition, she and her mother were very close, even though they lived a fair distance apart. Her mother had written often and come to visit twice before Christmas. Both stays were brief. But during the holidays she'd tarried a whole fortnight. What a wonderful Christmas season it had been!

After the loneliness of being only children, Kacy and Clay were now the center of a large extended family. All who dwelt at Havenhurst, be they servants or tenants, were included.

A knock on the door interrupted her thoughts.

"Who's there?" Clay asked and Kacy smiled in the dark. She hadn't realized he too, was awake, but she should have known he'd awaken when she did because they were so finely attuned to each other.

"It be Montfort, milord. Ye have visitors."

With his arm already wrapped around her, Clay drew Kacy closer, pillowing her head on his bare shoulder.

"Come in and tell us who they are."

Montfort opened the door. He carried a moderator lamp. "The man be Mr. Rey." Out of respect Montfort kept his gaze on the blue carpet beneath his feet. "And his companion be her ladyship's Aunt Fey."

Kacy turned a happy smile to Clay. "They promised to come for the birth of our baby."

"Babies," he corrected gently.

"The Countess's mother be with them," Montfort said.

"How wonderful!" Kacy exclaimed.

"Tell them we will be right down," Clay instructed.

"I awakened Cook Edna Mae and Ellen. Coffee and tea shall be ready in a thrice," Montfort promised, lighting two wall sconces before he left the master suite.

Clay placed a hand carefully on Kacy's stomach
and was rewarded with the movement that made his heart thump. "One of our babies moved," he said huskily.

Kacy gave him an unfathomable look. "You've never told me why you think we're going to have twins."

"Fey told me, after I dreamed it, just as I dreamed we'd be uncommonly happy and she confirmed that as well." He dropped a kiss on Kacy's forehead, then climbed out of bed and reached for her robe.

In his opinion, she was unduly self-conscious about her appearance and did her best to keep her body covered, even when they went to bed. But every morning her nightwear was hiked above her waist and his arm circled her bare middle. He missed seeing all of her. The thought of her flesh swollen with his seed made him exceedingly proud. But he wouldn't force her to let him look at her without clothes. Just as there were times when his wife was very improper, there were times when she was remarkably prim. He wouldn't change one single thing.

"You want to see me, don't you, Clay?"

She must have read his mind. He knew his surprise showed as he nodded.

"Go ahead."

When his eager hands reached to uncover her, she stopped him saying, "I've kept my body hidden because I feel so unattractive. I didn't do it to cheat you of your husbandly rights."

"You haven't cheated me of anything, love. I've held your bare flesh close every night."

She smiled then, not her usual sun bright smile, but a warm and tender one. "I love you, Clay and I have a feeling I won't look like this much longer. Gaze to your heart's content."

With a feeling of reverence, he drew the bed covers away.

Although her nightdress fit loose, it wasn't one of the modest crushed cottons she'd started to wear a few months past when her middle began to bulge. Made of sheer, delicate fabric, this nightdress covered her to her knees. Beneath the soft folds of the gown he saw her full rosy tipped breasts. A surge of possessive male pride that she belonged to him coursed through his veins. His hungry gaze drank their fill of her lovely full twin peaks and rounded middle. Never had he seen a more beautiful sight. Even swollen with child, her body was exquisite.

Had candlelight been created to illuminate her beauty? "You're beautiful, Kacy. Thank you for sharing yourself with me."

Because she seemed to have trouble sitting up, he helped her, then held her robe open. While she fastened the butterfly at the top, he donned trousers and a robe of his own. He kissed her forehead, drawing her close, then offering his arm. Slowly they walked out into the corridor.

At the top of the staircase Kacy emitted a small startled gasp.

Ever concerned, Clay asked, "What is it, love?"

"I had a backache last evening," she admitted. "I suspect my time is near."

With deepening concern, Clay slipped his arm around her waist. His smile was strained.

So was Kacy's. The pain had begun low in her back. As she stood there, immobilized, it moved higher, then traveled around to her stomach and held her in its grip for a few breath stopping moments before it pushed down upon her, announcing the commencement of labor.

"I think it's time," she breathed.

"I'll put you back in bed." Clay scooped her up and carried her back to the master suite. He removed her robe the way he did everything else. By taking charge. Then he slid his eyes down her swollen body once more.

Pride gleamed in his green eyes. "You have never looked more lovely, Kacy." As he patted her middle tenderly, it hardened with another contraction. He waited until it ended before he asked, "Do you wish to change bed gowns before I summon your mother?"

Kacy nodded. Her mother had been a doctor in a previous life and she insisted she be the one to assist with the delivery. She couldn't think of anyone she'd rather have.

Changing the translucent nightgown took longer than expected. Twice contractions forced them to stop. "Those were close," she gasped as Clay drew the sheets up to her waist.

"I know. I'll summon your mother."

When he returned a few brief moments later, she knew he must have run all the way down and back up the stairs.

"Your mother is washing her hands. She and Fey will be here soon."

Kacy stared at him in bemusement. Concern and love lurked in his green eyes as he approached the bed. "Should I tell you what I see right now?"

"Please do," she invited.

"The embodiment of everything I've ever wanted. My wife. My countess. The mother of my children. The lady I have loved for almost eternity."

Kacy's bemusement dissolved into a loving smile, which faded as another contraction began. After it ended and she regained her breath, Clay sat down on the edge of the bed and kissed her like a man should kiss a woman but seldom did. With tenderness, passion and love.

The door opened without a knock. Kacy's mother, who had assumed Eliza's identity, walked in along with Fey and Rey. "How close are the contractions?"

"Not more than a couple of minutes apart." Kacy gave her mother, Fey and Rey a quick, welcoming smile, which they all returned with love in their eyes.

"You must leave," Eliza told Clay. "We must prepare for the birthing."

"I'll be close by if you need me," he promised.

Kacy knew he didn't want her to face this without him. "Why don't you stay?"

Although Clay looked pleased with her suggestion her mother said, "A husband watching his wife give birth in the nineteenth century isn't done."

"I want him to share this. He shouldn't be left out."

"Men don't belong in birthing rooms. Do you want to shock the servants?"

"They'll understand." Gripped by another very strong contraction, Kacy had to wait to remind, "In the future men are with their wives all the time during delivery."

Her mother smiled. "Very well. It's your show, darling. If you want him here and he wants to stay, it's no skin off my nose."

"Who will keep Rey company?" Fey wanted to know.

"No need to worry about me," Rey said. "I shall know when the business at hand has been accomplished and I shall return."

As he started toward the door, Kacy asked, "Will we have twins, Rey?"

"You shall know before dawn." He smiled then, a benevolent smile, which he aimed at Clay. "You have nothing to worry about, Claythorne. Labor is hard work, but it isn't impossible. Kacy belongs to you now. She won't be taken away again."

Another contraction gripped Kacy. Squeezing Clay's hand, she bore down with all her might, gasping for air when it ended, praying the pain would end soon.

"A couple more like that and I think we'll be ready for novocaine, Fey," Kacy's mother said.

"I'm ready now," Kacy gasped, wondering if she could endure another contraction without passing out.

"We'll give you the injection just before the walls of your uterus collapse. If the pain is unbearable, I'll also give you a local to help deaden the pain."

"It can't get worse," she complained. Just when she thought she couldn't stand anymore, her mother picked up the syringe and lowered the covers. The novocaine relieved some of the pain, but Kacy still struggled through each contraction. *Would the delivery never end?*

Holding her hand, Clay did his best to hide his anxiety. When she pulled against him, her strength was as fierce as ten strong men. He suffered through each pain with her, cursing himself for being responsible for putting her through such agony.

"How do you feel?" he asked, some fifteen minutes later.

"Like I'm having a baby," she panted. Perspiration peppered her brow, the skin above her upper lip and her forehead.

"I wish I could take your pain from you."

"It's labor," she said, trying to act brave. "And some of the pain has been deadened."

But it hurt a lot, he could tell. More than she wanted him to know. The pressure mounted. He saw that in her eyes. She closed them. He feared she had blacked out because she didn't pull on his hands.

"It hurts," she whimpered.

"I know and I'm sorry." Clay had to call on all his willpower not to groan. Damnation. Maybe witnessing the birth wasn't such a brilliant idea. He hated to see her suffer.

"It isn't like what I imagined," she said unexpectedly.

"Why not?" Tenderly he wiped tiny drops of perspiration from her brow and face.

"It's as though everything has more feeling."

He didn't ask if that meant more pain. He couldn't bear to have his suspicion confirmed.

She gasped and got down to the very serious business of giving birth. She pushed, and panted, tried to breathe easier and said, "I wish I could faint," then reversed it, "I hope I don't…"

Finally, an hour later, it ended. The occupants in the master suite breathed collective sighs of relief. The countess had delivered Havenhurst's heir, a dark-haired boy two inches longer and a pound heavier than his blond-haired little sister.

Bertha and Maisy changed the bed sheets. Both babies were held, examined and bathed. As Kacy held one in each arm, an aroma as sweet and gentle as baby powder wafted to her. Thinking Fey must have provided a few items from the future, Kacy smiled and winked at Fey. Fey winked back.

Both babies fell asleep in Kacy's arms. "I guess they're ready for the new twin cradles you ordered
from London," she said to Clay.

Taking their daughter, he laid her tenderly in the pink cradle. Then he did the same with his son, in the blue cradle.

A moment later Rey returned to the bedroom. "How do you feel?" he asked Kacy.

She couldn't help but smile. "Like a mother."

"And how did your husband fare during the ordeal?"

"It was pure torture," Clay answered. "But I wouldn't have missed it." He sat by the bed again, reaching for Kacy's hand. "How may I thank you for bringing Kacy to me?" he asked Rey.

"It isn't necessary."

"How are Catharine and Jennifer?" Kacy asked then.

"Content at the moment," Fey said. "But I suspect they will one day yearn for more, as you did."

"I yearned for the universe." Kacy smiled up at Clay. "And now I have it."

"As do I," he said quietly.

She squeezed his hand. And a startling revelation leapt between them. Quick, clear, precise and as astounding as it was profound, the glimpse of eternity rocked them both. In other lives, they'd always allowed responsibilities and duties to take precedence. Now they discovered they would live out a natural lifetime together. And again after this life, in the future because they would be eternal partners. *Their love had and would transcend time.*

Sensing the revelation had come from Rey, Kacy turned her eyes to him. How many times had she looked into his wizened, ageless eyes and wondered why she was so lucky to have both a guardian angel and a fairy godmother?

"I love you, Rey, and I love you too, Fey."

"We know you do," Fey said, smiling.

Kacy turned her gaze to Clay. In his eyes she saw a look she'd seen before, in other life times and in this one as well. Deep abiding love. Yet now there was also a promise that he would be with her forevermore.

He raised her hand to his mouth and kissed it.

Thrilled beyond words, she smiled. She couldn't have asked for a more wonderful husband or eternal partner. He made her happy and their marriage spectacular.

Would he someday be a guardian angel?

Would she, too?

What marvelous possibilities to ponder into eternity.

Meet Evanell

Born in Utah, Evanell is the mother of three sons. She owned her own Oil & Gas Consulting firm in Denver, Colorado, prior to moving to England for four years. She now lives in Arizona during the winter and Utah in the summer. She loves to golf, read and travel, and spends more time in front of my computer than anywhere else.

Visit her web site: www.evanell.com

Works From The Pen Of Peggy P. Parsons & Evanell

Written as Evanell

Glimpse of Eternity

Startled, and still on the bed, his gaze level with hers, he said, "If you like my kisses, why did you stop me?"

"Because that's not why I'm here. And I'm sure my guardian angel wouldn't approve if we did anything more."

Clay breathed in and out, slowly. "Why then, did you thank me?"

"For the reunion."

Puzzled, he frowned. "The reunion?"

She nodded. "I think we've known each other before. In prior lives. But I don't expect to stay in this century. So I don't think we should kiss again. I He wanted to kiss her again. Giving in to the impulse, he lowered his head.

She thwarted him by scooting off his lap, jumping to her feet. Instead of dashing away, she stood before him, her mouth swollen from his prolonged kiss, her eyes blazing with unfulfilled passion. And then to his utter amazement, she said, "Thank you."

need to try to help solve your problems, not complicate them, so I can go home."

Glimpse of Forever

Having loved and lost Drake in other lives, including her current life in the twenty-first century, Jennifer is delighted when she finds herself catapulted into his life in the middle of the nineteenth century. Mistaking Jennifer for his intended, Drake finds her much easier to deal with after she falls from a tree in his woods. Although he thinks she tricked him into agreeing to wed her, he plans to have a marriage in name only. Now he discovers he wants her to be his wife in every way.

With her gift of sight, Jennifer knows Drake's charge is impersonating her in the future. When she convinces Drake she isn't his intended, he promises they will fight the evil wizard who wants her soul together. Then he is thrown from his horse and wounded. Fearing the wizard will never let them live in peace, Jennifer returns to the future only to discover the girl impersonating her is dead and she has no life to reclaim.

Glimpse of Never Ending Love

Still standing close but no longer touching, Catharine said, "Tyler?"

"Yes?"

"Will being together be this exciting if we are married?"

"Yes," he promised. "We'll make it this exciting or more."

Neither said another word, but both knew a commitment of sorts had been made.

He reached inside his breast suit coat pocket and removed the betrothal ring. "You'll let me know when you're ready to wear this, won't you?"

She nodded, staring at the huge diamond solitaire sparkling up at her.

Written as Peggy P. Parsons

One Stolen Night

Having broken up with her high school sweetheart after graduation, Pamela Tate follows her dream of attending the University of Hawaii where she meets the legendary Robin, who steals more than her bruised heart.

Yours Till Niagra Falls

Embarrassed by her attempt to warn Jade about a conniving college classmate, Kia flees to her beloved Camp in the Adirondack's to mourn the loss of her family. When Jade shows up uninvited and unexpected, she agrees to let him stay in one of her log cabins. Although she isn't ready for love, she wants to trust Jade, but his association with her unscrupulous ex-boyfriend, makes it difficult to believe he isn't there for a sinister reason.

Paper Marriage

Chandler's eagle gaze checked Analyn's compact living room. "Is your whole apartment decorated in red, white and blue?"
"What if it is?" He'd broken her heart. Would he insult her taste, too?

Yesterday's Secrets

Story begins with Janalou boarding a bus in Spartanburg, SC. She meets seven people and they form a friendship and stay together after they transfer to a different bus. That evening Janalou has an attack of appendicitis and is rushed to the hospital, then ends up traveling by car across the country with Kree to give her body and her facial bruises time to heal before she meets his family and starts to work with them.

When Janalou discovers her father/papa and stepmother have been arrested for her murder (even though no body was found--there was blood in the house), she feels compelled to return to Spartanburg. The next day at the court house she meets her real family, including her identical twin, and discovers she was kidnapped when she was four. Her twin tells/reminds her that for their last Christmas together they were given twin dolls, and dresses in their own size to match the dolls.

Letter to Our Readers

Enjoy this book?

You can make a difference

As an independent publisher, Wings ePress, Inc. does not have the financial clout of the large New York Publishers. We can't afford large magazine spreads or subway posters to tell people about our quality books.

But we do have something much more effective and powerful than ads. We have a large base of loyal readers.

Honest Reviews help bring the attention of new readers to our books.

If you enjoyed this book, we would appreciate it if you would spend a few minutes posting a review on the site where you purchased this book or on the Wings ePress, Inc. webpages at: https://wingsepress.com/